STARFULLY YOURS

A SWEET CELEBRITY ROM-COM

CELEBRITY LOVE IN NEW ORLEANS
BOOK 2

KATIE TALBOT

LAKE VISTA
PRESS

Cover design by Beck and Dot Book Covers

Published by Lake Vista Press

ISBN 978-1-969144-00-4 (e-book)

ISBN 978-1-969144-01-1 (paperback)

First edition, 2025

To the city of New Orleans. You inspire me.

1

ANNA

YOU'D THINK after ninety-nine rejections, I'd stop checking my email at work.

But there I was at Muses Bar, elbow-deep in cocktail napkins and flaming shots, waiting for a miracle. Or at least a tip of over five dollars. My phone buzzed in my apron pocket. I already knew it wasn't good news.

The subject line confirmed it: *Thank you for submitting your story. It was a unique concept, but unfortunately...*

The dreaded *unfortunately*. I didn't bother reading the rest. I knew exactly how it ended.

I'd written ten novels and four short stories in the past five years: romance, cozy mystery, literary fiction, dystopian horror, ghost pirates, even a retelling of *Great Expectations*. A few had earned polite interest, but each one had ended up here, in my inbox of rejections.

The first one had stung. The ninety-ninth felt like the universe was sending a clear message: *give it up, Anna.*

Behind me, my friend's familiar voice sliced through my sulking. "Anna, please tell me you're not looking at another rejection email. If you cry into someone's margarita, I'll charge you for it."

"I'm not going to cry." I shoved my phone into my apron. "But yes, it's another rejection."

The voice belonged to Marie Antoinette, my co-worker and best friend. She sauntered over, waving a towel dramatically. She insisted that everyone call her by her full name, claiming that *if you're named after royalty, you don't do anything halfway.*

"Was that the big one hundred?" She narrowed her perfectly lined eyes at me. "Have we hit triple digits yet?"

"No, it was ninety-nine."

She leaned against the bar as if she had all the time in the world. "Oh, honey. That's a milestone. We should celebrate. Champagne, maybe? Or cake? Let them eat—"

"Don't say it," I warned, grabbing a dirty martini glass and shooting her a look.

She sighed dramatically. "Fine. But are you still planning to quit at one hundred rejections?"

"I am." I set the glass down harder than I intended. "One hundred rejections, and I'm done. No more writing. I'll officially retire my pen, or keyboard, or whatever."

My friend arched a skeptical eyebrow. "But what about that fancy award you won in college? What was it called again? You were supposed to be the next big thing."

The reminder stung more than I wanted to admit. "It was the National Emerging Writers' Prize. And that was years ago. I peaked at twenty-two. All downhill from there. I'm a failure."

"Failure, schmailure. You know what I always say: I haven't failed. I've just found 10,000 ways that won't work."

"Who said that?"

"Me. And Thomas Edison."

I didn't respond. The truth was, I had won the National Emerging Writers' Prize for a deeply personal story about my mom, who died when I was young. It was raw, emotional, and the most vulnerable thing I'd ever written. People loved it, but I hadn't been able to replicate that magic.

Marie Antoinette studied my face, her teasing tone softening. "You'll get there." For a second, I almost believed her.

But before I could respond, reality crashed in, reminding me that the rejection letter wasn't even the worst part of my day. I groaned and rubbed my temples. "Oh, and get this—I need to find a place to stay. My cousin Lucy's having another baby, and apparently, they need the nursery back."

She arched an eyebrow. "Another baby? Is she starting a daycare or something?"

"Right?" I sighed. "My aunt and uncle said I could stay with them, but, uh, *no, thank you*. They'd turn it into a family intervention about how I'm the only Amato who isn't married with children. Aunt Dolores would spend all day giving me pointed looks about my *life choices*, and Uncle Ray would pull out his calculator to explain how much money I'm wasting not working a 'real job.' I'd rather live in the walk-in freezer here at Muses."

She whistled. "Ouch. Nothing like a family intervention to put the 'fun' in dysfunction. Honestly, the freezer might be the more comfortable option. Where are you going to go?"

"I'll figure something out."

The truth was, I didn't know what I was going to do, and the rejection email had just solidified the growing pit in my stomach. As much as I hated to admit it, I was running out of options.

Before Marie Antoinette could respond, Mrs. Brodie appeared, her turquoise earrings jingling as she carried a pitcher of sangria. She had a knack for showing up at just the right time. Or at least when you needed sangria. "I couldn't help but overhear. You need a place to stay?

I hesitated. "Uh, yeah. But don't worry, I'll figure something out."

"Nonsense," Mrs. Brodie said with a wave of her hand. "Topher's got a little cottage on the back of his vacation property right here in the Garden District. His last tenant moved out last year, and it's been sitting empty ever since."

"Oh, I wouldn't want to intrude."

She dismissed that with another wave. "It's no intrusion at all. In fact, you'd be doing *us* a favor, keeping it from falling into disuse. It's small, but charming. Needs a little fresh air and someone to open the curtains. You can stay as long as you need."

"Really?" I asked, a flicker of hope warming my chest. "I mean, if you're sure."

Mrs. Brodie beamed. "Topher's friend is staying at the big house, but I doubt you two will even cross paths. And don't worry about rent for the cottage. It's not like anybody's using it."

She gave me a wink, then added, "I'm heading out as soon as I deliver this sangria, but I'll get you the keys tomorrow."

As she floated off, I let myself smile. A cottage. In the Garden District. A little cottage on Mrs. Brodie's son's property was a far cry from crashing on someone's couch or dodging my aunt and uncle's "helpful" lectures. For the first time in a long time, something had gone right.

Maybe things weren't so bad after all. Sure, my latest story had been rejected, and I was dangerously close to giving up on writing altogether. But I still had one more try in me. And wouldn't it be something if my one-hundredth attempt at getting published was *the one*?

The story practically wrote itself: *"After 99 rejections, award-winning writer Anna Amato finally broke through and published the Great American Novel."* I could already imagine the headlines, the late-night interviews, and the Pulitzer acceptance speech, where I would charm the crowd with my tale of perseverance.

One more shot. One more story. And then I'd see what the universe had to say.

I was wiping down glasses when Marie Antoinette's sudden intake of breath caught my attention. She was staring at her phone, her expression a mix of dread and panic.

"What's that face?" I asked.

She pushed the phone into her apron. "Nothing," she said quickly. Too quickly.

"You're a terrible liar. Show me."

She sighed dramatically and handed over her phone. "Fine, but don't freak out, okay?"

My stomach dropped as soon as I read the headline: *Mardi Gras royalty to tie the knot: A love story for the ages.* And there he was— Theodore Beauregard IV. Better known as Beau, my ex. Grinning in a tuxedo, arm around the picture-perfect woman he'd left me for.

"Oh, come on." I shoved the phone back. "Couldn't they just headline it *'Local jerk to marry rich lady'* and be done with it?"

She frowned. "Are you okay?"

"I'm fine," I lied. "It's ancient history."

Except it wasn't. My chest tightened, an ache I tried to ignore. I'd spent five years pretending I didn't care, convincing myself I was over Beau. But seeing their perfectly staged engagement photo, complete with a glowing caption about love and destiny, made me feel small.

A love story for the ages. At least someone was writing a good story. Too bad it wasn't me.

I was wiping down a sticky part of the bar when the door swung open, and the atmosphere shifted. The hum of conversation softened, and a few heads turned.

I didn't look up at first, but I felt the energy change.

A tall figure stepped inside, hunched over as if he didn't want to be noticed. Marie Antoinette nudged me. "That's a look," she whispered.

He was wearing a baseball cap pulled low and sunglasses—even though it was well past sunset. His face was mostly obscured. He was clearly trying not to draw attention, which, ironically, only made him more conspicuous.

"Sketchy," she murmured.

I rolled my eyes. "Probably just a tourist trying too hard."

He approached the bar, glancing over his shoulder as if he expected someone to jump out at him. His blue eyes darted toward me. "Is Josephine Brodie here?" he asked, his accent crisp and undeniably English.

"She just left," I said. "Can I help you with something?"

"No, that's all right," he said, his hand twitching toward the door.

But before he could leave, a surge of people pushed in behind him—a rowdy, boisterous group blocking his escape route.

Trapped, he hesitated before reluctantly sliding onto a barstool. "Seltzer water, please," he said, avoiding eye contact like the crowd might swallow him whole.

I poured the drink, set it in front of him, and leaned an elbow on the bar. "And who should I say is asking after Mrs. Brodie?"

"Call me Nigel." He glanced behind me at the sign advertising Pimm's Cup. "Nigel Pimmington."

I raised an eyebrow. "Pimmington? That sounds... distinguished. Where are you from?"

"The English countryside."

I tilted my head, amused. "Oh, really? What part?"

"A quaint little village," he said, taking a sip of his drink.

I gave him a once-over. "So, Mr. Pimmington, when you're not sipping Earl Grey and strolling through the heather, what do you do for a living?"

He hesitated just long enough to be suspicious. "I'm a blacksmith."

I couldn't help but chuckle at what was so clearly a line. "A blacksmith? Like, with an actual forge and an anvil?"

He gave a tight nod, giving a nervous look at the gathering crowd before turning back to me. "Yes. It's a... respected trade in my village."

"Mmhmm." I leaned a little closer. "And what exactly do you forge?"

"Horseshoes," he said smoothly. "And... shields."

I tried not to laugh. "Shields? For what? Local dragon attacks?"

"For jousting," he said.

I blinked. "You're telling me jousting is still a thing in England?"

"It's a niche sport," he muttered.

"Well, if you're ever in need of a damsel to rescue," I said, my voice somehow going all coy without my permission, "I've been told I look good in distress."

What did I just say?

Heat rushed to my cheeks. I wasn't usually that girl who flirted so brazenly with customers. But something about him, whether his ridiculous story or his stupidly good posture, was throwing me off my game and replacing it with a completely different game.

His shades dipped low enough that I could catch the look in his bright blue eyes. He looked startled at first but then amused. "Do you faint easily? That's a key qualification."

"Only if someone's waving a sword at me," I replied, before I could stop myself.

Seriously, what was happening right now?

Was I... enjoying this?

Before I could process whatever I was doing or saying, something in the room shifted. Laughter dimmed. Chairs scraped. The air got tight, like a balloon stretched to its limit.

"That's him," someone whispered.

"No way," another voice gasped, breathless.

I glanced toward a nearby table. A woman was pointing at Nigel while her friend frantically typed on her phone. The others were already leaning in, laser-focused.

Nigel's posture stiffened. His eyes widened, and he clenched his jaw. His voice was low and urgent. "You have to hide me."

I raised an eyebrow. "What are you, the headliner at a Renaissance fair or something?"

He didn't laugh. He just looked at me, pleading. "It's... complicated. Please."

Something about the way he said it, with a hint of panic, his eyes not leaving mine, made my pulse skip a beat.

"Follow me, Lancelot." I gestured toward the back.

Then I held up a hand like I'd spotted something urgent up front. "Hey, everyone, someone left their phone at the bar, and it's been getting some *fascinating* texts from a girlfriend stuck at home!" I said it loud enough for half the bar to swivel their heads.

With the crowd distracted, Nigel slid off the stool, head down, as I eased him behind the bar and guided him through the back to a small office. Behind us, the crowd remained fixated on the fake misplaced phone, utterly oblivious to our escape.

Once the office door clicked shut, I crossed my arms and faced him. "So, Nigel Pimmington, care to tell me what you're really doing here?"

He sighed, rubbing the back of his neck. "Maybe we could skip the interrogation? I'm trying to lie low."

His English accent had vanished, and he pushed his sunglasses onto the top of his cap. My stomach flipped, and my brain put the pieces together. His jawline was sharp, and his dark blonde hair was tousled, giving him a rugged charm. His blue eyes were startlingly bright, framed by lashes that seemed unfairly long for a man, and the faint scruff on his face added to his appeal.

"You're Luke Fisher," I said, my voice barely above a whisper.

Hollywood's golden boy. And somehow, he'd ended up at my bar.

2

LUKE

I WAS TRAPPED.

I'd come to the bar to drop in on Mrs. Brodie, my best friend's mother, not to get cornered by fans, dodging camera phones and whispers like some fugitive. But now I was stuck in this back room, and the waitress who had shoved me in there didn't look particularly sympathetic to my plight.

She leaned against the wall, arms crossed, her dark eyes cool and assessing, like she'd already decided I was the problem. Her brown hair was pulled back into a messy knot, with a few strands curling rebelliously near her cheekbones. And her jeans were worn, clinging in a way that briefly made me forget my frustration.

She was gorgeous, but not in the polished, Hollywood way I was used to.

She tilted her head and looked at me. "Are we just going to stand here in awkward silence, or are you going to explain what you're doing in New Orleans? I guess you needed a break from... everything."

The way she said *everything* made my jaw clench. She knew. Of course, she knew. The entire world had seen the fallout. Why would I expect this waitress in a New Orleans bar to be any different?

I exhaled shortly, irritation bubbling up. "Trust me, I didn't choose to be here in this backwater place."

"Backwater?" Her eyebrows shot up, her arms folding across her chest. "What's that supposed to mean?"

The frustration spilled out before I could stop it. "I think 'backwater' is accurate. This city is loud, it's sticky, and the potholes could swallow a car."

Her expression turned icy, like I'd just insulted her grandma's gumbo recipe. "Wow. Insulting the city of New Orleans. That's a great look for someone who supposedly has come to the city and is trying to 'lie low.'"

The words stung more than I wanted to admit. Lie low. That's what everyone thought I was doing. Licking my wounds after Sienna broke up with me and started the public train wreck that was my life. But no one ever wondered if the spotlight itself was part of the problem. If maybe, just maybe, I wasn't the polished, charming star they expected.

I sighed, leaning back. "Touchy, aren't we?"

"Touchy?" Her voice was rising. "You're the one who called New Orleans 'backwater.' You're acting as if this place is beneath you. What, is New Orleans not good enough for you?"

"Let's be honest, the city has its... quirks."

Her eyes narrowed. "Quirks? Wow. What a brave take. How much of the city have you even seen?"

I shrugged. "I've seen enough to know it's... unique."

She scoffed. "Unique. That's what people say when they hate your outfit but don't want to start a fight." She looked at me pointedly. "Tennessee Williams said there are only three great American cities. New York, San Francisco, and New Orleans. The rest? Cleveland."

My lips twitched into a smirk. She was not letting this go. "New York's the capital of finance. San Francisco's the capital of tech. What's New Orleans the capital of? Sweat?"

Her eyes flared, but then she smiled. Slowly. Dangerously. "Jazz. Ever heard of it? You're welcome, America."

I leaned back, but my gaze stayed on her. "Fine. Jazz. What else?"

"Oh, where to start?" she said, arms crossing as she listed them off. "Mardi Gras. Frenchmen Street. Crawfish season. Beignets that taste like happiness. Music around every corner. People who talk to you like they've known you forever."

I raised an eyebrow. "Look, I'm just saying that parades and potholes aren't exactly my love language."

She stepped a little closer. "No city's perfect," she said, her voice a growl. "But here? We don't pretend to be. We decorate the potholes and throw parties to make light of an annoying situation. That's the beauty of New Orleans. We don't hide our craziness; we celebrate it by throwing a parade. We don't stuff our family skeletons in the closet; we bring them to Sunday dinner. I would *never* leave this place."

I dragged a hand through my hair. I needed to apologize for insulting New Orleans, which she clearly loved.

A lot.

I mean, I like my hometown of Boston, but would I defend it in a duel? Probably not. This hometown loyalty felt *a bit much* to me. Still, I got the feeling that this waitress would throw me to the wolves if I didn't apologize. "I didn't mean to insult New Orleans."

Her eyes flashed. "Well, you did. Am I getting this right? Your perfect life blew up, and now you're hiding out here because you didn't have anywhere else to go?"

Her words about my perfect life struck too close to home, and I didn't answer right away. My ex-girlfriend Sienna's voice echoed in my head, uninvited: *Everyone thinks you're perfect, but you're impossible to love. Impossible.* I glanced at the closed door, wishing for an escape route that didn't involve the crowd waiting outside.

When I finally spoke, my voice was quieter. "You don't know anything about me."

"I don't need to. You're exactly like every guy who walks in here thinking this city owes him something. News flash. It doesn't. But hey, if New Orleans is beneath you, the door's right there."

Her head tilted toward the door, where the muffled sound of voices grew louder. My escape route, as she well knew, wasn't an option. I couldn't leave. Not without blowing my cover, because the news had not gotten out that I was hiding in New Orleans.

She was still angry, still defiant. But something softer flickered underneath. Her passion radiated from her in waves. She wasn't just defending her city; she was *fighting* for it. It was the kind of raw, unfiltered loyalty I didn't see much of in LA.

"You always talk like that?" I asked, my voice lower now. "Like you're trying to win a debate?"

Her eyes didn't leave mine. "Only when someone's asking for it."

A beat passed. The air between us shifted. Something electric.

I opened my mouth to say something else, something I probably shouldn't.

But then there was a knock at the door.

"Anna? Are you in there?" came a bright, teasing voice. "Who was that guy in the baseball cap and sunglasses?"

I froze.

The waitress, who I now knew was "Anna," sighed, rolling her eyes as if she'd been expecting this. She pushed off the wall and cracked the door open just enough to peek out.

"Oh, hey, Marie Antoinette," Anna said casually. "It was just some random guy named, uh, Nigel Pimmington."

"Nigel Pimmington?" The woman's voice dripped with disbelief. "What kind of name is that? Sounds like he should be sipping tea in a cravat and complaining about the weather."

Anna didn't miss a beat. "Well, he *is* English. They all have names like that."

"Do they now?" The woman's voice was filled with mock fascination. "So, this *Nigel Pimmington* just happened to wander into our humble establishment? What was he doing here? Inspecting the quality of our biscuits?"

Anna shrugged. "It was packed out front, and he was feeling overwhelmed, so I helped him find the bathroom. Not sure where he went after that."

"Uh-huh," the other waitress said slowly, clearly not buying it. "And then you stayed in here because...?"

"I came in here to check the inventory of emergency napkins," Anna said with complete deadpan seriousness. "Obviously."

I bit back a laugh.

The woman at the door was still skeptical. "Funny, he looked an awful lot like Luke Fisher. That jawline, those cheekbones."

I bit down on my cheeks, nervous that Anna would give me up.

Anna, however, didn't flinch. "Nope. Nigel Pimmington is just a regular English guy. Very normal, very boring."

"Boring?" the woman exclaimed. "Honey, I saw you two talking. You don't blush over boring. There was *tension,* Anna Banana. The kind of tension that could turn a stiff upper lip into a trembling lower one."

My eyebrows shot up. *Tension?* I remembered the way Anna's lips curved when she teased me about being a blacksmith.

Tension.

Yeah. That's one word for it.

Anna groaned. "There was no tension. He was just... lost. It was so crowded in front, so I helped him find the bathroom, that's all."

"Lost, huh?" She was skeptical. "Well, next time, feel free to lose him my way. Nigel Pimmington sounds like the kind of man who'd recite Shakespeare to you at sunset."

"Yeah, I'm sure," Anna said dryly. "He seemed more like the type to complain about the font we use for the wine list."

There was a pause, and then the woman at the door sniffed. "Well, if he comes back, I call dibs on serving him. You can't just hoard all the posh accents for yourself."

"Fine," Anna said, clearly eager to end the conversation. "Now, don't you have tables to check on? The jukebox crowd looks like big tippers."

The woman sighed theatrically. "Fine. Hurry it up."

And then she was gone. Anna leaned back against the door and muttered, "That woman needs her own sitcom." Then she turned back to me, crossing her arms. Her expression was hard to read. "You're welcome for not giving you up," she said, her tone light, but with just enough edge to remind me she'd done me a favor.

I cleared my throat, looking away for a moment before meeting her gaze. "Thank you," I whispered, keeping my voice low. The words felt awkward in my mouth, like I hadn't said them in far too long.

Anna raised an eyebrow, the ghost of a smirk tugging at her lips. "Wow, an actual 'thank you.' Must've really cost you."

I sighed, dragging a hand down my face. "You win. Can we just wait until the crowd clears, and I'll be out of your hair?"

She studied me for a moment, her expression unreadable. I tried not to squirm under her gaze, but it felt like she could see right through me. Did she know how hard I worked to keep the cracks hidden? How much effort it took to pretend I was still the confident, charming star everyone thought they knew?

I hated the vulnerability creeping in around the edges of this moment. I hated even more that she might notice it.

Finally, Anna shrugged and leaned back against the door, her voice smoother but no less cutting. "Suit yourself. But if you hate it in New Orleans so much, maybe next time, stay wherever it is you think you belong."

She didn't say it outright, but the implication was clear: *It's not here.*

I stayed silent, leaning against the opposite wall and closing my eyes, trying to shut out the noise both outside and in my head. The crowd out there would move on eventually. They always did. And yet, I couldn't help but wonder if they'd still be interested if they saw the real me—the me that wasn't a polished, smiling persona crafted for the cameras. Probably not.

Anna broke the silence. "You're lucky I don't like chaos."

I opened my eyes, glancing at her. She was leaning against the doorframe, arms loosely crossed, her messy bun a little crooked. Somehow it worked. Her olive skin had a warm, golden glow, and her lips, even pressed together in an unimpressed line, looked soft. She was beautiful, the kind of pretty that made you notice, whether you wanted to or not.

"What do you mean by chaos?" I asked.

"You. Keeping your secret." She shrugged. "It's not for you. It's because I don't want a circus in Muses. This place is crazy enough without a mob scene."

I smirked faintly despite myself. "Well, thanks... for not letting it turn into one."

She shrugged again, but her gaze lingered on me for a beat longer before she looked away. "Just don't make it a habit, okay?"

I nodded, leaning my head back against the wall. "I'll try not to." I couldn't stop looking at her. Her presence was impossible to ignore.

The noise from the crowd outside remained a low hum, but I tried to focus on anything else, waiting for the chaos to die down and trying not to think about how I'd ended up in this.

3

ANNA

WHAT WAS LUKE FISHER, world-famous movie star, doing in New Orleans? And why was he standing in front of me, staring at me with those impossibly blue eyes that made women across the globe swoon?

I'd watched him win the hand of Lady Elizabeth and the hearts of women around the world, playing Sir Nigel in the historical epic *The Crown and the Anvil*. He'd portrayed a royal pretending to be a blacksmith, which explained his silly cover story at the bar. No wonder his English accent was flawless. There wasn't a woman alive who could forget that iconic scene where, to solve some period-appropriate dilemma, he had to spontaneously strip down and take a dramatic swim in a lake.

But for me, his breakout role in *The Boyfriend Test* had been even more unforgettable. That was the movie that not only skyrocketed his fame but also set an impossibly high standard for boyfriends everywhere. In the film, he embodied every romantic dream. In every scene, whether he was orchestrating a moonlit rooftop dinner or serenading his love with a ballad he wrote just for her, he embodied the perfect boyfriend. Watching him in that movie, you couldn't help but wish for a love story just like it, knowing full well that real life could never compare.

And yet real life had hit him back—hard. Even *he* hadn't passed the Boyfriend Test in the end. After all, movie star Sienna Hart had broken his heart in front of the entire world.

I stared at him, taking in the features that had been splashed across movie posters and magazine covers for years.

But as I looked closer, I realized he wasn't perfect. There was a small scar at his hairline, faint but visible. Freckles dotted the bridge of his nose. Freckles. I'd never noticed those before, even in high definition. He must use makeup to hide them. And then there were his sunglasses—slightly crooked and scratched across one lens, like they'd been hastily tossed into the bottom of a bag. The kind of tiny, real-world imperfection that would make any Hollywood handler cringe.

Somehow, though, all those flaws didn't detract from his looks. If anything, they made him more compelling, more human.

Grrrrr. I didn't want him to be more human, more relatable. He'd been a complete jerk about New Orleans. Loud, sticky, potholes, *blah, blah, blah.* Who even insults a city like that? It's like insulting someone's kid. He didn't want to be in the best city in the world, and, honestly, the feeling was mutual. He could take his swoon-worthy blue eyes and perfectly tousled blonde hair and leave. The sooner, the better.

"Are you going to keep glaring at me?" he asked, "or are you going to say something?"

Oh, great. It was as if he could read my mind. "I'm not glaring," I shot back, crossing my arms. "I'm thinking."

"Well, don't hurt yourself," he muttered, running a hand through his annoyingly perfect hair.

I rolled my eyes. "You're unbelievable."

A sudden swell of noise and a high-pitched squeal from outside the door caught my attention. The chatter and laughter from the bar had grown louder, with a new edge of excitement.

Luke's blue eyes darted to the door, then back to me. "I need to get me out of here," he said, his voice lower now, laced with desperation. "No one can know I'm in New Orleans. If word gets out..." He exhaled, then looked at his phone. "I texted my bodyguards, and they're waiting in a car outside. I'll have them come in and escort me out. Quietly."

My jaw tightened. This guy. *This guy.* I could let him fend for himself. I could tell Marie Antoinette exactly who he was and let her spill the beans to the rowdy crowd outside. I'd bet they'd love a selfie with Hollywood's golden boy. It would serve him right after all the insults about New Orleans.

But something about him made me take pity on him. Maybe it was the flicker of desperation in those gorgeous blue eyes.

"Luke, the only way out of this bar is the front door. If you bring in suited-up bodyguards to escort you out of here, everyone will know it's you. If I'm going to help you, we're doing this my way."

He tilted his head, eyes narrowing. "Your way?"

I held up a hand before he could repeat something stupid about my city. "Here's the deal. You'll have to be quick and avoid anyone who might recognize you. Can you manage that?"

"Do I look incapable of sneaking out of a bar?" His voice was full of disdain.

I gave him, his baseball cap, and his Ray-Bans a pointed look. "You're dressed like you're trying to avoid the paparazzi while also screaming, 'Look at me.' So, yeah, you look incapable."

He frowned. "I thought wearing a cap and sunglasses would be enough."

"It's not."

He opened his mouth to argue but seemed to think better of it. "Fine," he muttered. "What's your brilliant plan, then?"

I crossed the room and pulled open the bar's lost-and-found box. "You're about to become the most fabulous Bourbon Street fashionista anyone's ever seen. Don't thank me too quickly."

I rummaged through the box, pulling out a mishmash of abandoned accessories. One by one, I laid them out on the desk with a flourish. "Let's see." I held up a purple, green, and gold sequined jacket. "This is a start." I tossed it at him, and he caught it reluctantly.

"Are you serious?" he asked, looking at the jacket like it might bite him.

"Very serious." I held up the next item: a floppy straw hat with a giant, fake sunflower pinned to the brim. "This screams 'Bourbon Street tourist.'"

"You've got to be kidding me."

"Oh, we're just getting started." I yanked out a pair of giant, glittery flamingo-shaped sunglasses. "These are non-negotiable."

Before he could protest, I threw a feather boa over his shoulder and layered him with at least fifty strands of brightly colored Mardi Gras beads. By the time I was done, the beads almost entirely obscured his face, and the hat dipped low enough to hide his eyes.

I stepped back to admire my handiwork, biting the inside of my cheek to keep from laughing. "Perfect. No one will recognize you."

"I look like I belong in a parade," he grumbled, adjusting the boa.

"That's the point." I stifled a giggle. "Now, you can walk right past everyone in the bar, and they'll think you're just another overzealous tourist who lost their group. Trust me, you'll blend right in."

He sighed, glancing down at himself. "This is ridiculous."

"This is New Orleans," I shot back. "Are you ready to escape or what?"

He groaned but nodded. "Fine. Let's get this over with."

I peeked out the door, making sure the coast was clear. The crowd was still rowdy, but most people were preoccupied with their drinks and each other. I motioned for him to follow, and we weaved our way past the crowd and out the front door.

As he stepped into the street, he turned back to me, the feather boa swaying with every movement. "You have a cruel sense of humor." His voice dripped with reluctant gratitude.

I smirked, crossing my arms. "You're welcome. Get in your getaway car before someone spots you."

He muttered something under his breath, adjusted the floppy hat, and strode toward a sleek black SUV that was idling on the street.

The ridiculous outfit didn't quite diminish his natural air of confidence, though the beads clinking around his neck made it hard to take him seriously.

The car door opened, and he climbed in without a backward glance. The SUV pulled away smoothly, leaving only the faint echo of the engine behind.

For a moment, I stood there, leaning against the doorframe and shaking my head.

4

LUKE

I SANK into the plush leather seat of my SUV and pulled off the absurdly oversized feather boa.

From the front seat, Hal, one of my bodyguards, turned halfway around, trying—and failing—to hide his smirk. "So, uh... interesting look you've got going on there, boss. New character research?"

Tom, the driver, snorted. "Yeah, what is your next role exactly, Mardi Gras king or a guy who lost a bet?"

I sighed, glaring at the back of Tom's head. "Very funny. You two done?"

Hal grinned. "You're the one who walked out looking like a parade float, mate."

I leaned my head back, groaning. "Blame the waitress. She was the one who came up with the disguise."

Tom shot me a glance in the rearview mirror. "Maybe you should hire her as your stylist."

Tom and Hal were the best at what they did: keeping me safe. Even if I didn't always make it easy.

I'd been in New Orleans for days, and I was going stir crazy. Tonight, I'd snuck out in the hopes of seeing Mrs. Brodie, which led to that near-meltdown with the bar crowd. But at least they didn't give me lectures. Even if they liked to joke at my expense.

I ignored them, staring out the window as we turned onto a quieter street. Topher's mansion was only a few blocks away. The idea of finally peeling off this ridiculous outfit and retreating into solitude should have been comforting, but I couldn't shake the thought of her, Anna.

She wasn't like anyone I'd met before. Most people either fawned over me or tiptoed around me. But Anna? She didn't care. She talked back, rolled her eyes, and seemed completely unimpressed with the idea of me.

I didn't like it.

But her quick thinking that got me out of the bar without causing a stampede? I had to admit, I was grudgingly impressed. Not many people could make that happen.

Still, it didn't matter. I'd never see her again. It was fine. Great, even.

The SUV rolled to a stop in the circular driveway of Topher's mansion, the oversized gates clicking shut behind us. The house loomed ahead, a Southern colonial birthday cake of a house, the kind of place that screamed money and power. I climbed out of the car, clutching the feather boa in one hand and the goofy sunglasses in another.

As I made my way up the front steps, I dialed my best friend Topher. He picked up on the second ring, his voice tinged with amusement.

"Luke," he said, dragging out my name, "Hal just texted me a photo of your 'disguise.' What, are you preparing for a second career as a Bourbon Street mascot?"

I groaned, yanking open the front door. "Tell Hal I'm going to fire him. And for your information, it was the waitress's idea. This getup helped me blend in so I could get out of there. Your mom wasn't at Muses, by the way. I guess she'd just left."

"Well, that waitress made sure you certainly blended into something," Topher replied, laughter in his voice. "You could start a side hustle as a human parade float."

I shoved the door open, stepping into the sprawling entryway. The place was pristine, of course, with perfectly arranged art pieces and furniture that looked like no one had ever dared sit on it. "If you're done mocking me, maybe you could tell me how I'm supposed to survive this circus."

Topher didn't miss a beat. "The same way you always do—by pretending you love the attention and smile for the cameras."

"Yeah, except the whole point of this exile is to avoid the cameras," I shot back, heading for the kitchen.

Topher's voice shifted into what I'd dubbed his *Wall Street Warrior* tone, the one he used when closing a deal. "Look, you're lucky the studio didn't pull your contract after you punched Dylan. They're giving you this chance to lie low and prove you're more than just a tabloid headline. And any time you're about to blow your cover, think about that role in the new Gerald Fargo movie. It's exactly what you want—a meaty part that could redefine your career. But you've got to show them you've got depth. And that means keeping your cool."

Directors saw me as the poster boy, as Hollywood's favorite heartthrob. It wasn't hard to get roles; they lined up for me. But they were all the same role, for a charming, shallow, pretty face. I wanted more. I *needed* audiences to see that I understood real stories, real pain, real depth.

I pulled a bottle of water from the fridge and pressed it to my forehead. "I'm keeping my cool," I muttered.

"Are you? Because, from what I hear, you're dressed like a budget Mardi Gras clown."

"Says the guy who thinks work-life balance is rowing on an erg machine between conference calls."

"Hey, that erg machine keeps me fit." He was dead serious. "Seven hours of sleep per week, and I'm still outperforming everyone in the game. Efficiency is key, my friend."

I laughed despite myself. Topher and I had been best friends since our college days at Brown, where we'd both suffered through endless rowing practices and learned to survive on sheer willpower and caffeine. He'd taken that discipline and turned it into a billion-dollar empire, making him some wunderkind genius in the business world. I, on the other hand, had taken my talents straight to Hollywood.

"Toph, you're one missed nap away from a total meltdown."

"Maybe, but I'm too rich to care," he joked. "Now, about this waitress. What was her name again?"

I hesitated, gripping the bottle a little tighter. "Anna."

"Wait, *Anna Amato*?" Topher's voice perked up, practically crackling with intrigue. "Gorgeous, brown hair, outspoken?"

I couldn't help but smirk. "Outspoken? She could give a TED Talk on being outspoken."

Topher continued, undeterred. "Everyone was into Anna back in high school. She was that brainy, outspoken girl who didn't even realize how cool she was. And you? You're just the latest in a long line, my friend. Honestly, it would be a nice change from the type of women you've been dating since your ego—sorry, I mean your *career* —took off."

"I'm sick of the type of women I've been dating," I blurted before I could stop myself. The admission hung in the air for a second, so I scrambled to clarify. "But for clarity's sake, I'm not interested in Anna."

"Oh, sure. I totally believe you," Topher said, his voice dripping with mock sincerity. His tone softened slightly. "Look, man. I know things with Sienna wrecked you more than you let on, but I don't want Anna to be your rebound. She's been hurt before, and she's too sweet to be toyed with. Also, she's from a big New Orleans family, and I'd prefer not to have a dozen of her cousins gunning for me."

She'd been hurt before... I wondered how, but then shoved the question away. "As I said, *not interested*. And I *will* figure out how to play this role."

"Good," Topher replied, the faint clatter of a keyboard in the background, "because the studio's watching. If you can't figure out how to play a real person who struggles in life, they'll find someone else who can. Get to know some real people. This is your shot. Don't blow it."

The line went dead, and I stood there staring out at the moonlit backyard.

A real person. Right.

The role was a calculated risk. I would be playing a wealthy man who returns to his small hometown to serve court-mandated community service after a public scandal costs him his wealth and his family. It was the kind of story that would force an audience to see me as something other than a headline. *If* I could pull it off.

Success came easily to me. Maybe too easily. I never slept on a couch. I never wondered where my next meal was going to come from. Stardom felt like destiny rather than a hard-earned ascent. That meant I skipped the part where real people grow through struggle, and I didn't understand them.

And that was the problem. I didn't know anything about being a real person. A person who worked two jobs to make ends meet, who had no time for fame or ego. People would look at me and see nothing but another spoiled, rich jerk trying to play their lives like a role.

Topher was right. I'd spent too long surrounded by handlers, too insulated in my Hollywood bubble to understand what real struggle even *looked* like. And now I was supposed to become a guy who shoveled dirt, patched fences, and shook hands with neighbors.

I let out a long breath, pressing my forehead to the cool glass. *Get to know real people.* Easier said than done.

This exile was going to be unbearable. But if I wanted to save my career, I'd have to start somewhere. And that somewhere, apparently, was here.

5

ANNA

LIVING in a tiny cottage on the grounds of a sprawling estate wasn't exactly the worst outcome for someone teetering on the edge of failure.

However, it was my third day there, and for all the charm and postcard-perfect scenery, I still couldn't write. Not a word.

It turns out that writer's block isn't picky. It doesn't care that you've fled to an impossibly cute cottage. It doesn't care that no little nieces are banging on your door demanding snacks or that you're not vacuuming instead of working. Writer's block follows you, stubborn and smug, no matter how far you run or how many distractions you leave behind.

I'd tried everything the experts recommended. Scribbling whatever came to mind to get the words flowing. Writing prompts. I took walks, hoping the steady rhythm of my footsteps would unlock some brilliant idea. I meditated because, apparently, clearing your mind is supposed to make room for creativity, though all it did was make me acutely aware of how quiet my brain actually was. I even tried the age-old trick of switching to pen and paper, thinking maybe the tactile experience of writing would somehow coax the words out. It didn't.

I pushed away from the cute little desk, frustration bubbling, and wandered to the big picture window. Maybe the grounds outside would inspire me. Or at least give me a moment to clear my head.

The view offered more than I expected.

There was Topher's pool, glittering under the midday sun. My pool too, technically, for as long as I was staying here. And then I saw him.

The mystery guest.

Mrs. Brodie had said he was a "friend of Topher's" staying at the mansion for a month or so. No hints about who he was, but the luxury SUV in the driveway and the careful secrecy surrounding his presence told me he was someone important.

He was swimming, sleek and effortless. And then, as if on cue, he climbed out of the pool, his back to me.

Water streamed down his shoulders and muscled back. His muscles may well have been sculpted by an artist who took their job very, *very* seriously.

His swim trunks clung low on his hips, droplets falling lazily from the hem as he reached for a towel. The sun caught his golden skin just right. His blonde hair was plastered to his neck, sending tiny rivulets of water running down his corded throat.

I should've looked away. I really should've. But my brain stalled, and I stood there frozen, clutching my coffee like a lifeline.

Finally, I snapped out of it. What was I doing? Peeking out from behind glass like some creeper? No. I was better than this.

With a deep breath, I set my coffee on the windowsill and headed outside. The air hit me like a wall, thick and warm, carrying the scent of chlorine and jasmine. As I rounded the corner, he was toweling off, his head dipped forward.

"Hi." My voice was steady, but my pulse was not.

He glanced up, his eyes meeting mine. They were bluer than the pool behind him, piercing in a way that made it impossible to look away.

My brain tried—and failed—to process what my eyes were seeing.

It was him. *Luke Fisher.*

World-famous movie star Luke Fisher.

The smug jerk who'd insulted New Orleans, my entire existence, and everything I held dear four nights ago.

"You've got to be kidding me," I muttered.

His reaction wasn't much friendlier. His eyebrows shot up as recognition dawned. "You?"

I'd seen him on screen up close, in high definition, so many times, that it felt almost surreal for him to be standing there, in front of me, staring *back* at me with those beautiful blue eyes. The kind of eyes that could make you forget your own name if you weren't careful.

And then, in that very recognizable, very sexy, world-famous movie star voice, Luke Fisher said, "Are you stalking me?"

My mouth clamped shut. *The nerve of him.* Did he think he owned the place? Did he think everyone wandered around in his orbit, just waiting to be graced with his presence? I straightened, summoning every ounce of righteous anger I could muster.

"No, I'm not stalking you. I'm staying in the cottage. I heard someone in the pool, and I came by to say hello. Then I saw your body—I mean, I saw *somebody.*" My cheeks burned as I stumbled over the words, one clumsy syllable at a time. "Anyway, what are *you* doing here? I thought a friend of Topher's was staying here."

He raised an eyebrow, like he couldn't believe someone didn't know. "I'm the friend. Topher and I went to Brown together."

Oh. Wow. Okay. That was... a lot to process.

Luke Fisher—the *actual* Luke Fisher—was standing there, dripping water, looking like he belonged on the cover of a magazine even while trying to accuse me of stalking him. Apparently, in real life, he was far less charming than in the movies.

"Guess we're neighbors," he said, like it was no big deal.

Neighbors. *Neighbors.*

I blinked at him. Then, at the mansion behind him. And then back at him, because my brain refused to process what it was seeing. This couldn't be real. This had to be some cruel, cosmic joke.

"Small world, huh?" he said, his grin widening like he was thoroughly enjoying the horror etched on my face.

Small world? No. This was a *tiny* world. A shrinking, claustrophobic world where I was now somehow neighbors with *Luke Fisher*.

Panic rose in my chest like a flood. *Leave. Move your feet. Go. Move.*

I forced a smile that felt like it belonged to a hostage. "Right. Well... enjoy your swim. I, uh, have work to do. Very important work."

I turned on my heel, flip-flops smacking far too loudly as I bolted. I needed to go somewhere. Anywhere. Grabbing my keys, I marched to my car, threw myself into the driver's seat, and started the engine like I was escaping a crime scene. I didn't have a plan. I just needed to *move*.

"Where to?" I muttered to myself, pulling out of the driveway. The gas tank warning light blinked on. Perfect. *Fine.* I'd go fill up the car with gas. Filling up the tank was something normal people did, right? Not running. Not fleeing. Just responsible car ownership. I could do that.

And then I'd come right back, because where else was I going to go? I figured I'd be able to sneak in without seeing Luke again.

I sighed as I turned onto the road, gripping the steering wheel like it might steer me away from my mounting embarrassment.

How was I supposed to focus on writing? I was already up against a block so big and high that not even three days in a cute cottage had been able to fix it. It could only get worse knowing I was staying across a yard from a Hollywood heartthrob who thought I was a lunatic stalker.

6

LUKE

I'M NOT USED to women running away from me.

Usually, they're running *toward* me, camera phones out and squealing.

But Anna ran like I'd accused her of grand theft, not stalking. Which, in hindsight, probably wasn't my smoothest opening line.

Never thought I'd see the day when *I* was the one left standing, speechless and stunned. Welcome to rock bottom, Luke.

I wiped water from my face, grabbed the towel I'd left by the pool, and wandered toward the pool house.

A shower sounded good. A little peace before I figured out how to deal with my unexpected "neighbor," who, for some inexplicable reason, had run away from me like she'd seen a mouse.

The inside of the pool house was small but neat. I tossed my towel onto a chair, kicked off my flip-flops, and headed straight for the shower.

The place was stocked with fresh towels and fancy soaps. Nice touch. Probably the housekeeper's doing. Honestly, I respected the effort.

A few minutes later, I stepped out of the bathroom, still damp, wearing just a towel. I headed toward the chair where I'd left my clothes. That's when I noticed it.

The wall.

I froze mid-step.

It was *covered* in paper.

Dozens of sheets of paper, maybe hundreds, pinned in rows like a bizarre art exhibit. I squinted at them, water still dripping off me onto the floor.

"Thank you for your submission..."

"Unfortunately, we are unable to accept..."

It was a *wall* of rejection letters. A sea of polite "no's."

And some that were not so polite. One with a handwritten *P.S.:* "*This gave me flashbacks to high school English. That's not a compliment.*"

A particularly crumpled letter read: *"Your protagonist was certainly unique. I hated him immediately."*

I blinked at the wall, unable to stop myself from reading more. There were rejections for *everything.*

A story about a cursed lighthouse? Rejected. A submission about a girl who fell in love with a ghost pirate? Hard pass. Something described as *"Kafka-esque, but the Russian greats would be rolling in their graves?"* Yep, rejected.

It was a staggering collection of failure. I couldn't tell what type of writing the author specialized in because the genres bounced from romance to dystopian horror to whatever one letter described as *"a bold reimagining of 'Great Expectations'... but with robots? Please don't contact us again."*

I couldn't help but stare. The sheer *volume* of rejection was almost impressive. Whoever the writer was, they'd tried everything, and the universe just kept sending back a firm *no.*

The salutations were missing from the rejection letters, leaving me to wonder who had written these doomed manuscripts. Were they Topher's? He was always full of business plans. But creative writing? Not a chance. My best friend's idea of a gripping story probably involved a spreadsheet showdown and a shocking twist about market trends.

Maybe they belonged to the housekeeper. Could she secretly moonlight as a novelist?

Or Anna. She had the wit to pull off being a writer. But if they were hers, why would she hang up rejection letters in the pool house?

"WHAT are you doing here?"

I spun around. Anna was standing in the doorway, her eyes wide and accusatory.

My infuriatingly judgmental, very real neighbor, holding a coffee cup in her hand. It was shaking slightly, like she couldn't decide whether to throw it at me.

What was I doing there? "Uh... showering?" I gestured to the towel like it wasn't obvious.

Her jaw dropped. "*In my shower?*"

"I thought this was the pool house," I shot back defensively, though I wasn't sure that excuse was helping.

She crossed her arms, her coffee mug wobbling dangerously. "It's *not* the pool house."

I glanced around, taking in the tiny space. The desk, the wall of rejection letters, the distinctly *non*-pool-house vibes, and I blurted, "But it's too small for someone actually to *live* here."

Her eyes narrowed into a glare so sharp I almost took a step back. "Well, someone *does* live here, and you're dripping all over my floor."

I glanced down at the puddle forming beneath me and winced. "Right. Sorry about that."

Her glare could've peeled paint. "Get. Out."

I grabbed my clothes from the chair, backing toward the door like a man escaping an active crime scene. "You've got quite the setup here." I gestured toward the rejection letters. "Are you a writer?"

Her eyes narrowed. "No, I just like collecting rejection letters for fun."

"I didn't mean—"

"Just go," she interrupted, her tone leaving no room for argument.

The door slammed behind me with impressive force, leaving me standing on the porch in a towel, holding my dry clothes and wet swim trunks.

I stared at the door for a second, still not quite sure how things had spiraled so quickly. But as I turned to leave, my eyes flicked back to the cottage, to the wall of rejection letters I'd seen.

Something about it wouldn't let me go. Maybe it was the sheer *volume* of rejections. There was enough to wallpaper a room. Or perhaps it was the determination of someone who'd been told "no" so many times and still got up every morning to try again. But mostly, it was the notes themselves. A theme had started to jump out at me, scribbled in red ink and typed in tidy little platitudes: *"Write what you know."*

I remembered her at the bar, so fiercely protective of New Orleans, a city she'd clearly loved like it was part of her soul. I could still hear her voice, so defiant and dripping with pride. *I would never leave this place.*

It hit me then, hard and sudden: *she's a real person.* Like Topher had told me that I needed to find.

Not someone trying to get something out of me. Not someone who cared about who I was or what I'd done. Just a woman stubbornly chasing a dream that wasn't handing itself over without a fight.

And wasn't that precisely what I was supposed to be doing? Getting to know *real* people? People with grit, stories, and something to say?

I stopped, turning back to the door. This was an opportunity. One I couldn't ignore.

I knocked once, a little too loudly.

The door flew open, and she stared at me with an expression that said she was two seconds from launching her coffee at my face. *"What now?"*

"I have a proposition for you."

Her eyes narrowed, suspicious. "If it involves you showering here again, the answer is no."

"Relax." I held up my hands in surrender. "I've got an idea you might like."

She stared at me, torn between curiosity and her apparent desire to slam the door.

"Just hear me out," I said quickly. "You're a writer. You've got rejection letters from half the country telling you to 'write what you know,' and I know for a fact you know this city better than anyone."

She blinked, clearly caught off guard. "And?"

"And for my next movie role, I need to get to know *real* people. Real stories, real places. If you act as my tour guide and help me see this city the way you do, maybe you'll be inspired, too. Then you'll be able to write what you know about: *this city.*"

She stared at me. "You think dragging you around New Orleans is somehow going to help *me*?"

I shrugged, smirking just enough to keep it light. "It's worth a shot. You clearly love this place. Maybe you need a reminder of why it's worth writing about."

Her lips pressed into a thin line like she was considering all the ways that this could blow up in her face.

"Of course," I added, "I'll have to be in disguise. Can't exactly go wandering around looking like, well... me."

Something shifted in her expression. Her eyes narrowed, but not in anger this time. It was almost like inspiration. Like I'd just handed her a plot twist she hadn't seen coming.

And that's when I knew I had her convinced.

7

ANNA

IT'S a maxim every writer knows: when inspiration strikes, don't ignore it.

And it struck—right there in the doorway of the cottage, standing across from a movie star wearing only a towel. It was the first spark of inspiration I'd felt in months.

"Fine." I pointed my coffee mug at Luke as if it were a weapon. "I'll show you around New Orleans."

He looked entirely too pleased with himself. "See? I knew you'd come around."

I didn't bother telling him that what I'd *actually* write about wasn't the city. No way. Because standing there, dripping water onto the ground, and talking about disguises, this golden god was basically begging to be turned into a character. Into the character of a man who didn't want anyone to know who he really was.

Let him think he'd convinced me to write some love letter to New Orleans. That was fine. I'd write my story. The one I didn't even know I'd been waiting for until now.

This would be the end of my writer's block. And if I had to show around a conceited movie star to make it happen, well, so be it.

Luke grinned that perfect smile, and I tilted my head, feigning indifference. "Meet me at the front gate tomorrow morning."

"Fine," I said. "Tomorrow. And please wear clothes." I shut the door before he could respond, but I couldn't help smiling as I turned away. Maybe this deal wouldn't be such a disaster after all.

By the time I arrived at Muses for my shift that night, my brain was still tangled up in the possibility of writing about Luke Fisher. A fictional Luke Fisher, of course.

The warm glow of Muses' neon sign lit up the sidewalk, and as I pushed open the door, the familiar scent of citrus cleaner, stale beer, and a hint of something smoky hit me like a weirdly comforting slap. Behind the bar stood Marie Antoinette, red hair piled on top of her head in an elaborate bun, with a few curls escaping to frame her face. She was wearing a T-shirt that read "Let Them Drink Rum" in sparkly gold letters.

"Anna Banana," she called, her Louisiana drawl rolling out as she slid a fresh cocktail to one of the regulars. "You're late."

I glanced at the clock and frowned. "It's 6:02."

My friend leaned over the bar, narrowing her cat-like green eyes. "Exactly. That's two minutes of valuable gossip time wasted. Now, tell me everything about the mysterious Englishman. What did you say his name was? Nigel... Brandywine?"

I grabbed an apron from behind the bar. "Pimmington."

She froze mid-motion, her hand clutching a shaker. She stared at me like I'd just told her the ghost of Marie Laveau was mixing drinks in the back room. "Pimmington? What is he, the long-lost heir to the Pimm's Cup empire?"

"Pretty sure he's just a regular guy," I lied, though my voice wavered slightly. "Well, sort of regular."

She cocked her head. "*Sort of?* Oh no, Anna Banana, you don't get to drop breadcrumbs like that and not deliver the full loaf."

I ducked my head, pretending to focus on organizing the glasses behind the bar. My cheeks burned at the thought of Marie Antoinette finding out the truth. She'd probably declare it the most significant scandal to hit New Orleans since the pirate Lafitte smuggled goods into the French Quarter.

"Nothing to spill," I said quickly, waving her off. "Hey, are you still doing those ghost tours in the Quarter?"

Her eyes narrowed, but her lips twitched like she was trying not to smile. "Why do you ask? Thinking of joining my merry band of haunted historians?"

I smirked and shook my head. "No, just curious. What's the weirdest thing that's ever happened on one of your tours?"

Her entire demeanor shifted, her green eyes lighting up as she leaned on the bar. "Oh, baby, where do I even start?" Her drawl practically dripped with drama. "There was the guy who claimed a ghost slapped him on the butt outside Lafitte's Blacksmith Shop. He yelped so loudly, I thought he saw a real banshee. Then there was the tourist who fainted after swearing she saw Marie Laveau herself crossing the street. And my all-time favorite? The guy who tried to bribe me into 'summoning a ghost' for his girlfriend. He pulled out a hundred-dollar bill and said, 'Just make something float or something.' 'Honey,' I told him, 'This is New Orleans, not Hogwarts.'"

I laughed, wiping down the bar. "You're making that up."

She raised a perfectly arched eyebrow. "Darlin', I don't have to. The truth in this town is stranger than fiction." She tilted her head, giving me that all-knowing tour guide look. "Speaking of truth, what are you digging for? You didn't just ask about my stories for fun."

I deflected with a shrug. "What's the most popular tour you lead these days? Still the spooky stuff?"

"Ghosts always sell." She straightened her posture, as if she were addressing a crowd. "But the real money's in the scandals-and-secrets tours. People love dirty laundry. Whether it's old-money feuds, cursed inheritances, or dueling politicians. I tell them about a society belle sneaking off with her lover while her husband's throwing a masquerade ball, and suddenly everyone's hanging on my every word."

I nodded, pretending to focus on restocking cocktail napkins. "So, if someone's new to New Orleans, what would you tell them to check out first? You know, if they're more into people-watching than scandals or ghosts?"

She didn't miss a beat. "The French Market." She twirled a bottle of rum like a baton. "If you want to see New Orleans in all its messy, colorful glory, go there. You'll see it all—the locals, the tourists, the artists, the street performers, and, of course, the food. You'll get a little bit of everything, like Cajun spices, Creole crafts, and enough personality to fill a riverboat."

"That's a good tip," I admitted, tucking the idea away in my mental notebook.

She leaned closer, her grin widening. "You thinking of taking this Pimmington fella there? You know, showing him the *real* New Orleans?"

I choked on a laugh. "Absolutely not. He's not exactly French Market material."

She laughed, too, shaking her head. "Honey, everyone's French Market material."

I smiled, my mind still spinning with possibilities. Marie Antoinette didn't know it, but she'd just handed me exactly what I needed.

8

LUKE

WHY DID I think this would be a good idea?

I stared at my reflection in the bathroom mirror while I waited for Anna to ring the doorbell. I had to admit, I'd outdone myself. The disguise was perfect. A battered straw fedora tilted just so, dark aviators covering half my face, and a thrift-store Hawaiian shirt that screamed, *"I'm definitely not famous."* That, paired with khaki shorts and flip-flops, and I was practically unrecognizable. Just another middle-aged dad on vacation.

As soon as Anna spotted me, her eyes flicked up and down, and a smirk tugged at the corner of her mouth. She tilted her head as she took in the full glory of my disguise.

"You look like you just stepped off a Bourbon Street party bus. You'll fit right in. Everyone'll think you're a tourist here for a bachelor party."

I stared at her, unsure if she was serious. "Is that a compliment or an insult?" I asked, tugging at the collar of my Hawaiian shirt.

"It's an observation. But"—she gave me a pointed look—"we're not going with your bodyguards."

"Yes, we are." That wasn't negotiable.

She rolled her eyes. "This is New Orleans. They'll stand out more than you do."

"They'll be inconspicuous," I argued, pulling out my phone to text them.

"Inconspicuous? They're built like tanks. You'll get *more* attention with them trailing behind you."

"They're not just for show. If something goes sideways, they can handle it. Crowds getting too close? Fans figuring out who I am? These guys get me out of sticky situations before they escalate."

Anna raised an eyebrow. "Do you think people are going to swarm you at the French Market? This isn't a red carpet."

"You'd be surprised. I've been mobbed at a gas station before. One photo gets out, and it's chaos. Trust me, these guys have saved me from more than one awkward escape. And they're trained to be subtle."

Anna shook her head, slinging her bag over her shoulder. "Fine. Bring your tanks. But don't say I didn't warn you when everyone in the market starts whispering about the linebacker squad shadowing Hawaiian Shirt Guy."

AN HOUR LATER, Anna and I stood at the edge of the French Market, the scent of fried dough and spice wafting through the air. Hal and Tom trailed behind us. They wore cheap sunglasses and held café au lait cups as props.

"See?" I gestured toward them. "Totally inconspicuous."

"If you think two guys the size of refrigerators wearing 'I Heart Bourbon Street' T-shirts are inconspicuous, we need to talk."

I ignored her, focusing on the market ahead of me. It was a feast for the senses. Colorful stalls overflowed with beads, paintings, and food; the buzz of voices mingled with the wail of a saxophone; and the rich aroma of pralines mixed with the tang of hot sauce.

Anna weaved through it all like she owned the place. I followed behind, trying to look as casual as possible. That's when I saw someone pointing.

A woman near a booth of hand-painted masks was nudging her friend, her eyes fixed on me. My pulse spiked.

"They're pointing," I hissed to Anna, my voice low.

She barely glanced at them. "They're pointing at the masks being sold over there. Relax."

"No," I insisted, leaning slightly closer to her. "They're pointing at me."

Anna stopped walking, her hands on her hips. "Luke, you're wearing sunglasses that could double as ski goggles and a hat that looks like you bought it on Canal Street five minutes ago. No one thinks you're famous. They think you're a lost tourist."

But I couldn't shake the feeling. Another nudge from the woman, followed by another glance in my direction. I had to act. I pretended to browse a display of decorative vases at the nearest stall.

The problem? These vases were balanced precariously on a rickety wooden table.

The second my arm brushed the edge, the whole display wobbled. My attempt to steady it only made things worse, and in slow-motion horror, I watched as one vase toppled, setting off a chain reaction that ended with half the table's contents shattering on the ground—probably a dozen vases.

Anna whipped around at the sound of breaking pottery. "Oh my gosh," she muttered, rushing back to the stall. Hal and Tom were close behind.

The vendor was a wiry older man with a weathered face. He glared at the destruction, his jaw tightening. "What in the—"

"I've got it covered," I said quickly, holding up a hand. "Hal. Tom."

Hal stepped forward. "Yes?"

"Pay him," I whispered, gesturing to the vendor, whose face hardened, his arms tight over his chest. "Cover everything. Whatever it costs."

The vendor's eyebrows shot up. "Whatever it costs, huh?" He let the words hang in the air like a challenge, his weathered face betraying no amusement.

Anna groaned audibly, dragging her hands down her face. "What a disaster," she muttered before turning to the vendor. "I'm so sorry about this."

Hal stepped forward with his wallet, looking as awkward as someone who had just walked into the middle of a family argument. "Uh, how much are we talking about here?"

The vendor tilted his head. "These were hand-painted vases. Genuine work by a local artist. Let's say... a hundred bucks each." He gave a slow, deliberate shrug. "That would be a steal."

Anna winced, crouched, and picked up one of the unbroken shards. She flipped it over. "Made in China," she read flatly. "Local artist, huh? I wouldn't pay more than twenty dollars per vase. And that's generous."

Hal froze, a credit card suspended in the charged air between them. "Sooo... what do I do?"

"It's fine," I said quickly. "One hundred dollars a vase is fine."

Anna shot me a look that could've turned me to stone. "Are you serious? You're just going to let him make up a number?"

"It's not like we have time to haggle," I said, glancing around nervously. The last thing I needed was for this little incident to become an internet sensation. I turned back to the vendor, who was leaning on his stall with a smirk, enjoying the show. "What's the damage?" I asked, keeping my tone casual.

"Two thousand," the vendor replied without missing a beat, folding his arms.

"Dollars? Two thousand dollars?" Anna looked like she was going to explode.

"Done." I turned to Hal. "Give him the card."

Anna's jaw dropped. "You're just going to hand over two grand like it's nothing?"

I shrugged. "I've spent more on a pair of shoes."

The vendor chuckled, swiping the credit card with a flourish. "Pleasure doing business, mister...?"

"Doesn't matter." I looked around to make sure no one was getting too curious.

As we walked away, the tension between Anna and me was palpable. I couldn't figure out why she was so upset. The vendor had probably made enough to pack up his table for the day. She spoke first.

"You didn't have to just throw money at the situation," Anna said under her breath, not looking at me.

"I fixed it, didn't I?"

Anna straightened, her expression somewhere between exasperation and resignation. "Next time, try not to destroy half the stall."

"Next time," I said, half-joking, "I'll shop online."

Her eyes narrowed, slicing through me like a warning. "This isn't a joke. You can't just buy your way out of everything. People here care about authenticity. If you keep this up, you're going to stick out like a sore thumb."

"Fine. I'll... try harder."

"Good." She was already walking away from me.

We walked on, passing a street performer juggling flaming batons while a small crowd cheered him on. Anna tossed a few dollars into his hat without breaking stride, her movements natural and uncalculated.

I wondered how she made it look so easy. For her, being part of this city seemed effortless, like breathing. For me, it felt like trying to dance to a rhythm I couldn't hear.

Finally, I broke the silence. "How much do you think those vases were actually worth?"

Anna snorted, shaking her head. "Not two thousand dollars, that's for sure."

I couldn't help but smile, even as the tension lingered. "Guess I overpaid, huh?"

"You think?" she shot back, a hint of a smile tugging at her lips.

I chuckled. "I'll let you handle negotiations from now on. Can you tell me more about this place?"

The French Market sprawled out before us, a kaleidoscope of

color, sound, and smells. Anna walked a step ahead, her voice carrying just enough over the din of the crowd to reach me.

"It's the oldest public market in the country." She glanced back to see if I was paying attention. "It's been around since the 1700s. Originally, it was a Native American trading post. Over the years, it's been everything from a butchers' market to a bazaar selling spices and coffee."

"And now?" I sidestepped a man selling feathered masks.

"As you can see, now it's a mix of everything. You can find anything here if you look hard enough."

We stopped near a stall selling colorful handmade pottery when I caught someone staring at me. A young couple, holding iced coffees and wearing matching sun hats, exchanged whispers before one of them pointed right at me. And they weren't subtle about it.

My stomach dropped. My heart picked up speed. They recognized me. The couple approached, and I braced myself. Here it comes. The awkward smile. The sheepish, "Are you...?" And then the inevitable selfie request.

"Excuse me," the woman said, her voice polite.

I gave a tight smile. "Yes, I am."

She looked confused for a second. "Uh, do you know how to get to Frenchmen Street from here?" she asked.

I blinked. "What?"

She tilted her head. "Frenchmen Street? We heard it's got great live music."

"Oh!" Relief washed over me so fast I almost laughed. They didn't recognize me. They thought I was a local. I could do this.

I straightened, trying to play it cool. "Yeah, absolutely. Frenchmen Street. Super close."

Or not super close. I had no idea where it was.

"So, uh, you just head that way." I pointed in the general direction of what I hoped was north, "Take a left. Or maybe it's a right. You'll see it. Can't miss it."

The couple exchanged a confused glance. Anna stepped in.

"Actually," she said, her voice cutting through my nonsense like a hot knife through butter, "Frenchmen is a bit farther. Go down Decatur, and you'll hit Esplanade. Turn left, and it's a few blocks up."

The couple looked relieved. "Thank you so much."

Before they could leave, I added, "And if you make it to Frenchmen without melting into a puddle, consider yourselves lucky."

Anna's head wheeled toward me, her expression caught between a raised eyebrow and a smirk. "Really?" she muttered under her breath.

The couple gave an awkward laugh and hurried off, leaving me with Anna's eyes narrowing slightly in my direction, though I could see the faintest twitch of a smile on her lips.

"What?" I said, lifting my hands in mock innocence. "It's hot enough out here to cook an egg on the sidewalk. I'm just being honest."

She shook her head, her expression hovering somewhere between exasperation and begrudging amusement. "Honest? You're just proving you can't help but comment on everything."

"Hey," I shot back, falling into step beside her again, "they'll thank me when they don't pass out on the way."

She rolled her eyes but didn't press the issue. For a second, I almost thought I'd done something right. Until we passed a hot sauce stall, and inspiration struck.

Normal people tried things, right? They were adventurous. Adventurous was real.

"I'll take your hottest sauce." I puffed up like a guy who knew what he was doing.

The vendor grinned. "Someone's feeling brave."

Anna's arms were crossed across her chest. "He's not brave. He's foolish." To me, she said, "Don't do it."

"Watch and learn." I grabbed a cracker loaded with fiery red sauce.

The second the hot sauce touched my tongue, my brain short-circuited. Every nerve in my mouth lit up like a fire alarm, and my lungs betrayed me by demanding air in loud, desperate coughs. My eyes watered, and I'm sure my face turned a shade that should only exist on stop signs.

Anna handed me a bottle of water. "You're trying way too hard."

I sipped my water, still trying to cool my burning mouth. "What's that supposed to mean?" I felt myself getting defensive.

"Everything about you screams 'performance.' You need to be real."

"I'm not performing." But deep down, wasn't I? The charm and confidence were all a mask. People liked that version of me, the one who always seemed sure of himself. As for the real me? Even I wasn't sure there was much worth liking. It was easier to stick to the act and let everyone believe in it.

Anna turned to me, her expression unreadable. "Time to go." She started walking without waiting for me to follow.

I stared after her, catching the edge of her annoyance in her voice. This was not going well.

9

ANNA

WHY HAD I agreed to this?

I guess it was because I thought playing tour guide to a movie star would jump-start my writing career. Well, that plan had gone down in flames faster than Luke had after a single drop of hot sauce.

I stopped walking and glanced back at him, now doubled over, wheezing and attempting to down a bottle of water like it was his lifeline. His Hawaiian shirt was rumpled, his straw hat sat at a ridiculous angle, and sweat poured down his face as if he'd just run a marathon.

I could already see the opening of my novel. It would be a thinly veiled fictionalized account of a movie star in disguise, trying to blend in among regular people. Except the whole premise would collapse if my protagonist did what Luke was doing now: loudly drawing attention to himself with every step, mimicking locals as if he were auditioning for a sketch comedy show. Somehow, he managed to look more conspicuous in his attempt to hide than if he'd just strolled in wearing a tuxedo.

No one would believe it. I mean, I was living it, and I couldn't believe it.

I guess I would have to find another topic to write about. I couldn't get rejected again. I don't think I could take it.

I walked back to him. And instead of focusing on my failures, I focused on what was right in front of me. I folded my arms. "Let me see if I've got this straight. Your idea of blending in was to wear *that* shirt, take down a vendor's stall, lead some tourists astray, and guzzle the hottest hot sauce in town?"

Luke, his face still red, managed to croak, "I was... embracing the culture."

"You were embarrassing the culture."

He opened his mouth to defend himself, but I cut him off. "And seriously? Dropping two thousand dollars like it was confetti at a parade? While so many people around us are struggling?"

He blinked, caught off guard.

His bodyguard named Hal stepped forward, concern etched on his otherwise stoic face. "Boss, you okay?" The man, who looked like he could bench-press a car, held out a monogrammed handkerchief. "You're sweating like you're auditioning for *Survivor*."

The second bodyguard, Tom, balancing a comically small café au lait in one massive hand, nodded in agreement. "You should've stuck to the mild sauce. Heck, I think you're more of a 'lemon pepper' guy."

Luke shot them both a withering look. "I don't pay you to critique my spice tolerance."

"That's a shame," I muttered under my breath. "You might get your money's worth."

Luke straightened, likely trying to salvage what was left of his dignity. His face was still an alarming shade of crimson, and his eyes were watering so much I half-expected him to start crying actual tears. "You know what? Maybe I'm trying too hard because—" He paused, wiping his face with Hal's handkerchief. "Because there's not exactly a lot to work with here."

I felt my spine stiffen. "Excuse me?"

"I mean, look around." He gestured wildly at the French Market, nearly smacking a woman carrying a bag of beignets. "It's the same twelve songs on repeat, drunk people stumbling around at eleven in the morning, and vendors selling garbage with 'Made in China' stickers they forgot to peel off. You keep acting like this place is sacred, but it's basically Disneyland with worse parking and more vomit."

Tom's café au lait stopped halfway to his mouth. Hal's eyes went wide, and he took a subtle step backward like he was trying to distance himself from the impending explosion.

My jaw clenched so hard I thought my teeth might crack. "Disney-land with worse parking?"

"I just mean—" Luke started, his voice slightly hoarse from the hot sauce damage.

"No, no, please. Continue." I crossed my arms tighter. "Tell me more about how the city I love is basically a tourist trap with better music."

"That's not what I—"

"And for your information, those 'twelve songs' you're complaining about? They're classics. They're the soundtrack of this city. People have been playing those songs for generations because they *matter*. But I guess when you're used to Auto-Tuned pop garbage, you wouldn't recognize real music if it hit you in your sunburned face."

Luke opened his mouth, then closed it. His face was now red for an entirely different reason.

"And those 'drunk people'? Some of them are musicians who've been playing since dawn. Some of them are locals who actually live here and don't need your permission to enjoy their own city. And yeah, some of them are tourists, but at least they're *trying* to have a good time instead of—" I gestured at his entire outfit, "—whatever disaster this is supposed to be."

"I was trying to blend in!" Luke's voice cracked slightly, either from defensiveness or from lingering hot-sauce trauma.

Hal cleared his throat. "Maybe we should—"

"And another thing," I continued, on a roll now, "you waltzed in here with your bodyguards and your credit card, thinking you could just throw money at everything and make it go away. That's not how this works. That vendor knew *exactly* what he was doing when he saw you coming, and you know what? Good for him. You want to act like you're better than everyone here? Then yeah, you can pay the idiot tax."

Luke's jaw tightened. "I never said I was better than anyone."

"You didn't have to say it. It's written all over your face. All over that ridiculous outfit. All over the way you keep looking around like you're afraid someone's going to mug you for your flip-flops." I took a breath, my chest heaving. "This city has survived hurricanes, floods, and centuries of people trying to tell us we're doing it wrong. We don't need some Hollywood pretty boy in a tacky hat telling us we're not good enough for him."

The words hung in the air between us.

Luke's expression shifted—hurt flickering across his face before he schooled it back into something neutral. "Right," he said quietly. "Got it."

Tom muttered under his breath, "This is going well."

Hal shot him a look that could've melted steel.

I took a step back, suddenly exhausted. "Luke, this isn't working."

He stopped, frowning. "What isn't?"

"This. You. Me. All of it." I gestured between us. "You're not the lie low and disappear type, and that's fine. But trying to make this arrangement work? It's not happening. I think we need to cut our losses before you insult jazz music or call gumbo 'swamp soup' or whatever's next."

His jaw tightened, and for a second, I thought he might argue. Push back. Maybe even apologize. But then he shrugged, his expression carefully blank. "So, what? You're saying we call it quits?"

I nodded, ignoring the unexpected twist in my chest. "Yeah. No harm, no foul, right?"

Tom muttered under his breath, "Plenty of foul. That shirt alone—"

Luke shot him a glare before turning back to me. "If you think that's best."

"It is." I kept my voice steady even as something inside me wavered.

See? He wasn't even going to fight for this. Not even a token protest. The ease with which he gave up shouldn't have stung, but it did.

"Great," I said, my voice coming out sharper than I intended. "Enjoy the rest of your stay. Try not to destroy any more local businesses."

Luke's mouth twitched like he wanted to say something, but instead, he just adjusted his ridiculous hat and turned toward where the car was parked.

As we walked back in tense silence, Hal and Tom trailing behind us like the world's most awkward funeral procession, I tried to ignore the hollow feeling settling in my chest, brushing it off as relief. He wasn't rejecting me. This was a mutual agreement. Logical. Practical. The right thing to do.

But my thoughts wouldn't stop spiraling. If he'd fought harder, would I have relented?

No, I told myself firmly. This was the right call. Better to end things now than to risk letting him see just how much the possibility of rejection terrified me.

10

LUKE

BEING EXILED to New Orleans wasn't the punishment I expected. It was worse.

Anna had already written me off. One bad outing, and she was ready to throw in the towel on our arrangement. It stung more than I wanted to admit, even though I couldn't blame her. So far, I'd been a walking disaster.

I dialed Topher's number, pacing the room as I waited for him to pick up.

Topher didn't know about Anna or the mess I'd made of our agreement. But he knew enough about the rest of my life—the exile, the studio's doubts, the storm of pressure I was under. That's what happened when you trusted your finance guy with more than just your bank account.

"This isn't working," I said the moment he answered. "New Orleans? It's not happening. I need to get back to Hollywood."

"Stop right there," Topher cut in, his voice clipped. "Given the small fortune the studio spent turning my house into Fort Knox, I'd say you're not going anywhere, buddy. Seriously, it's New Orleans, not solitary confinement. You've only got a few weeks left before you're back on set. Can't you lie low until then?"

"It's not about lying low," I snapped, instantly regretting it. "It's about everything. This city doesn't exactly scream 'low profile.' When I try to avoid attention, I'm not blending in—I'm standing out."

Topher sighed, and I braced myself for what was coming.

"Luke," he said, his tone almost apologetic, "the studio's nervous. They've started looking at someone else for the role."

The words hit me hard. "What? Who?"

"Doesn't matter. What matters is they want someone polished enough to sell the movie but gritty enough to make it believable. Someone real. And right now, they don't think you're it."

"How do you even know that?" I asked.

Topher hesitated for half a beat. "Because they contacted me about analyzing the risk if they go with someone else. They want to know how much money they'd lose if they pulled the plug on you now. They're asking questions they don't usually ask unless they're worried."

I frowned, my grip tightening on the phone. "Why would they ask you that? You're not their employee."

"Businesses sometimes tap me for outside assessments. I told them I couldn't work with them because it would create a conflict of interest. But trust me, Luke, they wouldn't be consulting with anyone unless they were seriously considering a shift."

I pressed the phone tighter to my ear, trying to process what he was saying. Topher wasn't just my financial consultant. He was the one person in my life who didn't sugarcoat anything. That's why I called him when everything went sideways—because he told me the truth, even when it hurt.

"I can handle the role." My words felt hollow.

"Then prove it," Topher replied. "You've got to audition for this movie within the next three weeks. It's their insurance policy. After what happened, they want to make sure you're worth the investment."

My stomach churned. Of course. The audition. I had to *earn* the role after the PR nightmare I'd caused.

"They're protecting their investment," Topher continued. "If you flub this, they've got other people lined up. People who don't need a crash course in how to act like a normal human being."

"I get it." My chest squeezed. I couldn't let someone else step into that movie role. It was supposed to be *mine*.

"Do you?" Topher pressed. "Because from where I'm sitting, it sounds like you're more interested in complaining than doing the work. You're not just playing a part here, Luke. You've got to *be* the guy. You want a real connection? Start by being real yourself."

I was quiet as the words sank in.

Topher continued, "You've got three weeks to prove to them—and to yourself—that you can pull this off. So, stop making excuses and figure it out. Because if you quit now, you're handing the role that you deserve to someone else."

Three weeks. That was all the time I had to salvage my career.

Topher was silent for a beat, but then his face shifted, as if he was going into problem-solving mode. "Okay, go see my mom at Muses. She's not going to fix your life or anything, but she's a friendly face. And honestly, you could use one right now. This time, make sure she'll be there. Text her and let her know what disguise you'll be wearing."

After we said goodbye, I tossed the phone onto the couch and stared at the ceiling. Another guy. They were already looking at another guy for my role.

But Topher was right. Complaining wouldn't fix this.

I looked out the window again and imagined the chaos of New Orleans. The music, the laughter, the life. It wasn't Hollywood. But maybe, just maybe, it could be precisely what I needed.

If I didn't screw it up again.

11

ANNA

I NEVER THOUGHT BEING a tour guide to a movie star, if you could even call it that, would change my life. But after one outing, I was sure: I would never, ever do it again.

Marie Antoinette popped up from behind the bar as I walked into Muses for my evening shift, her red hair a fiery halo in the dim light. "Anna, darling," she said with her trademark smirk, "tell me all about the date."

I froze. "Date?"

"Don't play coy." She wagged a finger at me. "You don't fool me. Sparks were practically flying between you and Nigel, or as I like to call him, *Sir Swoons-a-Lot*. The heat between you two was so palpable that you could've fried a full English breakfast on the bartop."

Determined to change the subject, I rolled my eyes. "He's probably on a plane back to England by now. Like you always say, 'There's no point in waterin' last year's crop.'"

I pretended to busy myself cleaning pint glasses, but my hands trembled slightly. What would she say if she knew that the man People magazine had once declared the "World's Most Eligible Bachelor," was staying just a few streets away from this bar? Just the thought of it sent a shiver down my spine.

But it didn't matter. Luke and I had agreed it wouldn't work. The arrangement, the partnership, whatever you wanted to call it, was doomed from the start. My time was too important to waste on someone who, for all his charm, was just an out-of-touch, rich guy who wouldn't know how to interact with real people if his life depended on it.

"Oh, poor Luke Fisher," Marie Antoinette said suddenly, drawing my attention.

My head popped up, and I sloshed soapy water onto the counter. "What? Where?"

The bar went silent as every head turned toward me. I winced, realizing I'd shouted.

She raised an eyebrow. "Relax," she said, pointing at the TV. "Luke Fisher's on the screen, not in the room."

I followed her gaze to the television, where Luke's too-familiar face filled the frame. A moment later, it was replaced by an image of Sienna Hart draped over her new flame, Dylan Sanders.

"Sienna must've lost her mind," Marie Antoinette said, shaking her head. "Imagine breaking up with Luke Fisher."

Suppressing the irritation building inside me, I muttered, "Seems even the world's most beautiful woman can see through his act."

Marie Antoinette turned to me, her eyebrows raised in surprise. "Well, someone poured vinegar in your sweet tea. I think Sienna's a fool. As they say, 'Beauty is only skin deep, but ugly cuts clean to the bone.'"

"Who said that?" I asked, narrowing my eyes.

"Me. And Dorothy Parker," she replied with a wink.

Before I could respond, her attention shifted to the entrance like a heat-seeking missile. She fanned herself dramatically with both hands. "Would you look at that specimen of manliness? My, my, my. If he's interested in a fling, I say get ready to get flung."

I followed her gaze, curious despite myself. A brown-haired man with a face straight out of a Hugh Grant movie stood in the doorway, his posture casual but commanding. He wore sunglasses indoors, which was an automatic red flag, and carried himself with a kind of effortless charm that screamed *not from around here.*

"Who even looks like that in real life?" Marie Antoinette whispered, clutching her chest. "It's not fair."

"Stop drooling," I said, though I couldn't look away either.

As if summoned, Mrs. Brodie hurried up to him and clasped his arm like they were old friends. She led him toward the back office, chatting animatedly.

We caught snippets of a strong Irish brogue.

"Gorgeous *and* Irish," Marie Antoinette murmured, swiping at an imaginary tear. "Oh, come to mama. He's the pot of gold at the end of my rainbow."

I rolled my eyes. "He's probably here to sell whiskey or something."

Just then, the bar was hit by a sound that made my teeth ache. "Today's ALL about ME!"

The screech was followed by the arrival of a bride-to-be, charging into Muses like a glitter bomb with legs. Her white tank top declared in cursive letters *"Queen of the Day,"* as if there was any doubt.

Trailing behind her was her entourage, all in matching black tanks with their designated roles blazoned across the front: *"Sister of the Queen," "Known the Queen Since Kindergarten,"* and my personal favorite, *"Barely Tolerating the Queen."*

I snorted, unable to help myself. "That last one's got a story."

Marie Antoinette leaned over the bar, her eyes sparkling with mischief. "I'll bet ten bucks *Barely Tolerating the Queen* is the first one to lose her mind tonight."

"You're on," I said, wincing when the group commandeered three tables with the precision of military generals.

"Where are my shots? I want them now!" the bride demanded, her voice like nails on a chalkboard.

I grabbed a tray and started loading it up, bracing myself for whatever chaos they were about to unleash.

And chaos they delivered.

The first thing they whipped out? Straws. But not just any straws.

These featured a rather *notable* part of Michelangelo's David, if you catch my drift.

Of course.

They didn't just take their shots; they sipped them through those straws like it was some kind of twisted tea party. The bride held hers aloft like a royal scepter, her laughter loud enough to drown out the band.

The chaos reached a fever pitch when the bachelorette party set their sights on their next victim: the pool table. Two bridesmaids climbed up, turning it into a makeshift stage. They danced like they were auditioning for a music video.

The band faltered, patrons groaned, and I was mentally drafting my resignation letter when I spotted the young Hugh Grant look-alike from earlier, apparently finished with his discussion with Mrs. Brodie. The guy shifted, sunglasses still on, and started edging toward the door with the kind of practiced nonchalance that screamed *I'm not trying to sneak out, but I'm absolutely sneaking out.*

My brain made the leap instantly: *Luke.*

Then immediately rolled its metaphorical eyes: *Oh my gosh, get a grip. Not every tall guy in aviators is your movie star crush.*

That's when the bride noticed him. She had been enthusiastically cheering on her friends' dance moves, but when she saw the Irish-man, she froze mid-cheer. Her eyes locked onto him like a predator spotting prey. Without hesitation, she charged toward him, a cocktail sloshing precariously in her hand.

"You're the spitting image of Hugh Grant," she announced, her voice carrying over the band and the general chaos.

The man offered her a polite smile. "Ah, cheers," he said.

The bride's eyes widened. "No way, are you *Irish*? I am *obsessed* with Irish guys."

Before he could formulate a response, the floodgates opened. Bridesmaids swarmed like moths to a flame, circling him with giddy laughter and overly familiar grins.

"I'd do *anything* for a bit of Irish luck tonight," one cooed.

"If he's the leprechaun guarding the pot of gold, I'm ready for a chase," another one quipped, sending the group into fits of giggles.

To his credit, the man remained polite. "You ladies look like you're having a grand time. The evening must be treating you well."

He spoke calmly, but I caught the slight edge to his tone, and his jaw tightened as his eyes darted toward two large men in the corner who were completely engrossed in the bridesmaids' impromptu dance routine on the pool table.

The man was looking for an exit. With his sunglasses still on, he moved toward the door, his movements deliberate but subtle, like someone trying to escape a crime scene without drawing attention.

That's when I looked more closely at the two hulking men who were staring at the dancing bridesmaids, and even though they were wearing baseball caps, I recognized them as Luke's bodyguards.

Was Luke trying on an Irish accent that night? I stepped into his path, tray balanced precariously on one hand and looked up at him.

Even wearing a brown wig and his face hidden by shades, those piercing blue eyes were unmistakable.

12

LUKE

It was only a matter of time.

The bridesmaids' attention on me was snowballing, their shrill laughter and flirtatious remarks escalating as the bride grabbed my arm and declared, "You *have* to dance with us."

I shot a desperate glance at Hal and Tom, my so-called body-guards, but they were utterly useless, transfixed by the bridesmaids on the pool table. At this rate, my disguise was as good as finished. The studio would love a viral video of their supposed-to-be-behaving-himself lead getting dragged into a bachelorette party conga line.

And then, like an unexpected plot twist, *her* voice cut through the clamor.

"Mr. O'Toole, there's a call for you."

My head jerked toward her. Anna. Of course, it was Anna.

"It's urgent." She jabbed a finger toward the bar. "From Ireland."

The bridesmaids and the bride reluctantly parted. "Who does she think she is?" one of them muttered, glaring daggers at Anna.

I barely had time to register my relief before Anna turned her gaze on me, her eyes flashing with something I couldn't quite place. "Well? Are you coming, *Mr. O'Toole*?"

The words startled me into action, and I followed her, weaving through the crowd. On the way, she stopped at Hal and Tom's table, their eyes still locked on the gyrating women. Her voice was steel. "Gentlemen, are we forgetting who you're here to watch over?"

They jumped to their feet, looking sheepish.

"Right. Of course," Hal muttered, while Tom adjusted his sunglasses.

By the time I reached the safety of the bar, my heart was still racing from the near disaster. I turned to Anna, trying to put all the gratitude I felt into words—or at least into my expression.

"You're a lifesaver," I said, my voice low. "That was... intense."

She squinted, her expression unimpressed. "I'm just doing what I said I'd do and keep your identity a secret. You're welcome, by the way."

The bride's shrill laughter pierced the air again, and I winced. "I'm already wearing a disguise," I muttered, tugging on my brown, Hugh Grant wig. "I need a disguise for this disguise."

Anna raised an eyebrow, the corners of her mouth twitching with amusement. "Wait here," she said, disappearing into the back room.

"Should I be worried?" I called after her, but she was already gone.

She returned, thrusting something lavender and fluffy at me. "Here."

I blinked. "What is this?"

"It's my hoodie," she said matter-of-factly. "Put it on."

I held up the purple hoodie, which featured an embroidered golden fleur-de-lis in sequins. "This is... very purple." I tried to suppress a laugh.

"Exactly." Anna's tone dared me to argue. "No one will expect Luke Fisher, Hollywood's golden god, to be wearing *this*."

She wasn't wrong. With a sigh, I tugged it on. It fit surprisingly well, and it smelled like Anna. Cinnamon with a trace of jasmine.

"Wow," I murmured. "This is comfortable."

Anna rolled her eyes. "It's not a fashion statement. It's a disguise on top of your already terrible disguise."

"Noted." I tugged the hood up over my wig. "How do I look?"

"Ridiculous," she replied, but there was a flicker of amusement in her eyes.

Hal walked up to us. "We've got a clean path to the car. Let's move."

"Thanks for the save," I said to Anna, pausing for a moment.

She gave me a look I couldn't quite decipher, then nodded. "Don't mention it. Literally. Don't."

"Time to move," Hal muttered, his voice low as he clapped a hand on my shoulder.

Tom flanked me on the other side, his expression deadly serious despite the ridiculous tourist sunglasses still perched on his nose. "Let's go before they connect the dots."

I didn't argue. The two of them ushered me toward the front door, cutting through the crowd with surprising efficiency. I caught a glimpse of the bride craning her neck to look for me, her friends buzzing around her like a swarm of bees.

"Keep your head down," Hal instructed, his bulk acting as a human shield as we slipped out the door.

The second the steamy night air hit my face, I exhaled a shaky breath, relief washing over me. I leaned back against the wall, trying to make sense of everything. The humid air clung to my skin, but my mind was elsewhere, still back in that chaotic bar, back on Anna.

She hadn't just saved me. She could have walked away, let me crash and burn, but she didn't.

Why?

I glanced back toward the bar, and there she was, framed in the doorway, scanning the street like she wanted to make sure the coast was clear before heading back inside.

She caught my eye across the alley, and the rest of the city seemed to blur.

My throat tightened. I cleared it and looked away, but my chest was still racing.

Before I could tell if she felt it too, she turned and disappeared back into the bar, and I was left staring at the empty doorway, my chest tingling with something I couldn't quite place.

For the first time since I got to New Orleans, I didn't feel entirely out of my depth. More and more, it seemed like having Anna show me the city, and help me figure out how to connect with real people, wasn't just a good idea; it might be the *only* idea.

She didn't want to be my tour guide, though. That much was clear. But I could be persuasive when it mattered. And right now, it definitely mattered.

13

ANNA

My story was practically writing itself.

Each keystroke brought the reluctant superhero to life. A man torn between the safety of his disguise and the risk of revealing his true self. It was clever, it was cunning, it had depth. This story felt like it could be something big.

And the truth? Luke Fisher was my muse.

There. I said it. I wasn't proud of it, but there it was. Every smirk, every infuriating comment, every moment he seemed almost real—that's what fueled my creativity. He was the blueprint for the complicated, charming disaster I was pouring into my pages. It was like he'd stepped out of the story and into my life, bringing both inspiration and chaos in equal measure.

And that was why it was so unfortunate that I'd told him I wouldn't show him around New Orleans. I'd slammed the door on any possibility of spending more time together.

We'd agreed to part ways, and in my heart, I knew it was the right call. He was spoiled, a wealthy playboy with an ego bigger than the mansion he was staying in. He wasn't the kind of person who stuck around, and I wasn't the kind of person who wasted time on someone like him.

Still, I couldn't shake the memory of the way he'd looked at me the night before outside Muses. His look was intense, almost like I was the only person in the world. It lingered in my mind, sending an unexpected warmth curling through me, the flicker of a spark I wasn't ready to acknowledge.

My thoughts were interrupted by the ringing doorbell. My young cousins Therese and Amelia burst inside, followed by their mother, my cousin Lucy. "Aunt Anna," the girls yelled, flinging themselves at me.

"Hey, you two," I said, kissing the tops of their heads.

"Thank you so much for watching the girls while I shop," Lucy said. She set a bag down on the counter, giving the room a once-over before raising an eyebrow at me. "You know, having to announce myself at the gates of this place makes me feel like I'm visiting Buckingham Palace. Should I have worn a fascinator?"

I snorted. "You in a fancy, stuffy hat, a la Audrey Hepburn in *My Fair Lady*? Now *that* I'd pay to see."

She grinned. "How's mansion life treating you, Your Highness?"

I shrugged, trying to sound casual. "It's convenient. Close to Muses."

"Mmm." She dragged the word out like she didn't believe a word I was saying. "So, do you ever go into the main house? Or is that off-limits?"

I avoided her eyes, suddenly very interested in rearranging the pastries she brought. "Someone's staying there. I haven't been inside."

Lucy didn't say anything for a beat. Then she leaned against the counter, arms folded, her expression amused. "Wait. Is this one of those situations? Like... a mysterious stranger in the big house? You catch glimpses of him swimming shirtless in the pool while dramatic cello music plays in the background?"

"What? No." My voice cracked, which didn't help my case. "That's ridiculous."

Her eyes widened. "Oh my gosh. *There is someone.* You're blushing right now."

"I'm not."

"You so are." She pointed at me like she'd won a game. "Anna, what are you not telling me?"

I sighed. There was no keeping anything from Lucy. "Fine. I met the guy staying in the main house. He's charming and handsome, but he's also a ladies' man. And spoiled."

"What's spoiled?" six-year-old Amelia asked, tugging on my sleeve.

"It means he gets everything he wants," I replied.

Therese, four years old, bounced on her toes. "I want to be spoiled."

Lucy grinned. "So, is this mystery man good-looking?"

I snorted. "He might be *too* good-looking. Like 'People Magazine's Sexiest Man,' good-looking."

Lucy gave me a playful shove. "What's the problem?"

"The problem is that I don't have time to get involved with anyone. I'm making progress on my writing, and that's what matters."

Lucy wagged a finger at me. "Don't ignore romantic possibilities. This could be like a rom-com. You, the hardworking writer, and him, the—what is he again? A secret prince?"

"Luce, this is real life, not the Hallmark Channel. Don't you have shopping to do?"

"Fine." She grabbed her purse. "Girls, be good for Auntie Anna. I'll be back in an hour."

After she left, the girls kept me busy with books and games for about half an hour, until the doorbell rang again. Expecting Lucy, I swung the door open. "Wow, that was the shortest—oh, it's you."

Luke stood there, looking sheepish and entirely out of place. My heart skipped a beat. "The shortest what?" he asked, tilting his head.

I swallowed hard. "I thought you were my cousin."

He nodded. "I brought your purple hoodie."

I waved a hand dismissively. "You didn't have to do that. It's way too big for me, anyway. I just kept it at Muses in case I got cold, but I never wear it. Pretty sure it's stained from when a customer spilled a rum and Coke on me."

"Well, if that's the case, maybe I'll keep it. It's surprisingly comfortable."

The way he said it, so casual and self-assured, made it hard not to smile. This was the Luke Fisher who made romantic gestures look easy on film, the same Luke who could turn wearing a lavender hoodie into an effortlessly cool moment. And, annoyingly, he knew it.

"By all means." I assumed he had to be joking. "Consider it a gift. You'll be the most stylish guy at your next movie premiere."

"Obviously." The corner of his mouth twitched.

Before I could respond, the girls peeked out from behind me. "Who are you?" Therese asked.

"I'm Luke." He crouched to their level with a warm smile that seemed genuine. "I stay in the big house over there."

"Are you the president?" Amelia asked, her wide eyes sparkling with innocent curiosity.

"No, but I have been to the Oval Office."

I folded my arms, giving him a skeptical once-over. "Oh?"

He straightened up with an air of exaggerated nonchalance, as if he hadn't just dropped that bomb casually. "Yeah, for a movie. *The Terrorist*. Played a Secret Service agent. Maybe you've seen it?"

I mean, everyone had seen it. It had been one of the highest-grossing films of last year, and his chiseled jawline had been plastered on billboards from here to Tokyo.

And yet, there he was, standing on my doorstep, larger than life, as if he'd stepped out of one of the very scenes I'd been writing all morning. The irony wasn't lost on me. I'd been trying to envision him while working on my story, and now, here he was in the flesh.

He hesitated, his gaze steady, and was that sincerity I saw there? "In addition to returning your hoodie, I wanted to thank you. For yesterday."

"It's no problem. It's my job."

He frowned, tilting his head slightly. "It's your job to rescue people who get trapped by bachelorette parties?"

"Uh, yeah. Happens all the time."

He nodded slowly, as if sincerely trying to decide whether I was serious or not. Then, he flashed his signature lopsided grin, the one that made women across the world swoon. It was the kind of grin that made you feel like you were the only person in the room, even if you were in a crowded theater.

Just then, Amelia tugged on my sleeve, her small voice cutting through the silence. "Aunt Anna, is he going to read with us?" Her wide eyes brimmed with excitement.

Therese piped up before I could respond, bouncing on her toes. "Auntie Anna does all the voices. Can you do voices, too?"

I hesitated, glancing at Luke. There was no way he'd say yes, right? He was Luke Fisher, the guy whose face was plastered on billboards and magazines, not someone who'd willingly dive into a Seuss performance for a couple of kids.

"Oh, no, he doesn't have time for—"

"I might have just enough time." Luke arched his eyebrow, and an amused grin tugged at his lips. "What story are you reading?"

Amelia held up the book as if it were a golden ticket. "*The Cat in the Hat*. And Auntie Anna makes it really funny."

Therese nodded eagerly. "You can be the cat."

The girls were already grabbing his hands and tugging him toward the couch. I stood there, frozen, unsure if I should intervene or just let it happen. Luke Fisher, movie star, sitting on my couch, reading Dr. Seuss? The absurdity of the situation hit me like a tidal wave. He cleared his throat like he was about to perform on Broadway.

"Well," he said, flipping to the first page, "I hope you're ready for the greatest rendition of the Cat you've ever heard."

I stood back, arms on my hips, watching him. He was good at this. And not just at making the girls laugh, though he had them in the palm of his hand. No, what struck me was how at ease he seemed, as though he had dropped some charade that he was always playing at.

He glanced up mid-sentence, his eyes meeting mine, and there was something almost proud in his expression, like he was enjoying the chaos he was creating. How could someone like him, someone so polished and untouchable, look so completely comfortable in this little slice of my world?

Holding the book high like it was a sacred text, he intoned dramatically, "I have some tricks. Very good tricks. And your aunt? She'll be *totally* fine with it."

Amelia shot her hand up like a tiny crossing guard. "That is *not* what it says."

Luke blinked, pure innocence. "It's not?"

"No," she giggled, lunging to take the book. "It says *Mom*. Not aunt."

He tapped the page, squinting like a scholar. "Hmm. Are you sure? M-O-M... that looks like Aunt to me."

Amelia collapsed into laughter. "That spells *mom*. MOM!"

"Well," Luke said, shrugging with mock gravitas, "maybe you're right. You *are* very smart. How old are you again?"

"I'm six," she declared proudly, puffing up like she'd just won a spelling bee. "How old are you?"

"Six? That explains everything," he said, nodding solemnly. "I'm thirty."

Not to be outdone, Therese climbed into his lap and grabbed his face with both hands. "You *have* to keep reading," she ordered, her voice full of fire and four-year-old authority.

"Yes, ma'am." He saluted and dove back in, now armed with voices so over-the-top they belonged on a stage.

By the time he moved on to *Green Eggs and Ham*, the girls were thoroughly entranced, hanging on his every word. Even shy Therese, who usually took time to warm up to people, was giggling and chiming in.

I leaned against the doorway, watching the scene unfold. This was a different side of Luke than I'd seen before. His air of ego and self-importance had vanished, replaced by someone funny, lighthearted, and entirely at ease.

It was... unexpected.

Therese snuggled into Luke's side, tilting her head with the solemn curiosity of a courtroom judge. "Auntie says you're a lady man."

I froze, my brain scrambling for damage control, but it was too late.

Luke's eyebrows shot up, and a slow, amused grin spread across his face. "A what? A lady man?"

Amelia, the self-appointed expert, chimed in, her tone dripping with authority. "No, Therese. Auntie said he's a *ladies' man*."

If I could have evaporated on the spot, I would have. Luke glanced at me, his grin widening like he was thoroughly enjoying the show.

"Well, I've been called worse." His voice was light and teasing.

Amelia tapped his shoulder, her eyes wide with earnestness. "You're so lucky. You're spoiled."

Luke clutched his chest as if he'd been shot. "Spoiled? Did you call me spoiled?"

"Shhh, Amelia," I pleaded.

But Amelia wasn't done. "Auntie Anna said it. She said you're spoiled, and it means you get everything you want. I think that's lucky. I want to be spoiled."

"Amelia." My voice hit a pitch reserved for fire alarms, but the damage was done.

Luke turned to me, his expression the very picture of gleeful mischief. "Did you really say that?"

Amelia, traitorous to the end, nodded vigorously. "She sure did."

Luke leaned forward, his blue eyes sparkling. "So, what else does Auntie Anna say about me?"

Amelia wasn't done. "She also said—"

"Nope. That's it." I interrupted. "Let's let Mr. Luke go, shall we?"

Luke raised an eyebrow, clearly relishing every second. "Go? But I'm having such a great time. I could listen to this all day."

I shot him a glare that said, *Please don't encourage them,* but the amused sparkle in his eye made it hard to stay mad. The girls giggled, and Luke finally shifted his weight, giving me a break from his teasing grin.

He glanced toward the window, then back at me. "I saw a flyer earlier for some street market? Music, food, people dancing in the middle of the day like it's a perfectly normal thing?"

I tilted my head. "Sounds like New Orleans."

"That's what I figured," he said, leaning casually against the arm of the couch. "Anyway... it reminded me that I had a question for you."

I narrowed my eyes, wary. "About what?"

He cleared his throat. "You showing me the city." His gaze met mine, steady this time. "I think we should pick that back up."

My heart stuttered. Wait. Was he serious? This was exactly what I needed. My brain immediately sprang into overdrive, mapping out potential ideas for my story. A little voice in the back of my head was practically shouting, *This is perfect. This is it. You can keep writing.*

I didn't want to get too excited, in case he pulled back. "Really? I thought we agreed it wasn't going to work."

He shrugged, his gaze steady. "We did. But I've been thinking about it, and maybe I wasn't giving it a fair shot. And I promise to do a better job of blending in."

I bit my lip, torn between yelling, *yes, yes, yes,* and playing it cool. This was the best news ever. He'd practically handed me my story on a silver platter. *Be cool, Anna. Don't look desperate.*

"Fine," I said slowly, dragging out the word like I wasn't already mentally planning how to incorporate our outings into my superhero novel. "But this time, you're going to follow my lead."

"Absolutely." He nodded, clearly trying to play along. "So, what's the plan? Where are we going?"

My mind raced as I thought about the perfect way to dive back into this arrangement. I needed something that would allow Luke to blend into the New Orleans scene without standing out. Something loud and busy enough that no one would give him a second glance, yet also steeped in the kind of culture and chaos that made this city so uniquely alive.

I had an idea.

I smiled to myself. This was going to be good. It was the perfect way to show him the real New Orleans. Not the glossy version tourists post on Instagram, but the heartbeat of the city. He wouldn't know what hit him.

"It's a surprise," I said, keeping my tone light. "Be ready by two o'clock. Wear comfortable shoes. You'll be on your feet a lot."

"On my feet?" he repeated. "What exactly are we doing?"

I gave him a mysterious smile. "You'll see. Just trust me. Oh, and maybe bring a hat. Something that'll help you blend in but won't block your view. Sunglasses wouldn't hurt either."

A grin spread across his face, his blue eyes lighting up in a way that made it hard to look away.

"You really need to go now," I said, trying to keep my tone firm even as my heart skipped a beat. "My cousin's going to be back any minute."

He nodded but crouched down to Amelia's level, his expression playful and conspiratorial. In a stage whisper loud enough for me to hear, he asked, "Amelia, can I count on you to be my secret agent? Find out everything your auntie says about me and report back?"

Amelia's eyes lit up with the gravity of the mission, and she saluted him with a giggle. "You can count on me, Mr. President."

I groaned. "Amelia, don't you dare. Your allegiance is supposed to be with me."

Luke smirked, throwing a wink my way. "Guess we'll see about that." For a moment, his gaze lingered on me. "Good to see you."

My heart gave a giddy thud, and I barely managed a nod before I ushered him out the door.

And it wasn't a moment too soon. Lucy waltzed in only about five minutes later.

"Mommy, mommy! We met the president. The man who lives next door." Therese spoke with the excitement of a game-show contestant.

Lucy's eyebrows shot up. "You did? Is he cute?"

"I don't know," Therese said. "But when he read, he did the words funny."

"We told him that he was spoiled," Amelia said. "And Therese told him that he was a lady man, but I said it right. Ladies' man."

Lucy's face was a picture of horror. "You didn't," she groaned, shooting me an apologetic look. "Did they?"

"Oh yes, they did." I shrugged. "He took it in stride. Said he's been called worse."

Lucy sighed. "I'm so sorry. Girls, that was naughty."

Amelia looked up in surprise. "Why was it naughty? It's like saying congratulations on getting all the toys you want."

"Time to go, girls," Lucy said, hastily gathering their things. "We'll have a chat in the car."

She glanced back at me. "I'm glad he has a sense of humor."

My cousin ushered the girls out the door, their chatter trailing behind her. Once the house was silent again, I leaned against the counter, replaying the morning's chaos in my head. Luke's laughter, the girls' relentless honesty, and his disarming way of rolling with it all showed that maybe he wasn't entirely impossible.

But there wasn't time to dwell on that now. I was about to drop Luke right into the beating heart of New Orleans. Something so vivid, so alive, it might crack his polished Hollywood shell and force him to see what was right in front of him.

That is, if he could handle it.

14

LUKE

THE MUSIC HIT like a tidal wave as soon as we turned the corner. Brass instruments wailed, drums thumped, and the unmistakable hum of a crowd in sync with the beat filled the air.

I hesitated, glancing around at the revelers. People of all ages were moving to the music, some with umbrellas spinning in the air, while others waved handkerchiefs in time with the music. They weren't coordinated, but it was messy and alive and completely unselfconscious.

Anna walked next to me, her step light and confident, like she belonged here. She was completely at ease. I, on the other hand, felt like a cat dropped into a dog park.

"What is this?" I dodged a kid with a balloon who nearly barreled into me.

She turned to me, a knowing smile tugging at her lips. "It's a second-line parade."

"A second... what?" I scanned the scene like it might somehow explain itself.

Anna stopped and turned to face me, raising her voice slightly to be heard over the music. "It's a New Orleans thing. The brass band up front is the first line, and everyone who joins in behind them is the second line. It's a celebration of life. You don't need a reason to join. You follow the music and let go."

The heat of her proximity made my pulse quicken. I frowned, trying to focus. "Let go of what?"

She laughed, and the sound was low and intimate despite the chaos around us. "Whatever's holding you back."

The crowd thickened as we moved closer to the band, and I instinctively glanced over my shoulder. Hal and Tom weren't far, keeping their distance but clearly on high alert. They were dressed to blend in and tried to remain inconspicuous as they scanned the crowd for threats.

Anna pressed closer as someone jostled past us, her shoulder against mine, her hip bumping my thigh. She handed me a handkerchief. Her fingers grazed my palm as I took it, and our eyes locked for a beat longer than necessary. "Here. You wave this while you dance."

I glanced around, my hand tightening on the handkerchief she'd handed me. "I'm not exactly known for my rhythm. And I'm worried someone might recognize me. I mean, this crowd..."

"No one's looking at you," she interrupted, stepping close until I could feel the heat radiating from her body. "Here, no one's concerned with anyone else. They're too busy living in the moment."

I scanned the mass of people dancing, laughing, and cheering around us. A man spun an umbrella in time with the music, kids darted between his legs, waving tiny handkerchiefs, and an older woman twirled with surprising energy. None of them even peeked in my direction.

"You're serious?"

"Completely." Anna stepped closer still, close enough that her chest nearly brushed mine when she breathed. "You're just another face in the crowd here: no cameras, no headlines, no expectations. Just let go. I promise, no one's judging you."

I let her words sink in, looking around again. She was right. No one cared who I was or what I was doing. They were all too wrapped up in the music, the energy, the moment.

"Wave the handkerchief," Anna added with a playful nudge. "Move your feet."

I huffed a laugh, the tension easing just slightly. "Fine." I raised the handkerchief tentatively, then swung it in time with the music. It felt ridiculous at first, like I was a kid at a birthday party, but Anna's cheers were oddly encouraging. Slowly, I started to loosen up, moving my feet and trying to match the rhythm of the brass band.

Anna shot me a glance. "See? Not so bad."

I grumbled something under my breath but couldn't stop the faint smile tugging at my lips. She was right. No one was watching, and I felt like I didn't have to perform. I could just be.

The band surged forward, and the crowd pressed along with it, sweeping us into the flow. I followed Anna, trying not to bump into anyone, still gripping the handkerchief.

We stopped near the middle of the parade, where a group of kids twirled umbrellas and an older man spun a woman half his age in an elaborate dance move that had everyone cheering. The energy was infectious. Even I could feel its pull.

"Why New Orleans?" Anna asked suddenly, her tone light.

The question caught me off guard. "What do you mean?"

"I mean, out of all the places you could've gone, why here?"

I hesitated, choosing my words carefully. "Let's just say, people aren't exactly thrilled to see my face right now." Her eyebrows lifted, inviting me to continue. "I needed to lie low. And Topher offered me a place. End of story."

She didn't push. She just nodded and gestured at the scene around us. "Well, maybe this is exactly what you need."

I hesitated before finally giving in, waving the handkerchief in time with the beat. Dancing without a care in the world—or trying to. "So, what about you?" I stepped a little closer to her. "You're obviously passionate about New Orleans. Why don't you write about it?"

Her smile froze, faltered, and then quickly shifted into something guarded. "That's a loaded question," she said lightly, but her voice had an edge to it.

"Is it?" I tilted my head at the color-drenched scene around us. "You say you're never going to live anywhere else, and you talk about this place like it's magic. Seems like it'd be a gold mine for a writer."

Her laugh sounded forced. "Not everything's as easy as it looks."

Before I could push further, she spun away, waving her handkerchief as though the conversation hadn't just shifted. "Come on," she called over her shoulder. "The band's moving. Don't get left behind."

I watched her for a moment. Clearly, I'd hit a nerve I hadn't meant to. But she was already disappearing into the crowd, and I had no choice but to follow.

I caught up to her just as a woman near us twirled her umbrella with dramatic flair and called out, "Come on, handsome. Show us what you've got."

Anna glanced back at me, her earlier tension replaced by a broad, genuine smile that seemed to light up the entire street. "See?" she said, her voice lilting over the music. "You're almost blending in."

"Almost?" I echoed, the beginnings of a grin tugging at my lips as I waved my handkerchief in an exaggerated flourish.

She smirked, tilting her head as if sizing me up. "You could use a little more hip action."

"Hip action?" I attempted what I thought was a sway, moving my hips in what probably looked more like a broken washing machine than dancing.

Anna's hand flew to her mouth, but she couldn't contain the laugh that burst out. "Oh my gosh, no. Stop. You're going to hurt yourself." She stepped closer, and before I could protest, her hands were on my hips, guiding them in the actual rhythm. "Like this. Feel the beat, don't fight it."

The contact sent a jolt through me that had nothing to do with the music. "I'm feeling something," I murmured, and she either didn't hear me or chose to ignore it.

"There," she said, stepping back to admire her work, though her cheeks looked slightly flushed. "That's almost acceptable."

"Almost?" I challenged, feeling emboldened. "Watch this—I'm

practically a local now." The band had shifted to something slower, more soulful—a trumpet crooning over a steady, hypnotic beat. Anna swayed with it, and without thinking, I pulled her closer, attempting what I hoped looked like a proper dance move.

I went for a dip, like I'd seen in old movies. Somehow, miraculously, I didn't drop her.

"Practically a local," she repeated, her voice barely above a whisper as I pulled her upright.

That's when I spotted a street photographer with a camera the size of a small cannon, swinging it in our direction. My instincts kicked in before my brain could catch up.

"Down!" I grabbed Anna's hand and pulled her behind a group of enthusiastic dancers waving oversized umbrellas.

"What are you—" she started, but I pressed a finger to my lips.

We crouched there, her shoulder pressed against mine, both of us trying not to laugh as we peered through the forest of legs and umbrellas. The photographer panned across the crowd, oblivious that I was hiding three feet away.

"This is ridiculous," Anna whispered, her breath warm against my ear. "The photographer's not from a tabloid. He's just from the local newspaper covering the parade. We look like we're in a spy movie."

"I'm trying to maintain a low profile," I whispered back.

"By army-crawling through a second-line parade?"

A kid with a balloon peered down at us curiously. I waved my handkerchief at him in what I hoped was a casual, "nothing to see here" gesture. He giggled and ran off.

"The photographer's gone," Anna said, pulling me up by the hand. Her eyes were bright with barely suppressed laughter. "You know, for someone trying not to draw attention, you're doing a terrible job."

The band suddenly launched into something fast, energetic, all horns and drums demanding movement. The crowd erupted with fresh enthusiasm, and Anna turned toward it like a flower to the sun. She spun her handkerchief with abandon, her laughter spilling out like a melody of its own, completely unselfconscious.

I stood there watching her, this woman who moved through the chaos like she was part of it, like she and the city spoke the same language. In this place, there were no scripts, no lines to memorize. Just life, messy and vibrant. Maybe that's why I was here. Not to escape my life but to reinvent it.

15

ANNA

THE SECOND-LINE PARADE yesterday had gone better than I could have imagined. Seeing Luke finally relax and let loose made me realize there was more to him than his Hollywood persona. It was fun watching him get caught up in the music and energy.

And today, I was about to spend an entire day showing a movie star around New Orleans. Just casually hanging out with someone who'd been on more magazine covers than I'd read in my lifetime.

He was wearing a ridiculous disguise—a wig with wild, springy black curls and a pair of oversized glasses without lenses.

As Tom drove, we passed a pothole that had been turned into a makeshift fishing pond, complete with stuffed animals holding fishing rods. A plastic alligator was caught mid-escape at the end of one pole. The sign next to the pothole declared, "Welcome to Lake Pothole. Good things come to those who bait."

Luke stared. "Do you guys decorate every pothole in this city?"

"It's New Orleans. We lean into the weird."

We pulled up to St. Louis Cemetery Number One. "Normally, you'd need a guide to get in," I explained as we stepped out. "But my family's been here since the 1800s. We have a pass."

Luke followed me through the narrow pathways between weathered tombs, his footsteps echoing slightly off the stone. He slowed at each turn, eyes scanning the names and dates etched into crumbling marble and faded plaques.

"This is... different," he said finally, his voice low, almost reverent.

I smiled, though there was something solemn in it. "Welcome to the city of the dead."

He glanced around, eyebrows lifted. "Okay, but... why are we in a cemetery? Is this a thing people do here? In LA, we don't go sight-seeing in graveyards."

"It's not only sightseeing. It's history." I gestured to the maze of tombs rising all around us. Some were elaborate, featuring columns and angels that reached skyward. Others were simple, just brick and mortar, names erased by time.

"The water table here makes underground burials impossible," I explained. "Try digging six feet down, and you're basically building a coffin-sized boat. During floods, they'd just... float back up."

Luke blinked. "That's horrifying."

"So, the city adapted. Tombs above ground. Generations of families in the same vault. These places are like neighborhoods. That one's from the 1800s," I added, pointing to a tomb with iron gates and a carved fleur-de-lis at the top. "That one's recent. You'll see Mardi Gras beads on some, photos tucked into cracks, candles still burning."

He looked around again, more slowly this time. "It's beautiful. In a haunted, Tim Burton kind of way."

Our footsteps carried us deeper into the cemetery. The air smelled faintly of flowers left too long in the heat. When we reached the tomb of Marie Laveau, I pointed out the offerings scattered around—coins, beads, and even a bottle of rum. "That's the Voodoo Queen," I said in a hushed tone. "People still leave gifts, hoping she'll grant their wishes."

His eyes widened. "Voodoo? That's a thing here?"

I shook my head. "I don't know anyone who practices voodoo, not for real. I feel like it's more of a story for tourists. Take Marie Laveau. She's known now for voodoo and healing the sick with her mysterious potions. But when she lived more than a century ago, she was also a devout Catholic. That's the thing about New Orleanians. We're a mess of contradictions."

In that way, I was a lot like New Orleans. There I was, dreaming of writing a novel, yet there was that nagging understanding that everything I knew, everything I was, was rooted right here. I was sure that I would never live anywhere else, no matter how much I sometimes wanted to. Something was holding me here. It was a strange sensation, feeling tethered to a place while yearning to break free—just like the city's own blend of tradition and transformation.

As we wandered, Luke asked questions, surprising me with his interest. He was attentive, absorbing the history and stories.

After we left the cemetery, I offered to take him to the French Quarter. "The oldest bar in the U.S. is in the Quarter, Lafitte's Blacksmith Shop. They say that the pirate Jean Lafitte ran a blacksmith shop there, but only as a front to sell stolen goods."

Luke nodded. "Lead the way, Professor New Orleans."

We wandered through the Quarter, the streets buzzing with tourists, locals, and street performers. I pointed out landmarks and tossed out bits of trivia as we walked. Tom and Hal stayed close, their presence subtle enough to avoid drawing attention.

We stopped at the St. Louis Cathedral, the towering spires gleaming in the sunlight. "This is the oldest cathedral in the country." I motioned toward the impressive structure. "But see those apartments with the cast-iron balconies? That style is a signature of the French Quarter, all thanks to the Baroness de Pontalba. She brought it over from France about a century and a half ago. The whole look and feel of the Quarter? Credit goes to her."

I led him toward an apartment complex near the cathedral. "The baroness was born here in New Orleans. She fell in love with a local boy who didn't have a penny to his name, so her family whisked her off to France and married her off to her titled cousin. Little did they know, he was broke and only in it for her fortune."

Luke raised an eyebrow. "That's... dramatic."

"Oh, it gets better." I leaned in for effect. "Her husband and his father constantly plotted to take her money. When she resisted, they locked her away in their château near Paris. One day, her father-in-law shot her four times in a fit of rage before turning the gun on himself."

Luke looked stunned. "And she survived?"

"Not only did she survive, but she got a divorce and came back here to New Orleans. Once she was free of all that dead weight, she shaped the French Quarter into what we see today."

I glanced at him and saw something in his expression shift, like the story had struck a chord. He studied me for a moment. "Have you ever thought about being a tour guide?"

The question caught me off guard. I let out a small laugh, suddenly aware of how much I'd been talking. "Not really. I guess I just remember the story from school."

We stepped into Jackson Square, where the atmosphere was alive with tarot card readers, street musicians, and artists showcasing their work. The air hummed with energy, and I couldn't help but feel the tug of possibility.

Luke turned to me, his eyes sparkling with curiosity. "How about we get our fortunes told?"

I hesitated, looking at the colorful array of fortune tellers set up around the square. "You know, I've never actually done that. Do you believe in that stuff?"

He shook his head. "Not really, but it seems like the thing to do here. You in?"

I grinned, already scanning the options. "Why not?" Leaning closer, I whispered, "Who should we pick?"

Luke pointed toward a woman adorned in a vibrant head wrap and an outfit that seemed to belong on a movie set. "How about Madame Aphrodite over there?"

I led the way, trying not to laugh at the exaggerated way she gestured us over. "Hi there. My friend here is curious about a tarot-card reading. How much do you charge?"

She sized us up, her oversized feather boa brushing against the

cards laid out on her table. "For you, a suggested fifty-dollar dona-
tion," she said, her voice dripping with drama.

I choked a little, blinking. "Uh, do you take credit cards?"

She rolled her eyes, waving her hand dismissively. "Darling, do I
look like I have a card machine hidden in my turban? Next, you'll ask
if I take crypto."

Luke pulled out a bundle of bills as if it were nothing. "I've got
cash."

I grabbed his wrist, whispering, "Put that away. Do you want to
get mugged?"

Madame Aphrodite beckoned us with a dramatic flourish. "Sit,
my darlings. We must build a fortress of energies to protect us."

Luke murmured, "Protect us from what, exactly?"

Madame Aphrodite shot him a look of dramatic disdain. "From
malevolent spirits, of course. Now, sit."

Luke immediately gestured to me with a sly grin. "Ladies first."

I stared at him flatly but relented with a sigh. "Fine."

I'd always been skeptical about tarot-card readings. Growing up
in New Orleans taught me to respect the unexplainable. Madame
Aphrodite waved her hand over the deck, sprinkling herbs that
smelled suspiciously like my aunt's kitchen. Her bangles clinked
loudly as she spoke, her voice dripping with drama. "What question
would you like to ask the cards, my dear?"

I hesitated, trying to keep things light. "What does the future hold
for me?"

Her eyes sparkled as though I'd just handed her a lottery ticket.
"Ah, an excellent question." She spread three cards face down with
deliberate flair. "These cards represent your past, your present, and
your future. Let's begin. Flip the first card."

I flipped it over and saw an image of a lone figure walking away
from a scattered arrangement of cups.

Madame Aphrodite leaned in as if she were about to divulge the
secret of life itself. "Behold, the Eight of Cups. This card speaks of
moving on. It's time to leave behind the energy-draining ties of the
past." Her gaze bore into me. "You're carrying guilt, aren't you?"

I froze for a breath, then forced a laugh. "Well, there *was* that time I told my cousin the ice cream truck only played music when it was out of ice cream."

Madame Aphrodite didn't flinch. "This isn't about your cousin. This is guilt's shadow—fear. Fear is what's anchoring you. Fear of rejection, fear of the unknown, fear that you'll try and still fall short." Her voice softened, but the words landed like thunder. "You tell yourself it's only guilt. But that guilt leads to fear."

My chest burned. She wasn't wrong, and I hated how seen I felt.

As if he could sense it, Luke jumped in, his voice light and airy. "Fear? Anna? Nah. She faces down tourists at Muses without even blinking."

Madame Aphrodite smiled faintly, letting the moment settle. "Shall we move on to the present?"

I turned over the next card, revealing a woman calmly holding a roaring lion at bay.

"Ah, the Strength card." Madame's tone was theatrical. "It tells me you have the courage to face adversity, but not in the way you think. It's not brute force. It's quiet strength, the kind that comes from trusting yourself."

Luke leaned back, smirking. "Quiet strength? That's a fancy way of saying stubborn, isn't it?"

Madame's painted eyebrows arched higher. "The strength is there, whether or not she chooses to use it."

I resisted the urge to roll my eyes but said nothing, flipping the final card. It was a serene woman pouring water beside a shimmering pond beneath a glowing star.

"The Star," Madame whispered reverently, her tone dipping into mystery. "Hope. Renewal. A guiding light toward brighter days." Her voice dropped low with warning "But fear is stubborn. It will whisper doubts in your ear, telling you that you're not enough, that you'll fail. Only by confronting it can you step into the future you deserve."

I stared at the card. Her words felt too close to home, like she'd reached into my chest and plucked out all my buried insecurities. Strength, renewal, and courage sounded so absurdly out of reach. But part of me—the part I tried to silence—longed for it to be true. What would it be like to believe in that kind of promise, to imagine a future brighter than my fears?

"Well," I finally said, my voice shaky, "that's a lot to unpack. Do I get a user manual for all that strength and renewal?"

Madame Aphrodite chuckled. "You don't need a manual, my dear. You need to trust that the story you want to write is worth telling."

I wasn't so sure. But as I placed the cards back on the table, a tiny ember of hope flickered.

16

LUKE

IT WAS MY TURN.

I settled into the chair across from the fortune teller while she waved what looked like a bundle of herbs over the cards.

"Cleansing the space," she explained, her bracelets jangling with every motion. "Now, tell me, what do you wish to ask the cards?" Her tone invited me to whisper secrets I didn't know I had.

I hesitated, masking my discomfort with a casual shrug. "Am I going to win a big award next year?"

Madame Aphrodite clicked her tongue in mock disapproval, shaking her head. "No, no, no. Dive deeper. Ask a question that will guide your soul." Before I could think of a sarcastic comeback, she added, "We will ask the cards how you can rediscover joy in your life."

My stomach twisted slightly, and I shifted in my seat. Joy? That felt like a tall order. But her gaze held me captive, so I nodded.

She placed three cards face down in front of me, her bangles chiming like tiny gongs. "These cards reveal your past, present, and future. Go on, flip the first one."

I reached out, my fingers brushing the worn edge of the card before flipping it over. A regal woman seated on a throne stared back at me, her crown adorned with stars.

"Ah, the Empress," Madame Aphrodite declared, her voice dropping into a hush. Then her gaze narrowed as she leaned in, tapping the card with a finger adorned in rings. "But... she is reversed. This suggests a void, an emptiness in your past. Perhaps someone you once relied on left a mark? An absence you've yet to reconcile."

My throat constricted. My mom's face flickered briefly in my mind, unbidden and uncomfortable. But no. This must be about Sienna. It had to be her. She'd been the one who left me spinning, hadn't she?

Although if I were honest, Sienna hadn't crossed my mind recently. And the thought of my mother clung to me like a burr, making me squirm.

"Come on now." Madame Aphrodite's voice broke through my unease, light and coaxing. "Don't linger too long on the past, darling. Let's see what the present holds."

I turned over the second card, revealing a skeletal figure atop a horse carrying a sickle. The image sent a shiver down my spine. "This... doesn't look good," I said.

Madame Aphrodite rolled her eyes with flair. "It's Death," she said dryly. "But don't be so dramatic—this isn't about literal death. It's the end of something that no longer serves you. A door that must close so a new one can open."

I exhaled, letting her words sink in. Transformation. Ending something. This time, the message seemed clear: Sienna. But if I hadn't thought about her in days, my relationship with her was already over. Did that mean something else was ending?

"Finally, the grand finale." Madame spoke with theatrical anticipation. "Flip the last card to uncover your future."

I turned over the final card and stared at the image of a man in ragged clothes, barefoot, carrying a stick slung over his shoulder. "Wait, am I about to become the world's worst-dressed hiker?"

Madame Aphrodite cackled, clearly amused by my discomfort. "No, dear. This is The Fool." She leaned in, her tone serious. "The

Fool represents a fresh start. A journey into the unknown, full of possibilities. It's about trusting your instincts, even when others don't understand."

I stared at the card, feeling a strange mix of hope and dread. A fresh start sounded good on paper, but what if I messed it up? What if I wasn't enough?

Madame Aphrodite's eyes twinkled. "Of course, fear will cling to you like a shadow. It always does. But the question is, will you let it decide your path?"

I didn't answer. I couldn't. She was asking about something that I wasn't ready to confront.

As we rose to leave, her knowing gaze followed me. "The universe speaks in mysterious ways." Her voice sparkled with mischief.

When Anna and I reached the door, Madame Aphrodite leaned in close, her eyes glittering with sudden intensity. "Beware the place tall shadows lean," she whispered. "For when the ground trembles and silence is keen, it's the tree that falls, not the scene."

Anna tilted her head, her playful sarcasm vanishing. "What does that mean?"

Madame Aphrodite offered nothing more than a cryptic smile, her painted lips curving into an enigmatic grin.

I forced a laugh, trying to shake off the strange reading. "Well, I was kind of hoping for a card that said, 'Congratulations, you'll win an Oscar.'"

Anna snorted beside me. "With my luck, I'm surprised I didn't draw a card saying, 'Congratulations, you've won... jury duty.'"

As we walked away, the fortune teller's words followed me like a shadow I couldn't outrun. A fresh start. Trusting my instincts. Letting go of fear. They sounded simple enough, but deep down, I knew better.

17

ANNA

WE WERE DONE with the tarot-card reader, and I needed a drink—or maybe an exorcist—to shake off what had just transpired.

Or at least some comfort food.

"Do you want to go to Pat O'Brien's and have a hurricane? It's a sweet rum drink that's a New Orleans specialty," I said.

Luke offered a small, easy smile. "I don't drink. But if you want one, go for it."

"How about Napoleon House instead? They've got incredible muffuletta sandwiches. It's classic New Orleans."

Luke tilted his head, intrigued. "Napoleon House? Sounds fancy."

I grinned. "It's not. The building's over two-hundred years old, and the story goes that the owner wanted it to be a refuge for Napoleon Bonaparte after his exile. He never showed, obviously, but the name stuck. Now, it's one of the most iconic spots in the city."

"I'm sold."

With its dark wood and peeling paint, Napoleon House possessed a weathered charm. Stepping inside felt like stepping back in time. Luke slipped into a dramatic French accent, likely because he was worried about being overheard.

"You can call me Jacques Laurent," he declared, gesturing grandly toward a corner table. *"Assieds-nous et commandons ivrognes."*

I nearly dropped my bag as I burst out laughing. "Oh my gosh. What?"

His expression turned mock offended. "What? What did I say?"

Through my giggles, I managed to explain, "You just said, 'Let's sit and order drunks.' I think you were going for *boissons.* Drinks."

He sniffed, feigning indignation, though the glint in his eye gave him away. "You know, usually my French wows people. Okay, maybe not native speakers, but still. Don't tell me, you're fluent?"

"I minored in French in college." I tried to sound casual. "When I have time, I meet with a group of French speakers at a coffee shop uptown to keep it fresh. It's for when I finally visit Paris, which I fully intend to do. *Respirer Paris, cela conserve l'âme."*

Luke blinked at me, his face blank. "Uh, okay, what now?"

I smiled. "To breathe Paris preserves the soul."

As Luke and I settled into the cozy corner booth, the atmosphere lightened. Luke was back to his exaggerated French persona. *"Très bien,"* he said. Then he raised an eyebrow. "Alright, what's so funny? You've been holding back a laugh since we sat down."

I pointed to his head, grinning. "That wig. It's so convincing, I almost asked for your autograph, thinking you were an '80s rock star."

He smirked. "You ain't seen nothing yet. My stylist has an entire wardrobe of these."

"Your stylist? How very Hollywood." I imagined him surrounded by racks of wigs and disguises, someone on speed dial for every possible look. *What must that be like—having people whose entire job is making sure you look perfect?* "You're like a spy."

He leaned in, lowering his voice, letting me in on a secret. "Okay, random fact, did you know the CIA studied Hollywood costume designers and makeup artists? Like, they legit used movie tricks to help create spy gear."

I tilted my head, intrigued. "That's actually... not surprising. Makes sense."

"Right? Wearing disguises isn't exactly my idea of fun, but it keeps the paparazzi on their toes. If I ditched this wig, I'd probably cause a fan stampede."

A fan stampede. The image was almost comical—crowds of people shrieking and chasing after him like he was made of gold. But underneath the absurdity was something unsettling. *He can't even walk down the street without being hunted.*

"That sounds intense. Is getting mobbed by fans the worst part about being famous?"

Luke stared at his seltzer water for a moment, his easy demeanor slipping. "I think the worst part is having to always be 'on.' You can't have a bad day. You can't look less than perfect or lose your temper. And if you punch someone who deserves it..." He trailed off, his jaw tightening briefly. "Paparazzi are like vultures, waiting to catch you at your worst and blow it up for the world to see."

Something in his voice made my chest ache. I'd never thought about it that way—the relentless pressure, the constant performance.

I leaned back, studying him. "You have a pretty solid track record, though. I've never seen a bad picture of you. Have you ever taken a bad photo?"

He chuckled, the tension easing. "Oh, they're out there. But I've got a good publicist. I mean, she's probably more stressed than I am these days. I'm keeping her busier than she'd like."

"Sounds like you've got a small army behind you."

He nodded knowingly. "In this business, you don't always know who you can trust. But if you pay them well enough, you can usually trust them. At least until someone offers them more."

I grimaced. "That sounds exhausting."

And lonely, I thought but didn't say. *How do you build a life when everyone around you has a price tag?*

"It can be," he admitted, then his expression lightened. "But I'm luckier than most. I know that."

Before I could respond, a playful look lit his eyes. "It's not like I'm spoiled or anything."

I winced at his not-so-subtle jab at what I had told my cousin's daughters about him, but he quickly held up a hand. "Relax, I'm joking."

Then, in a move that caught me entirely off guard, he reached across the table and rested his hand briefly over mine. It was a simple, fleeting gesture, but it sent a jolt of warmth up my arm.

What was that? My pulse hammered in my ears. *Was it just... friendly? Or—*

He picked up his iced tea a second later as if it hadn't happened, but I sat there staring at the spot where his hand had been. Even with his hand gone, I could still feel his touch.

18

LUKE

MY FINGERS still thrummed from where they'd brushed against Anna's. I leaned back slightly, watching her as she spoke. There was something about her today—a shift, maybe. It could've been the sunlight slanting just right or the easy rhythm of conversation, but she seemed to glow with a magnetic, edgy charm.

"So, Topher mentioned you're from a big family?" I said.

"Yeah, my adopted family. My mom passed away when I was ten, and I ended up moving in with my Aunt Dolores and Uncle Ray. They had four children—two boys and two girls. It was an adjustment."

I caught the subtle hesitation in her tone, the way her fingers brushed against the edge of her glass. "That must have been a lot."

"I guess." She shrugged. "After my mom died, I got used to not being anyone's priority. Dolores and Ray were great, don't get me wrong, but with four kids of their own... You learn to fend for yourself."

She said it so matter-of-factly, like it didn't sting anymore. But it did. I could feel it in the way her smile faltered, the way her eyes darted away for just a second too long.

I wanted to say something to lighten the mood. But what could I say that wouldn't sound hollow?

Her words tugged at something deep inside me. I didn't have anyone who put me first either, I realized. Not since my dad died. He'd been the one person who always looked out for me, no matter what. And now? Now I was Luke Fisher, the face on the posters, the guy everyone recognized but no one knew. Everyone wanted something from me, but no one stuck around just for me.

The thought settled heavily in my chest as I looked at Anna. She brushed it off so easily, like it was nothing. But it wasn't nothing.

It was everything.

"So," she said suddenly, her tone lighter, like she'd flipped a switch. "Anyway, yes, my whole family's still here in New Orleans. They wouldn't dream of leaving. When Hurricane Katrina hit, that was the first time they'd even left the state."

I tried to wrap my head around that. "Wait. Katrina was their first time leaving Louisiana? Ever?"

She nodded, her expression pensive. "Yeah. For a lot of people here, evacuating for Katrina was the first trip out of state they'd ever taken. It's hard to explain, but New Orleans is everything to them. Most people don't have the means to leave even if they wanted to, and with so much family here, there's no reason to go."

"And you'll never live anywhere else, you don't think?"

She shook her head. "No, never, this is home."

I let that settle, trying to wrap my head around it, when there were so many incredible places in the world. "When you moved in with your aunt and uncle, what was it like being thrown into such a big family?"

She laughed, the sound warm and light. "Loud. Always loud. They're a loving bunch, but let me tell you, peace and quiet were never an option."

I thought of my own childhood, which for most of my life was just my college professor dad and me. "Sounds like you never had a boring day."

She smirked. "Not one. We didn't have fancy vacations or eat out at restaurants, but we always had what we needed. My aunt was also very involved in volunteering. It made me feel guilty sometimes for wanting more, you know? Seeing so many people who had less than we did put things into perspective."

Her honesty was disarming, and for a second, I felt a pang of guilt for holding back about my own family. She'd just laid it all out, and here I was, sidestepping the very thing I was asking her about. But diving into the layers of my history wasn't something I was ready for. The truth is, I was afraid—afraid that if I let her in, I'd lose control of the image I had so carefully built.

And so, I held back. Because opening up felt like stepping off a ledge I wasn't sure I could climb back from.

I gave her a small smile, deflecting. "Sounds like your aunt and uncle did an incredible job stepping in and raising you."

Anna nodded, but her eyes flickered with something I couldn't quite read, like she knew there was more I wasn't saying. I felt her gaze for a second longer than was comfortable. Then she looked away, the moment slipping by as effortlessly as the conversation had started.

We stepped out of the restaurant and into the warm, golden hush of early evening. Royal Street pulsed with charm. The windows of antique shops glinted in the fading light, and buskers played music low and sweet on a saxophone nearby. For a moment, I could almost forget who I was, or who everyone thought I was.

Then, the skies opened up, and a sudden downpour drenched us in seconds. "Classic New Orleans," Anna quipped, leading us to the shelter of an overhang. I scanned the street instinctively, my gaze darting to anyone who might recognize me. Tom and Hal had hung back half a block, giving us space to talk without hovering, though I had no doubt they were watching. Only when I was sure no one on the street was paying us any attention did I relax enough to peel off the now-soaked glasses and wig, giving it a good shake.

"It's all right." Anna took the wet wig from me and tucked it into her bag. "These showers are fleeting. It'll clear up soon."

But just as Anna finished speaking, a woman with an umbrella came to a sudden stop a few feet away. Her eyes widened like she'd just spotted Bigfoot in designer sneakers. "Wait a second... you're Luke Fisher."

My heart shot into my throat. Before I could even blink, Anna sprang into action. Her arm slid through mine, and her voice went full Broadway.

"*Darling,*" she gasped. "She thinks you're *Luke Fisher.* Can you *imagine?* Luke Fisher just strolling through the French Quarter? Without a publicist? Or a single bodyguard doing that weird earpiece squint?"

I tried to play along, nodding with a sheepish grin while Tom and Hal, standing a few feet away, watched closely but pretended not to know us.

The woman's expression wavered, excitement giving way to confusion. She glanced at me again, then back at Anna, recalibrating. "Yeah... you're right. That would be crazy," she said with an awkward laugh. "Sorry."

She hurried off, umbrella bobbing.

As soon as she was out of earshot, I turned to Anna. "I think you just saved my life."

She quickly dropped her arm, cheeks flushed, though it could've just been the humidity. "Geez, you weren't kidding about the whole getting-recognized thing. But I've got just the spot to lie low for a bit. I'm going to take you where William Faulkner wrote his first novel. Trust me, you'll love it."

She led the way, and we dashed through the rain. Faulkner House Books offered the perfect escape. I let myself relax as we hid in the stacks.

At one point, she picked up a vintage copy of *The Sound and the Fury.* "Confession time," she said, sheepishly. "I've never actually read Faulkner."

"Seriously?" I was genuinely surprised. "Faulkner's work is profound. I got into it in college."

She grabbed another book and held it up for me to see. *A Confederacy of Dunces.* "How'd you like this one?"

I shook my head. "Never read it."

Her eyes lit up. "Not reading this while you're in New Orleans is practically a crime. I'll get it for you. Once you've finished, we're having a book chat. Oh, and here's your wig. Sorry, it's not dry, but it's the best I can do."

She pulled the wig from her bag and leaned in to help me adjust it.

Our hands brushed, and I froze, caught off guard by the unexpected spark that shot through me.

My fingers lingered on hers a moment too long, and before I could stop myself, I glanced down at her. "Today has been... fun."

Her eyes lifted to meet mine, wide and searching, and for a second, the world fell completely still. The faint scent of jasmine clung to her, mingling with the musty aroma of old books, and the quiet hum of the bookstore wrapped around us, cocooning the moment.

Then, just as the silence began to crackle with unspoken tension, it shattered.

"Need any help?" The clerk's overly cheerful voice cut through the tension, making both of us jump. I stepped back so quickly that I nearly tripped over a stack of hardcovers, clearing my throat like I'd inhaled a whole library's worth of dust. Anna turned away, her cheeks pink and her hands fumbling with the book she'd been holding.

She raised *A Confederacy of Dunces* like a shield. "Just this," she blurted, her voice a touch too high-pitched as she bolted for the counter.

The moment we stepped outside, the humid air wrapped around us like a sticky blanket. But before we could take another step, a voice sliced through the air, pointed and dripping with familiarity.

"Well, isn't this unexpected?"

Anna froze mid-stride, and I nearly walked into her. Her whole posture changed. Her back was straight, her shoulders stiff, like a soldier preparing for battle. My gaze flicked toward the source of the voice: two women lounging at a table in the courtyard, their eyes locked on her like a pair of smug cats who'd cornered their prey.

The blonde, her smile as polished and fake as a plastic tiara, tilted her head. "Anna Amato, what an absolute delight." She nudged her companion, a brunette with a matching smirk. "Reagan, isn't this a treat?"

Anna stood her ground, but the faint flush on her cheeks gave her away. I could feel the tension rippling off her, sharp enough to cut through the humid air.

This was no casual run-in.

Reagan leaned forward, her voice syrupy sweet. "Anna, it's been forever. What are you up to these days?"

Anna squared her shoulders, her tone steady but tinged with defiance. "I'm a writer."

Reagan's brows shot up in mock surprise, her lips curling into a smile that didn't reach her eyes. "A writer? Huh. I thought you were waitressing." She laughed lightly, as though she'd just made the funniest joke of the evening.

Anna's jaw tightened, but her voice didn't waver. "Well, I do work as a waitress, but I'm also working on a novel."

The blonde cut in, her tone a shade too cheerful. "That's so... creative. I mean, it's good to have hobbies, right?"

Reagan chuckled, her eyes gleaming with mischief. "Speaking of hobbies, Beau and I are house hunting. We're back in town for a bit, getting everything ready for the big move. You know, after the wedding."

Anna's expression didn't flicker, but I caught the subtle way her hand clenched at her side. "When are you and Beau moving back?" Her voice was calm and polite, a masterclass in restraint.

"Oh, Beau's already staying with his parents," Reagan replied, flashing a dazzling smile. "After the wedding, he's taking over his father's business. I'll officially be leaving Manhattan in a couple of months to join him here. You must be so happy for us, Anna. Beau always said you had such a generous heart."

Anna's smile was strained, her words clipped. "Best wishes on the wedding, Reagan."

Reagan tilted her head, her mock sympathy practically dripping. "Thank you, Anna. You, of all people, would know how challenging it is to get Beau to commit."

The air between them felt like a rubber band stretched to its breaking point.

"*Bonjour, mesdames*," I said, stepping closer and wrapping an arm around Anna's waist. "I am Jacques. Jacques Laurent de Valois." My thick French accent turned the women's curious expressions into raised eyebrows.

Anna gestured toward them with a tight smile. "This is Chatterly, and this is Reagan. We went to high school together."

They looked at me skeptically, their gazes flicking between the wig, the oversized sunglasses, and Anna. They weren't buying it—*yet*.

"I'm visiting from my grand château nestled in the Loire Valley," I said, dialing up the accent and enthusiasm. "At Château de Valois, we've been perfecting the art of winemaking for generations. Our signature cuvée won the Crystal Cuvée Cup at the International Champagne Awards just last year. You must have heard the news here."

I turned to Anna as I brushed a damp strand of hair from her cheek. "My darling and I have spent many a starlit evening sipping the champagne on the terrace, overlooking the vineyards."

Her eyes widened in panic, her lips pressing into a tight line that clearly said *tone it down*. But her hesitation must have appeared to be bashful agreement because it worked in our favor, and the women's suspicion started to falter.

Reagan's voice was tinged with awe. "The Loire Valley? And the Crystal Cuvée? That's insanely prestigious."

"It must be a truly exquisite château, Monsieur de Valois," Chatterly added, blinking slowly. "How fascinating."

Their shift was almost comical. I leaned into the moment, turning back to Anna, my fingers brushing her cheek again, this time more deliberately. Her breath hitched, just enough to make my pulse skip.

"Darling," I murmured, low enough for only her to hear, "shall we show them how the French do romance?"

Her lips parted—maybe to protest, maybe not. I didn't give her time to make a decision. Tilting my head, I slid my hand to her jaw and closed the distance between us.

At first, it was all about the show: a performance, a carefully choreographed display of passion to silence our audience. I knew exactly how to draw her in, how to brush my lips over hers just enough to ignite curiosity, to tempt her into responding. I pressed closer, teasing her lower lip with the faintest bite, coaxing a gasp from her.

But as the seconds ticked by, the world outside began to blur. The watchful eyes of the two women, the rhythm of New Orleans jazz drifting from Bourbon Street, the distant chatter of the crowd, and the sweet scent of magnolia mixed with alcohol all faded to insignificance. The kiss deepened, becoming more intimate, more personal. The taste of her lips, the warmth of her breath, and the subtle traces of rain between us were all that mattered.

When we finally broke apart, I rested my forehead against hers, trying to catch my breath. Then I lifted my head to the two wide-eyed watchers. "Ladies, it's been enlightening."

I took Anna's hand, leading her away from the courtyard. Once we were out of sight, the tension broke, replaced by a shared, breathless exhilaration. Anna pulled away slightly, her cheeks still flushed. "That was... unexpected."

I grinned, leaning casually against a lamppost. "Well, it worked. You saw their faces."

She cleared her throat. "That was quite the story about your château in France."

"The château is real. And my champagne did win an award—though I couldn't tell you the name of the award."

She blinked in surprise. "Wait. You do own a château? And you make champagne?" Just then, her phone alarm beeped, and her face fell. "Oh, snickerdoodle. I've got to get to work."

"Let's go. Tom'll drive you," I said quickly, just as the black SUV pulled up to the curb.

Tom and Hal had been watching the entire performance from a distance, probably with matching expressions of long-suffering amusement. Tom gave me a look as he stepped out. Somewhere between *was that in the script?* and *you better be sure about this.*

We paused at the car door, her hand lingering on the handle, mine resting on the roof. Her eyes searched mine.

"I know that kiss was just for their benefit." Her voice was steady, but there was something she wasn't saying.

I nodded, though the words caught in my throat. "Right. Just part of the performance."

Her lips curved into a faint smile, one that didn't quite reach her eyes. "Well, you sold it."

Neither of us moved, and for a heartbeat, the world held its breath. Then she slipped into the car, and I stood still for a moment before I stepped inside, wondering how something fake could feel so real.

19

ANNA

LUKE FISHER JUST KISSED ME. Luke. Fisher. Just. Kissed. Me. Let's try that again. LukeFisherKissedMe. Luke. Freaking. Fisher. Kissed. Me. Me!

Fast or slow—it still made no sense. Did the laws of reality just glitch?

Sure, technically, it was for show, to throw off the mean girls—a little fake-out to make me feel better.

Except it didn't feel fake. At all.

Maybe he's just that good of an actor. Yeah, that's it. He's so talented that even his fake kisses deserve an award. And now, here I am, unable to stop replaying it in my head.

I'll let you in on a secret. I'd watched him kiss women on screen. Countless times. And yes, I'd imagined what it might be like, purely out of curiosity. But here's the truth: reality blew imagination out of the water.

As we drove back, my mind raced. Chief among the emotions was a touch of smugness at the jealousy on the faces of Reagan and Chatterly. Sure, they didn't know I'd kissed Luke Fisher.

They thought it was some black, curly-haired champagne baron.

Well, they could sit there with their fake smiles and passive-aggressive comments, but little did they know I was the one who'd just locked lips with a bona fide movie star.

I was mid-smirk when Luke's voice pulled me back.

"You're a great storyteller," he said, almost like he'd just realized it himself. "The way you talk about things—people, places, whatever—it's like you've got this gift of making everything sound alive. Like, when you were describing the baroness earlier, I could almost see her. Most people don't have that. It's natural for you."

A warmth settled in my chest. It didn't feel like one of those polite, throwaway compliments people give to fill silence.

I needed to say something—anything—to stop replaying that kiss in my head. "Thanks for stepping in back there," I said. "Every time I run into those women, it's like I'm sixteen again. Braces, insecurity, the whole awkward package. Ugh, listen to me. You probably have no idea what that's like."

Luke laughed, shaking his head. "Are you kidding? I was a total nerd in high school. Scrawny, constantly tripping over my own feet. I was invisible."

I raised an eyebrow. "Seriously?"

"Seriously," he said, grinning. "Then I shot up six inches the summer after graduation, joined the crew team at Brown, and suddenly people started looking at me differently. Still felt like the same dork inside, though." He rubbed the back of his neck, the corners of his mouth turning up with a sheepish smile.

I raised an eyebrow. Was he saying that to make me feel better? His sincerity seemed real. "Guess we both had our moments, then."

There was a brief silence before Luke said, "Speaking of the past, who was that Beau guy your old classmate mentioned?"

I smiled wryly. "Let me paint you a picture. Think high school rom-com. He was dripping in money and popularity. Me? I was the nerdy scholarship girl. At some point, he took off my glasses. Metaphorically. I don't wear glasses. He realized I didn't look so ugly after all. But plot twist. He still ended up with the popular high-society girl. And now they're getting married. End of movie. Roll credits. Cue sad trombone."

Luke held my gaze. "I don't think I'd watch that movie."

"Trust me, it wasn't a blockbuster experience from my end either."

I hesitated, unsure if I wanted to dredge up the past, but Luke's kind expression nudged me forward. "Those girls are the worst. In eighth grade, I got a scholarship to Collegiate. It's this fancy prep school in New Orleans, and I thought it was my big break. Before school started, my Aunt Dolores gave me some money to buy new clothes, and I found this Jill Stuart dress at the Junior League thrift store. It had a tiny tear, but she fixed it, and I thought I looked perfect."

Luke's brow furrowed slightly, but he didn't interrupt.

"First day of school, I showed up in that dress, thinking I'd nailed it. But the kids there weren't wearing fancy clothes. They were in jean shorts and T-shirts. One girl was even in pajama bottoms. I stuck out like a sore thumb." I laughed weakly, trying to downplay it. "And then Reagan happened."

"Reagan?" Luke murmured.

"She was one of the queen bees. She spotted me, smiled, and said she loved my dress. I believed her for a second." I swallowed hard, memories choking my throat. "Then she told me it used to be hers... until she donated it because of the tear. She pointed out the mend on the sleeve and laughed in my face. Everyone laughed." I forced a smile, trying to shake off the lingering sting. "It was humiliating. I was wearing her cast-off trash."

Luke's jaw tightened. "Kids can be brutal."

I nodded. "Yeah. After that, I just kept my head down and focused on school. I didn't want to give anyone a reason to notice me. Then, in junior year, I started spending more time with Beau. He was my debate partner. Rich, charming, popular. Somehow, he noticed me, and for a while, I thought maybe I belonged." I sighed. "Now he's engaged to Reagan."

Luke's voice was gentle. "And seeing her today brought it all back?"

"Yeah," I admitted, my voice barely above a whisper. "It's stupid, I know. I've moved on, but sometimes, it still feels like I'm that awkward girl in the thrift store dress."

"It's not stupid. That kind of thing sticks with you. Anyone who can't see your value isn't worth your time."

His words touched me deeper than I expected, and for a moment, I couldn't speak. Finally, I managed a small "Thanks."

But then a dangerous thought crept in. *What if I didn't let this moment pass?*

What if I put myself first? For once.

The idea alone was terrifying. I couldn't afford to lose my job. I'd never called in sick a day in my life. I didn't even know the procedure. Just the thought of dialing in made my stomach knot.

But even scarier was the thought that I might put myself out there... and he could turn me down, that this might all be one-sided. A misunderstanding. A moment I'd built up in my head.

I swallowed hard, then forced the words out before I could lose my nerve. "I can't believe I'm saying this, but... maybe work can wait. If you want to talk more and maybe hang out tonight."

Luke turned toward me, and for a fleeting second, hope flared. Was he going to say yes? Maybe lean in and kiss me again? This time for real? My heart pounded so loudly that I was sure he could hear it.

But then his face transformed, his easy charm replaced by a flicker of hesitation. "I have a lot to do." Gone was the easy warmth and curiosity he had shown before. He sounded cool and distant. "This script isn't going to read itself, and if I don't get through it, I'm screwed."

The rejection hit me like a sucker punch. The sting of sudden dismissal was so sharp that it momentarily stole my breath. His abrupt change of demeanor was like a neon sign flashing: *That kiss back there in the French Quarter? Meant nothing at all.* And there I was, thinking I could compete with Hollywood starlets.

I squared my shoulders, trying to keep the mood light. To look on the bright side. I showed a movie star around New Orleans. How many people could say that? Before the SUV could come to a complete stop, I flung open the door. "Hey, it's all good. Good luck with your script," I chirped, probably too cheerfully.

I was almost at my cottage door when I remembered something and headed back to him.

Luke was still in the SUV, a surprised look on his face as I approached. Marching up to his window, I rummaged through my purse. "Almost forgot to give you this." I handed over the copy of *A Confederacy of Dunces* from earlier.

Without waiting for a response, I pivoted and made my grand exit, head high, tears prickling the back of my eyes. I didn't look back. I couldn't.

20

LUKE

IT HAD TAKEN every ounce of my self-control to tell Anna I was too busy to hang out. How easy it would have been to stay with her, to give in to the pull I felt every time she looked at me. But something inside me wouldn't let it happen. Was it fear of rejection? Of letting her see too much of me?

The kiss had left me shaken. It wasn't just the way her lips felt against mine—it was what the kiss made me feel. Something raw, something real. Something I wasn't sure I could handle. I'd kissed plenty of women in my line of work, but Anna was different. She had this unfiltered warmth, a vulnerability that was both grounding and terrifying. She felt real. And that scared me more than I wanted to admit.

Because if Anna saw the real me—the broken parts I worked so hard to keep hidden—would she still look at me the same way? Would she still want anything to do with me? Probably not.

I threw myself into work, trying to drown out the thoughts of her that kept surfacing, no matter how hard I tried to push them away.

Spoiler alert: it didn't work.

Less than a day later, my resolve cracked.

It was the morning after the kiss when I finally called Bob Reardon, my manager. He had been trying to reach me for days to talk about my new role, and I hadn't felt up to it. He picked up on the first ring, wasting no time. "Luke, do you know why you're in this mess?"

I sighed, already regretting the call. "Yes, Bob, I know."

"Do you?" His voice dripped with sarcasm. "Because, in case you forgot, you punched a guy. In public."

"He was sleeping with my girlfriend!"

"It doesn't matter. You got violent."

"Thank you. Appreciate the trip down memory lane."

"Oh, don't mention it," he fired back. "I play the highlight reel every night before bed. It's like a bedtime story, only it ends with me needing Tums."

I groaned. "Can we skip the lecture?"

"Sure, but let's not skip the part where the studio is freaking out. They're convinced you're one headline away from becoming the guy who peaked with *The Boyfriend Test*. And instead of fixing it, you're hiding out in Louisiana like you're auditioning for *Swamp People*."

"I'm not hiding," I argued weakly. "I'm... regrouping."

Bob snorted. "Sure, if that helps you sleep at night. Meanwhile, Gerald Fargo, the director of this movie—the one that could save your reputation—wants to meet you. In LA. Face-to-face. You know, like normal humans do." Bob guffawed. "Let's be real: They want to see if you can still look them in the eye without punching someone."

I stared out at the pool, where Anna had just stepped out of the water, the sunlight catching her in a way that made the rest of the world seem irrelevant. Just then, I made up my mind. "I'll make them an audition tape. I'm not flying back to LA right now."

Bob bristled through the line. "What? Did you just refuse to fly to LA? We must have a bad connection."

I shrugged. "Can't you just tell them I'm focusing on the character?"

"You mean the character who's all about redemption and over-coming his demons? Oh yeah, hiding in Louisiana screams growth." Bob sighed loudly. "Luke, listen to me: you need this role. It's gritty, it's emotional, and it's the kind of thing the Academy loves. But they're not going to hand it to you on a silver platter. You need to prove you can deliver."

"I'll do the meeting with Gerald Fargo over Zoom."

Bob exploded. "Zoom? Oh sure, let's lean into this 'hermit in the bayou' aesthetic you've got going on. Maybe you can wear a swamp hat for effect."

"Bob—"

"No, no, you're right," he interrupted. "Why bother showing up at all? Let's send them a cardboard cutout of you holding a sign that says, 'Please trust me, I won't hit anyone this time.' That'll go over great."

I pinched the bridge of my nose. "Just set up the Zoom, Bob."

"Fine," he huffed. "But you'd better be charming. I'm talking peak Luke Fisher, the guy who could sell sunscreen in a rainstorm. Got it?"

"Got it," I muttered, hanging up before he could launch into another tirade.

I glanced through the window at Anna, who was now lounging by the pool with her nose buried in a book. Bob was right about one thing: I needed to figure out how to get this role.

But looking at Anna, I couldn't shake the feeling that I was figuring out something else, too. Something scarier than auditions and eccentric directors.

Something real.

I couldn't ignore the gnawing doubt in the back of my mind. Yesterday, in the car, I'd blown her off. Why? To avoid letting her see the mess underneath my carefully polished exterior? To keep her from realizing I wasn't as invincible as she thought?

Had I ruined something real before it even had the chance to begin?

I had to fix it.

21

ANNA

When I opened my door to head to work the evening after *the kiss*, my foot caught on something, and I nearly face-planted. A brown paper bag sat neatly on the mat. Picking it up, I spotted a handwritten card tucked inside.

Anna,

You have this incredible way of seeing the world. I hope this book makes you smile the way you make me smile.

Luke

Curiosity piqued, I carefully opened the bag, peeling back the tissue paper. It was a signed first edition of William Faulkner's *As I Lay Dying.*

"Oh, wow," I whispered, running my fingers over the worn leather cover, reverence taking over. This wasn't just thoughtful. It was extravagant. A gift so wildly unnecessary it made my head spin.

Why would Luke send me something like this? Especially after practically shutting me down the day before? My brain was a kaleidoscope of confusion.

But my watch yanked me back to reality. I was already late for work. With a sigh, I carefully closed the book and set it on the table, vowing to unravel the mystery of Luke Fisher and his baffling generosity later.

When I arrived at Muses, Marie Antoinette was practically vibrating with anticipation. She looked like she'd been holding in a secret for hours and might combust.

"Anna Amato," she said, arms folded, one perfectly arched brow raised. "You've been spotted in the French Quarter. With a *man*. A tall, mysterious, dangerously attractive *man*. And you didn't tell me?"

We were starting our shift, the bar mostly empty thanks to the looming rainstorm. A rival tour guide had seen me and Luke walking together and wasted no time feeding her the headline.

"It wasn't a big deal," I said quickly. "Very low key."

"Wait, was it the smoldering Brit? Or the charming Irish Hugh Grant lookalike?" Marie Antoinette quizzed.

"Nope, it was Jacques. The French romantic," I said with a grin.

Her eyes widened. "Come again?"

"Yep, Jacques."

She blinked in confusion. "Mercy! You're changing dance partners faster than I can keep track. This isn't like you at all. So, it's Jacques now? Fine. But if tomorrow you introduce me to an Italian named Giorgio, I'm holding auditions to find the real Anna Amato."

I exhaled deeply, trying to calm my emotions. "Listen," I began, gripping her shoulders. "Something *did* happen in the French Quarter."

"I'm listening."

"Well, we ran into these awful girls from Collegiate, and to make me feel better, Lu—Jacques kissed me."

She leaned in. "Was it a good kiss?"

"Yes. It was..." Earth-shattering, life-altering, weak-in-the-knees-inducing. "Good. It was a good kiss."

"That's great news. It's about time."

"But I don't know if it was just for show, because my high school frenemies were there," I admitted, heart sinking at the memory of Luke's change in behavior during the car ride. "Actually, I'm pretty sure it was just for show. Afterward, he said he had to read..."

Marie Antoinette leaned in like she was about to be handed state secrets. "Read *what*? His diary? A love poem? Don't leave me hanging."

My brain scrambled. I couldn't tell her that he needed to read a movie script. That would give Luke away. "An instruction manual," I said, cringing the moment the words left my mouth.

"He had to read a *what now*?" Her eyebrows shot up. "An instruction manual for what?"

"A blender," I improvised, glancing at the daiquiri machine.

"A blender? How long does it take to read a blender manual?"

I coughed. "Well, they're industrial-grade blenders."

"Industrial-grade blenders? Girl, that's just sad."

"Well, he had to read the manual for work." I felt a blush rise up my neck.

"For work? What does he do?"

I cleared my throat. "He's a kitchen-appliance efficiency analyst."

She shook her head, as though refusing to let her brain process this absurdity any further. "He's from France, and he's in America, reading about blenders. You sure know how to pick 'em, don't you?" She cleared her throat. "Anna, what Beau did to you was unforgivable. I know it scarred you. But you're strong. After all, women are like tea bags—we don't know our true strength until we're in hot water."

"Women are like tea bags? Who said that?"

"Me. And Eleanor Roosevelt. So, if Jacques doesn't realize how amazing you are, don't waste time on him. He may be French, but if you're feeling this conflicted after one kiss, I know your heart won't heal if whatever this is goes any further."

Marie Antoinette was right. That kiss had allowed me to hope, opened the door to new possibilities, and made it hard to focus on anything else. One kiss and I was already feeling things for Luke that I hadn't felt in years. Maybe ever. With Beau, I hadn't felt one-tenth of the glorious anxiety that had recently become my constant companion.

And the saddest part? It was a life-altering kiss from someone who didn't reciprocate my feelings.

Or did he? I wasn't sure anymore.

I'd put myself out there, only to feel the sting of rejection. But then he bought me that first-edition novel. It was a thoughtful, meaningful gift that left me completely confused.

Why would he do that if he wasn't interested?

Was he playing with my emotions, or was I just reading too much into everything?

Or maybe—and this thought made my chest tighten—maybe he felt sorry for me. Maybe the book was an apology gift, a "thanks for the tour guide services" parting present before he disappeared back to his real life.

The bell above the door jingled, and my heart skipped when I saw his familiar blue eyes. Luke stood there in a ridiculous black wig, stick-on mustache, and goatee.

Yanking him toward the private booth, I asked, "So, how did that script turn out? Is it a blockbuster?"

He rubbed the back of his neck, slipping into his French accent. "Ah, the script. Oui, I am still... wading through it." Then, almost tentatively, "Did you get the book?"

"It was too generous." The words came out sharper than I intended. "I can't keep it."

His face fell slightly. "Please keep it." His voice softened, dropping the accent. "I wanted you to have it."

I wanted to believe him. Man, I wanted to. But accepting expensive gifts from someone who'd blown me off felt like setting myself up for more heartbreak.

"I can't." My throat tightened. "It's too much, Luke. I can't accept something like that when I don't even know what we—" I cut myself off, aware of Marie Antoinette's increasingly obvious surveillance mission.

Out of the corner of my eye, I spotted her inching closer and closer to our table. She was trying to be stealthy, but it was like watching a bad spy movie. First, she adjusted the salt and pepper shakers at one table. Then, she rearranged a napkin at another table. She was on an eavesdropping mission, and she wasn't even subtle about it.

I lowered my voice. "I can't talk about this here. I need to get back to work."

I glanced over at my snooping coworker, who was now "casually" dusting off a completely clean chair.

As I walked to the bar, my friend followed. "That's Monsieur Jacques, right? Where did you say that you met him again?"

I was sick of all the lying. "At my Saturday French lesson."

"I thought that was all high schoolers and elderly people?"

"It was—until Jacques showed up."

She grinned. "I want to hear everything."

Fixing a drink for Luke, I replied, "I'll tell you later. I have work."

Her voice followed me. "Since when has *that* ever stopped you from gossiping?"

22

LUKE

I KNEW I'd messed up when Anna's smile didn't quite reach her eyes.

She walked toward me, a martini glass in hand, but something felt off. Had I blown it with the gift? It couldn't have been that bad. Right?

She set the glass down with a slight clink. "It's called a Cos-NO-politan, our nonalcoholic version of a cosmopolitan." Her voice was a little too casual. "So, do you always buy such extravagant gifts for your friends?"

"Not usually." I smiled, watching the faint blush rise on her cheeks. "But most friends don't make me laugh the way you do. Or call me out when I deserve it."

She looked at me then, long enough to make my chest tighten. Something flickered in her eyes, something unsure and maybe a little hopeful, but then she blinked and pulled back behind that practiced shrug. "Well... thanks," she said lightly, but the edge in her tone made it clear: I wasn't off the hook just yet.

Before I could say anything, she turned her attention to a group of three guys who had just stumbled in, their umbrellas dripping all over the floor. Judging by their slurred jokes and the way they leaned on each other, it was clear they'd been bar-hopping for hours. I gave them a once-over, silently pleading for Anna to let someone else handle the table. These guys had *trouble* written all over them.

But, unfortunately, Anna was on call. "Hiya, boys. How are y'all doing today?" She approached them with forced cheer.

The guy with the shoulders so broad that he must have bench-pressed kegs for fun, grinned like he'd just been served on a silver platter. "A whole lot better now that you're here." His eyes gleamed like a frat boy who'd just discovered a two-for-one special.

She took their order, and when she returned with their beer, one of the other men, Mr. Backward Baseball Cap, decided to kick things up a notch. He grabbed her waist, pulling her closer as if she were part of his order. "Hey there, darling. Why don't I help you out?"

Help her? Seriously? With what? Being a sleaze? My hand tightened on my glass, and my body tensed.

Anna didn't need me to intervene; I could see that in the way she deftly shifted her tray away and peeled his hand off with precision that screamed, *Don't even try it, pal.*

"I'm good, thanks." Anna's voice was sweet but edged with a warning. "How about you focus on the drinks, and I'll focus on the service."

I should have relaxed then. She had it handled. But my jaw stayed clenched, my fists balled under the table.

The third guy chimed in, his bark of a laugh cutting through the air like a car alarm. "I bet with looks like yours, you get tips just for smiling. How about I add a little something extra when you're done?"

Anna straightened, her composure unshakable. But Mr. Backward Baseball Cap wasn't done. He reached for her hand, lifting it as if inspecting it for a prize. "You don't look like the kind of girl who'd turn down a better offer." He grinned at his buddies. "Why don't you ditch this place and come party with us?"

That was my breaking point. I shot up from my seat before I even realized what I was doing. "Enough." My voice came out firm, stripped of any pretense or the French accent I had been using earlier. It was just me—raw and furious.

Anna whipped around, her eyes flashing a warning: *Don't make this worse.* But I couldn't stop.

"You don't grab someone like that. Show some respect," I shot back, glaring at the guy. Every muscle in my body was tense, ready for a confrontation.

Mr. Broad Shoulders raised his hands, pretending to be the picture of innocence. "Relax, man. We were joking around. No harm done." He turned back to Anna, his grin faltering but still holding onto his bravado. "Didn't realize she had a bodyguard."

"I'm not her—" I started, but Anna's hand shot up, cutting me off.

"Thank you, gentlemen," she said, her smile tight, with forced politeness. "Enjoy your drinks."

The guys took their drinks to go and slunk off after tossing a crumpled bill on the table, leaving behind a palpable tension. Car Alarm Laugh let out one last bark of his grating guffaw before the door slammed shut behind them.

Anna let out a long, frustrated sigh and turned to me, holding the crumpled bill in her hand. "Great. They gave me barely enough for a bottle of water."

"I'm sorry," I said immediately. "But those guys were way out of line—"

"I know they were out of line, Luke." Her voice was tight, controlled. "I deal with guys like that every shift. I had it handled."

"I know you did, but—"

"But what?" She crossed her arms. "You thought I needed rescuing?"

The edge in her voice caught me off guard. "I wasn't trying to rescue you. I was trying to help."

"Help?" She let out a bitter laugh. "You know what would've helped? Letting me do my job. Those guys were drunk and handsy, yeah, but they were also about to order another round. That's twenty, maybe thirty bucks in tips. Tips I actually need."

Guilt twisted in my gut, but frustration bubbled up alongside it. "So, what, you're supposed to just smile and take it? Let them treat you like that?"

She lowered her voice to a harsh whisper. "This is my job, Luke. This is how I pay my rent. And when some guy in a ridiculous disguise jumps in like he's my knight in shining armor, it makes me look weak. Like I can't handle myself."

"I just don't get why you have to flirt with guys like that for a few extra bucks."

The moment the words left my mouth, I knew I'd screwed up.

Her eyes narrowed, her anger hitting me like a punch. "Excuse me?" She crossed her arms, her stare withering. "In your world, you get paid millions to cozy up to your co-stars on screen, and you're judging me for a little banter?"

"I shouldn't have—"

She stepped closer, her voice dropping to something dangerous. "You show up here in your wigs and your fake accents, playing dress-up because you can afford to. You buy me an extravagant gift I can't accept, you kiss me and then pull away, and now you're lecturing me about how I earn my living? Who do you think you are?"

I winced. She was right. I had no ground to stand on, but the words had already escaped, and now they hung between us like a storm cloud.

Hal and Tom suddenly appeared at the entrance, their faces tight with urgency. "Weather's rolling in fast," Hal said, pointing at the darkening sky. "We need to get moving."

I glanced at Anna, a mix of guilt and something deeper twisting in my chest. I wanted to apologize, to explain that I hadn't meant it the way it sounded. That seeing those guys put their hands on her made something primal surge up in me, something I didn't fully understand.

But the storm outside gave me an out, and like a coward, I took it.

"I should go," I muttered, already halfway out the door.

"Maybe you should," she replied, her voice cold enough to make the rain outside seem warm.

I stepped into the brewing storm, Hal and Tom flanking me. But the icy silence I left behind was far worse than the weather.

23

ANNA

How dare he? I was fuming, wiping down tables in the now-empty bar, still stewing over my interaction with Luke. The nerve of him. Acting all protective, then throwing that ridiculous comment at me. Accusing me of flirting for tips. Seriously? My brain was stuck in a loop, replaying every infuriating second.

I scrubbed harder at an immaculate table, muttering under my breath. *Mr. Movie Star thinks he knows everything about real life? Please.* He probably had people hand-feeding him organic grapes while he casually dismissed real problems. I didn't even realize I was violently rearranging the salt and pepper shakers into angry little armies until Marie Antoinette interrupted my rage spiral.

"Hey, girl." She waved a hand in front of my face. "It's pouring out there. It's the kind of rain that turns streets into rivers. Mrs. Brodie called, and she wants us to close and head out."

I blinked, momentarily disoriented. "What?"

She threw her hands up in exaggerated disbelief. "You seriously haven't noticed the rain? It's like someone turned on a firehose in the sky." She pointed dramatically to the window, where rain poured down relentlessly.

I squinted at the downpour. *Huh. When did that happen?*

"I'll give you a ride."

She held an umbrella over both of us as we braved the rain. Luckily, she had a truck with tires high enough to handle stormwater. After a quick trip through the Garden District to drop me off, the rest of her drive would be on higher ground. She navigated her truck slowly through the streets, which were starting to fill with water.

When we reached the mansion, I was surprised to see that the gate was already open. The reason, I soon realized, was that Luke was sitting in his Lamborghini, ready to leave.

"Is that the guy who's staying in Topher's mansion? What is that fool trying to do?" Marie Antoinette exclaimed. Thankfully, there was no way she could tell it was Luke. She turned to me. "I have to get home before this rain gets any worse, but you have to stop him."

24

LUKE

THE RAIN HAMMERED against the windshield, loud and relentless, like the universe was trying to pound some sense into me. My grip on the steering wheel tightened, my knuckles stark white. I knew this was stupid. I knew driving in this storm was dangerous. I wasn't even sure the Lamborghini could make it a block without the engine flooding. But none of that mattered.

Anna wasn't home.

And she wasn't answering her phone.

I'd texted her twice. Short, direct. **Are you okay? Where are you?**

Nothing.

Every minute that ticked by churned through my mind, dragging with it thoughts I couldn't shake. What if she were stranded somewhere? What if the streets had flooded too fast, and she was stuck? What if she were hurt?

"Luke, it's not safe." Tom's voice was sharp as he stood just outside the car, umbrella useless against the deluge.

"I know it's not safe," I retorted, glancing toward the rain-soaked gates in front of me. "But sitting here while she's out there is worse."

Hal moved to block the car's path, his hand on the passenger door. "She's probably at work or waiting for the storm to ease. Just wait it out."

But waiting wasn't an option. My chest felt like it was going to explode. She was out there, and every instinct screamed at me to find her.

I threw the car into gear. "Move."

The Lamborghini inched forward as the gates began to slide open. Tom shouted something I couldn't hear, but I didn't care. I couldn't care. My only thought was to *find her.*

Then, through the rain, I saw her.

At first, I thought I was imagining it, that my brain was conjuring her up out of desperation. But no, it was Anna. She was running, her bag held over her head, completely soaked. Relief hit me like a lightning bolt, but before I could process it, she threw herself in front of the car.

"Anna." I slammed on the brakes, the tires skidding slightly on the wet ground. My heart slammed in my chest as she slammed her hands on the hood.

I threw the door open, the rain drenching me instantly. "What in the world are you doing?" I shouted, rushing toward her.

"What am *I* doing?" she screamed back, her voice cutting through the storm. "What were *you* doing?"

I grabbed her arm, dragging her to the porch, her wet shoes slipping against the concrete. She yanked away from me the moment we reached shelter, spinning around, her chest heaving.

Her eyes were blazing with anger. "Are you out of your mind?"

"I couldn't just sit here!" The words came out louder than I intended, my frustration boiling over. "You weren't home, Anna. You wouldn't answer your phone. I didn't know if you were safe. I couldn't just wait around while you might've been out there in danger."

"In danger?" She gestured wildly at the rain pounding against the pavement. "You were going to drive through *this*. You could've been swept away. You could've died."

"I was trying to find you," I shouted back.

"You could've died," she choked, her voice breaking. Tears

streamed down her face, mixing with the rain. "You could've died. You could've died."

She was distraught. My chest tightened, her fear and pain pulling me under. "Anna." I stepped closer.

She didn't move, just stood there sobbing, her shoulders shaking. I couldn't take it anymore. I reached for her, pulling her into my arms.

She collapsed against me, her hands gripping my shirt like I was the only thing holding her together. "I'm sorry," I murmured, stroking her rain-soaked hair. "I couldn't sit here, not knowing if you were okay. I didn't mean to scare you. I just... I couldn't do nothing."

Her sobs shook us both, the sound ripping through me. I held her tighter, letting her cry, letting her pour out everything she'd been holding in. The storm raged around us, the wind howling and the rain pounding, but it felt distant, unimportant.

All that mattered was Anna, safe and in my arms.

When her sobs finally slowed, she pulled back just enough to look at me. Her face was streaked with tears and rain. Her eyes burned with intensity. "You can't do that again." She spoke firmly, but her voice trembled. "Promise me, Luke. You can't."

I nodded, brushing a wet strand of hair from her face. "I promise."

And in that moment, holding her under the raging storm, I realized I meant it. For her, I'd do anything.

25

ANNA

WE STOOD there until my shaking stopped. I sniffled, feeling a wave of embarrassment over my emotional meltdown. "I, uh, need to get into dry clothes," I mumbled, glancing down at my soggy, tear-streaked mess of an outfit.

He nodded. "Let me get you an umbrella."

"I can make it." Using my bag as a makeshift cover, I hurried toward the cottage, desperate to escape.

Inside, I dropped my bag and flicked the light switch. Nothing. My breath caught in my throat. *Of course.* The generator for the main house didn't extend to the outbuildings.

I pulled out my phone, my trembling hands fumbling as I tried to turn on the flashlight. No battery. My lungs felt like they were shrinking, every breath a struggle. The exhaustion and the fear weighed me down like bricks. *What else could go wrong?*

A knock at the door startled me. I opened it to find Luke standing under a massive umbrella. "Why don't you sleep in the main house tonight?" His voice was steady and kind. "It has power." When I hesitated, he tried again. "C'mon, the place is big enough for both of us."

I sighed. There was no point in arguing. The cottage was a hot, sticky, miserable mess. "Let me get some dry clothes."

Using the flashlight on Luke's phone, I threw a few things into a bag and returned to the door, where he was waiting. "I know there's an umbrella around here somewhere," I muttered, more to myself than him.

"This one's big enough for both of us." He held it over me. "Can I help you with your bag?"

Even with the oversized umbrella, our arms brushed occasionally as we made our way to the main house. I tried to ignore the tingling sensation. Despite everything—his remarks earlier, his recklessness during the flood—a part of me was relieved to be in the mansion. Being alone in the cottage, with the storm raging outside, wasn't something I could handle tonight.

And, if I were being honest, it had felt good when he held me.

As we stepped into the house, the awkward silence grew thicker. It was made worse by Luke blushing and trying not to look at my chest. I looked down. My wet shirt clung to me like a second skin. I folded my arms, my cheeks flushing.

He dropped his eyes and cleared his throat. "You should change. Come with me. I'll show you to a room where you can stay for the night."

I followed him up a grand staircase and into a cozy chamber with a plush white bed and a small fireplace. He paused at the door, turning back to me. "Anna." His voice was low. "I'm sorry for what I said before at Muses. And for scaring you with the car."

As Luke's words hung in the air, a strange mix of emotions rippled through me. The sincerity in his voice caught me entirely off guard.

I nodded, unsure what to say.

He knocked lightly on the doorframe as a goodbye and disappeared down the stairs.

After showering and changing into dry clothes, I wandered downstairs and into a room that stopped me in my tracks.

Two stories of shelves stretched toward the ceiling, each lined with books that looked like they belonged in a museum. Ladders slid gracefully along polished wood rails, and the soft lighting gave the space a cozy, almost magical quality. For a moment, I just stood there, taking it all in.

Luke was sitting in a plush chair near the center of the room, casually flipping through a book. My heart quickened when I realized he was wearing my lavender hoodie from Muses—the one I'd shoved at him in a panic to help him escape that bachelorette party.

His gaze lifted, and he caught me staring. "Oh, this?" He tugged at the hoodie with a half-smile. "I've taken to wearing it around the house. It's ridiculously comfortable."

I felt a strange, inexplicable flutter in my chest. "Glad it's getting some use." I tried to sound casual.

He grinned and leaned back in his chair, gesturing around the room. "So, what do you think? Impressive, right?"

I glanced around again, my awe returning. "Am I in heaven?"

Luke chuckled. "Close enough. This is my favorite place. And believe it or not, all these books belong to Topher."

I raised an eyebrow. "Topher? I didn't know he reads."

"Shocking, I know." He pointed toward a spiral staircase that led to the second level. "You think this is impressive? Wait until you see upstairs. Rare manuscripts, first editions, and yes, there's a Shakespeare First Folio up there."

My jaw dropped. "You're kidding."

"Not at all," he said, his smile widening. "You're about to see history."

I was about to respond when my phone, now plugged into the charger, buzzed. "Excuse me," I murmured, answering. "Hi, Aunt Dolores."

"Are you somewhere safe? Where are you?" Her tone was edged with worry.

"I'm fine," I assured her. "I'm at Topher's main house. It's secure—bodyguards, whole-house generator, the works."

That seemed to make her feel better. "A whole-house generator? We might have to invite ourselves over."

I chuckled nervously, imagining the chaos of that. "How's the gang?"

"Knee-deep in jambalaya," she said before a baby's cry interrupted her. "Gotta go. Glad you're safe. Love you."

As the call ended, I turned to Luke, settling into the chair across
from him. The storm outside howled, bending trees and scattering
leaves against the windows. I hugged a blanket tighter around me,
grateful to be somewhere warm and safe.

Luke broke the silence. "Is this much rain normal here?"

I nodded. "We get storms like this every once in a while." I shiv-
ered, and before I could say anything, Luke grabbed a plush blanket
from a nearby couch and draped it over me.

Outside, the storm raged, trees bending in the wind while sheets
of rain lashed against the windows.

"I'm glad we're inside while all that's happening out there," he
said.

"Could we maybe find a spot with fewer panoramic views of the
apocalypse?"

"How about the home theater? It's a nice room, and the seats are
comfortable."

I followed him, still clutching the blanket, and as soon as he
opened the door, my jaw nearly hit the floor. "A *nice* room?" It was the
kind of space you'd see in a luxury magazine.

I dropped into one of the dozen leather recliners, which practically hugged me back. "Is that a massage function I'm feeling?" I
pressed the button and sank deeper. "And these"—I pointed at the
cup holders—"do they seriously heat or chill your beverage on
demand?"

Luke leaned casually against the wall, trying not to smile. "I did
say it was nice, didn't I?"

I bolted toward the snack corner. "No way. A legit popcorn
machine?" My gaze darted over the array of candy. "Twizzlers. Milk
Duds. And wait, is that a soda fountain?"

"You're easily impressed."

I grabbed a pack of Twizzlers with dramatic flair. "This isn't just
impressed." I twisted one of the sweet strands in my fingers. "This is
full-on *awe*."

He chuckled and dropped into the chair next to mine, glancing sideways like he was working up to something. "Hey, um..." He cleared his throat. "About earlier. At Muses. I'm sorry. I could've handled that better."

Something about the way he looked now, awkward and sincere, like a guy trying to fix something without fully knowing how, made it impossible to stay mad.

Honestly, I'd already forgiven him.

Not out loud, of course. That would've been too easy.

I sank back into my recliner, still fiddling with the Twizzler. "Honestly, if I had a dollar for every unsolicited comment or phone number scribbled on a receipt, I'd be rich enough to buy one of these theaters."

Luke laughed. "Okay, but what's the weirdest thing that's ever happened with one of your customers at Muses?"

I grinned. "Oh, that's easy. There was this regular who was completely convinced he was a time traveler."

Luke coughed. "You're kidding."

"Nope." I leaned in. "One night, he handed me a scroll. It was actual parchment, sealed with red wax like he's auditioning for *Game of Thrones*. Inside was a love letter written in Shakespearean English."

Luke's eyes widened. "What did you do?"

"Well, I'm not a monster," I said. "I wrote him a rejection letter in iambic pentameter."

Luke grinned. "Did it start with 'Shall I compare thee to a restraining order?'"

I laughed. "Something like that. Anyway, he said he'd return in seven days... and then he vanished."

Luke raised an eyebrow. "Maybe he leapt to another century."

"Exactly," I said. "I hope he's happy somewhere in 1623. Or maybe at the dive down the street."

Luke shook his head, laughing. "You win. My weirdest work story doesn't hold a candle to that."

"Oh, come on," I pressed. "You must have something."

"Fine. When I was a teenager, I worked at this burger joint. There was a woman who'd always order a cheeseburger... but with no cheese."

I blinked. "So... a hamburger?"

"Not in her world." He grinned. "She insisted it was a cheese-burger, *just without the cheese.* If you called it a hamburger, she'd lose her mind. One day, someone accidentally put cheese on her burger. She flipped out like we'd committed a crime against humanity. She waved it around, screaming, 'Cheese. Cheese. It's a scandal.' Then she hurled it at me like it was a grenade."

I was laughing so hard I had tears in my eyes. "What happened after that?"

"She came back the next week and ordered a veggie burger. Want to guess what she wanted on it?"

"No..."

"Cheese." He threw up his hands in mock despair. "Full circle."

I wiped my eyes, still giggling. "You need to write a memoir. *Cheeseburgers: The Luke Fisher Origin Story.*"

Luke smirked. "I think I'll leave the writing to you."

"Oh, yeah, because my glamorous life screams 'bestseller,'" I teased.

His expression shifted from teasing to something more serious. "No. You should be writing full time. You've got the stories, the voice —it's all there."

I rolled my eyes playfully. "My bank account has a different opin-ion. I mean, I've tried to write. I've written novels and submitted short stories to contests and magazines, pitched ideas to agents, and entered competitions. You name it, I've done it. And every single time, it's the same: rejection. Sometimes they're polite. Sometimes they're brutal. 'Not the right fit.' 'Lacks originality.' I once got a form rejection where they didn't even bother to spell my name right."

Luke winced. "I saw. That's rough."

"It is. I just haven't found my niche. Romance? I can't make it work. Fantasy? Nope. Thriller? Not my forte. And I've made a deal with myself that I'll keep going until I hit a hundred rejections. Then, if no one sees something in my writing by then, I'll give up. I'll accept it's not meant to be and move on."

His brow furrowed as if I'd said something deeply offensive. "A hundred rejections? That's your finish line? What number are you at now?"

I winced. "Ninety-nine. I figure one hundred is a fair number— enough to say I gave it everything. At some point, maybe I need to listen to what the universe is telling me."

For a moment, he didn't respond, just looked at me with those piercing blue eyes. Finally, he cleared his throat. "I bet this story you're writing now is your masterpiece."

I smiled, something bittersweet tugging at my heart. "You're awfully optimistic for someone who doesn't know if I'm any good."

Luke shrugged, a slow grin spreading across his face. "Maybe. Or maybe I know talent when I see it. Even if it's still waiting for its moment."

I looked away, trying to keep the warmth rising in my chest from showing too much. I snuggled the blanket tighter around me. "What about you? Is acting your calling?"

His expression shifted, a flicker of vulnerability breaking through his polished exterior. "Acting? Yeah, it's my thing. But the fame circus? That's a whole different story. It's like walking a tightrope, especially with relationships. Topher's always been an exception, probably because he knew me before all of this. But figuring out who's there for you and who's just along for the ride. It's tricky. Especially when it's family."

I noticed the hesitation in his voice, the unspoken words hanging between us. "Your parents?" I prompted gently.

"Not my dad—he was different. He was there for me until the end. But others... let's just say their support comes with conditions."

I didn't press, sensing the rawness of the subject. Instead, I shifted gears. "You've been all over the world, right? What's your favorite place?"

He chuckled, the tension easing. "Honestly? Wherever my shoes are at the moment. The beauty of my job is that it's like having a worldwide plane ticket. Sometimes, I even pick roles based on the shoot location. Settling down in one place? That's not my style."

I grinned. "Let me guess: you've got properties scattered across the globe?"

He shrugged, a faint smile playing on his lips. "A house in LA, the place in France. A penthouse in Manhattan. Investments, mostly. Topher's idea. But roots? Nah, not for me. What about you? What's your favorite place?"

That one was easy. "Destin, Florida. Every summer, it was just my mom and me. We'd rent this tiny condo with just a bedroom, a bathroom, nothing fancy. But it sat right on the beach. She stretched her budget to the limit to make those trips special. The last time we went..." My throat tightened. "It was just a few months before she passed away."

I hesitated, feeling the words catch in my chest. "In a way, that trip led to her passing."

Luke leaned forward, his blue eyes full of concern. "You don't have to talk about it if you don't want to."

There was something in his voice that made it feel safe to let down my guard. I hadn't planned to say more, but the words came anyway. "She didn't have any vacation time left after that trip, so when Hurricane Katrina hit, she had to stay and work. My mom was an incredible artist. Watercolors, acrylics... she could paint anything. But it wasn't enough to pay the bills, so she worked as an aide at a retirement home. She used to bring me to work with her, even though she wasn't supposed to. The rest of the family had already evacuated, so I stayed in her office while she worked." I swallowed hard, the lump in my throat growing. "Then, just hours before the hurricane hit, they decided to evacuate the nursing home."

Luke's brow furrowed. "Why did they wait so long?"

"It's not an easy decision," I explained, my voice steadying as I slipped into the memory. "Moving elderly residents can be dangerous. Some don't survive the stress. But as the storm's path became clear, staying wasn't an option anymore."

He shook his head in disbelief. "That must have been agonizing for everyone."

"My mom and I went home to pack, thinking we'd drive until we found a hotel. But by the time we were ready to leave, the roads were closed. The storm was almost here. We had no choice but to stay and ride it out."

Luke's gaze held mine, a mix of horror and empathy washing over his features. "That's terrifying."

"It was," I admitted, remembering the worst day of my life. "The storm itself was chaos. The wind, the rain... it was as if the world were breaking apart. But the real nightmare started after. The levees broke, and water started flooding the city. There wasn't a cloud in the sky anymore, but everywhere you looked, water was rising. Our house was one level. My mom knew we couldn't stay."

I took a shaky breath, my fingers curling into the fabric of my shirt. "We got in the car, trying to outrun the water. It felt like it was chasing us relentlessly. Everywhere we turned, there were downed trees and debris blocking the roads. But my mom kept going. She believed we'd make it to high ground. Then the car just stopped. Water started seeping in."

Luke's hand reached for mine and held it. "What happened?"

"My mom managed to force the door open against the pressure. She pulled me onto this makeshift raft. It was a door or something, I don't even know. But then she got swept away. I was alone, floating, until this man in a boat appeared and pulled me out."

I didn't realize I was crying until Luke handed me a Kleenex. "Anna... I'm so sorry."

His eyes were full of so much compassion that it made my throat ache. He didn't look away, didn't rush to fill the silence; he just held my hand. And for a second, I wanted to tell him everything. About the panic that grips me when I even think about leaving New Orleans. About how every time I pack a bag, I feel like the water's rising again, and I can't breathe. About how terrified I am that someday he'll finally see how broken I really am.

Luke's eyes stayed locked on mine. For the first time, I felt like I

could share my secrets with someone. I might have told Luke everything, right then and there, if the piercing wail of a siren hadn't cut
through the air.

26

LUKE

Tom burst through the door, his expression grim but controlled. "A tornado's been sighted a couple of miles from here. We need to get you both to an interior bathroom. Now."

I glanced at Anna, catching the flicker of fear in her eyes. She'd just opened up to me about her mom and shared pieces of herself I knew weren't easy to remember. And now this storm was bearing down on us, like the universe had decided she hadn't been through enough. My chest tightened, not from fear for myself but from the overwhelming need to keep her safe.

Without thinking, I squeezed her hand tighter. Her fingers were cold, and the slight tremble in her grip tugged at something deep in me. "We'll be fine." I kept my voice steady and calm. "We'll be fine." *I'll make sure of it. You have to believe that, Anna.*

All I wanted at that moment was to shield her from everything, to wrap her in something so solid even the storm couldn't touch her.

"Come on," I said, guiding her as we followed Tom. Her hand was still in mine, and I wasn't letting go. Not until I was sure she was safe. "Tom and Hal are pros. They've planned for every possible scenario."

The wind howled outside, shaking the windows. I glanced back at her as we moved, and something about the trust in her eyes, even through the fear, nearly leveled me. She didn't let go of my hand, and that simple act filled me with a determination I couldn't quite put into words.

Whatever happens, I'm not letting anything hurt her. Not tonight. Not ever.

Tom led us to a sleek, high-tech guest bathroom on the first floor. "You'll be safe here." He gestured toward the spacious, marble-clad room, then pointed to the sculpted bathtub at its center. "If you hear loud winds or crashing sounds, get into the tub. It's anchored and will give you extra protection."

"And you and Hal?" Anna asked.

Tom nodded reassuringly. "We'll be nearby, in safe positions, to monitor the property. Just stay here, and we'll let you know when it's clear."

I tightened my grip on Anna's hand as Tom left, the door clicking shut behind him.

Anna's eyes darted around the space, her shoulders visibly relaxing just a fraction. "Of all the places to ride out a tornado, this has to be the fanciest bathroom I've ever seen."

I scanned the bathroom, taking in the marble countertops, the gilded mirror, and the chandelier overhead. It was the kind of place that felt more suited to a palace than a house. "Yeah." I glanced up at the absurdly opulent light fixture before my eyes landed on something even more baffling—a plush ottoman tucked in the corner. "Why would you even need an ottoman in a bathroom? Are people just... lounging in here?"

She let out a laugh, the kind of laugh that snuck under your skin and made you feel like maybe things weren't so bad.

I stood and walked to a panel on the wall, my fingers hovering over a button. "What do you think this does?"

The room transformed instantly as I pressed the button. Soft LED lights embedded in the ceiling and floor tiles flickered to life, shifting through calming blues, vibrant purples, and warm golds.

I grinned. "It's like we're in a chic nightclub. Only it's a bathroom. Club Porcelain."

Anna giggled and then motioned toward an electronic panel on the opposite wall. "Let's see what else this place can do."

She tapped an icon that looked like musical notes surrounded by swirls. Instantly, the soothing sounds of a babbling brook and chirping birds filled the room, creating a spa-like ambiance. But then, a calm, authoritative voice boomed from hidden speakers: "Begin your journey to tranquility. Close your eyes and envision yourself as an oak tree."

Startled, I fumbled with the controls, but instead of silencing the voice, I cranked the volume all the way up. The voice exploded through the room, almost comical in its intensity. YOUR ROOTS DIG DEEP INTO THE EARTH, GROUNDING YOU.

Anna was shouting over the noise, her laughter bubbling up. "I think you've found the meditation program."

EMBRACE THE SOOTHING HUM OF THE UNIVERSE.

"How do you turn this off?" I yelled back, frantically pressing random buttons.

IMAGINE YOUR THOUGHTS DRIFTING AWAY LIKE AUTUMN LEAVES.

"Let me try this," she suggested, hitting a large button labeled "Stop." The voice cut off mid-sentence, leaving the room blissfully silent—except for our uncontrollable laughter.

"We might've been stuck in here until we both achieved nirvana," I joked, easing myself to the cool tile floor. She did the same.

We settled into a comfortable conversation, sharing thoughts on books we'd read recently, the ultimate comfort food, and our shared opinion that pineapple had no place on pizza.

It was one of those great, easy conversations where you don't worry about how you sound to the other person. I hadn't felt so comfortable in a long time. Anna was curled up on the ottoman beside me, legs tucked under her, a blanket draped over her lap. She looked so at ease.

I stared at the bathroom mirror. "You ever feel like people only want to know the polished version of your story?" I asked, not expecting an answer. "The PR-friendly one. With the clean lines and the perfect ending."

She glanced over, brow raised slightly. "Yeah. All the time."

I gave a humorless laugh. "Guess I shouldn't complain. I've been living inside the polished version for years."

She didn't say anything, just watched me. Not pressing. Just there.

I shifted, firelight throwing shadows across my face. "No one knows the full story about me and Sienna." I kept my eyes on the flames. "Not the real story."

She turned toward me, and I caught that smile. "What happened?" The way she pulled her knees up, settling in—it was like she was bracing for impact. That kind of attention could make a man say anything.

I ran a hand through my hair and laughed, but it came out wrong. "You know about Sienna. Her and Dylan Sanders. But nobody knows how it actually went down."

Anna's brow furrowed, but she didn't say anything. Just waited.

"We were supposed to go to Paris. First real break we'd had in months." I shook my head. "I planned this whole week. Rented an apartment in Le Marais with a balcony. Made reservations at all these restaurants she'd mentioned. Even learned some French because she always gave me grief about my accent."

Anna put her hand on my knee.

"I thought we needed the time away. Just the two of us. Turns out there were already three of us in the relationship."

Anna looked like she wanted to say something, but she held back.

"The day before we were supposed to leave, we had a talk show. Me, Sienna, Dylan—promoting the movie we were all in together. I got there early because I'm always early." My jaw tightened. "Walked into the wrong green room. Heard her voice and just... opened the door."

The memory hit me like it always did. "She was with him. And yeah, that part was bad enough. But it was what she was saying. The same things she'd said to me. 'You make me feel like I'm finally myself.' 'I've never felt this way with anyone.' Word for word. Like she had a script, and we were both just playing the same part in different takes."

Anna's hand found mine.

"I left before they saw me. Closed the door real quiet." I could still feel the doorknob, how my hands shook. "Then I had to go sit on that couch an hour later. Next to both of them. Smiling for the cameras like everything was fine. Because that's what you do, right? The show must go on."

I finally looked at her. Something about the way she was watching me made it easier to keep going.

"Then Dylan announces it. Right there, live. Takes her hand and tells everyone they're together." I let out a short, humorless laugh. "The host freezes. The crew doesn't know whether to cut or keep rolling. Half the audience gasps, half of them clap. And I'm just sitting there, trying not to look like I'm falling apart on national television—thinking about the plane tickets burning a hole in my wallet."

Anna's hand found mine and squeezed.

"So I hit him," I said simply. "Right there on set. Not my best moment, but I'm not sorry either. I've dealt with bad scripts, impossible directors, PR disasters. But that day?" I shook my head. "That day, something just broke."

Anna let out a breath. "After what you saw, I don't know how you even made it onto that stage. That took courage."

"Courage?" I laughed, sharply. "More like shock. And maybe I didn't want to give them the satisfaction." I turned back to the fire. "But I lost it anyway. Just did it on camera in front of millions of people."

Something about the way she listened to me without judging made my chest tighten. It was as if she saw me—the parts of me I worked so hard to keep hidden. Not the Hollywood version, not the polished, carefully managed persona. Just me.

I continued, "I don't miss her. I miss the idea of her—the comfort of having someone to take to premieres and talk about on talk shows. But deep down, I always knew we weren't right for each other. She wanted Luke Fisher, the movie star. Not me. But I stayed with her because I thought that's what I was supposed to do, play the role, keep up appearances."

I cleared my throat, glancing away. "Anyway, that's why I'm here. Not just to dodge the tabloids or the fallout. I needed some space. To figure out who I am when the cameras aren't rolling." I winced inwardly at my deflection, feeling the words ring hollow. Anna didn't need this canned explanation. She deserved more, but giving more meant unraveling parts of myself I wasn't ready to face.

Anna studied me for a beat, her eyes searching mine. I could feel her seeing through the cracks, and it was unsettling in a way I couldn't quite explain. I cleared my throat. "Okay, hypothetical, if you could have any superpower, what would it be?"

She smiled, as if she understood that I needed to move on, to stop talking about my pain. "The power to stop time. What about you?"

"Teleportation," I answered immediately. "No more red-eye flights. No paparazzi waiting at the airport. Now, tell me something about you that I don't know."

"I can hula hoop for hours."

I looked at her, surprised. "Really? That's pretty impressive."

She chuckled, nudging me with her elbow. "Your turn."

"I'm a pretty decent juggler."

"Really?" Her eyebrows shot up. "You've got to show me!"

"I don't know. It's been a while since I've juggled."

"Oh, come on. 'Pretty decent' jugglers don't just lose the magic."

"The magic fades without practice."

She stood up and looked around the bathroom with exaggerated determination. "Well then, let's see how much you've got left." She opened a drawer and started rummaging. "Aha!"

Out came a fancy bar of soap, a small decorative shell, and a toothbrush still in its packaging.

She handed them to me with a teasing smile, her eyes glinting with challenge. "Stand up and show me what you've got, hotshot."

I hesitated. "No promises. I haven't done this in years." I tried to sound casual while inwardly bracing myself for disaster. I weighed the soap, shell, and toothbrush in my hands, feeling like I was about to audition for the world's weirdest talent show.

I managed to get a few rotations going, and I thought I could pull it off. But the bar of soap was slippery, and the toothbrush felt weirdly off balance, as if it were defying the laws of physics to mess with me. My rhythm faltered. I lunged backward, desperately trying to catch the rogue toothbrush as it flew out of sync.

I lunged backward, arms windmilling like a cartoon character, and slammed into the sleek glass shower enclosure. My hand shot out to catch myself, only to find a touch-sensitive control panel.

The rain showerhead erupted above me.

"No, no, no—" I slapped at the panel. Side jets fired horizontally like I was in a car wash. A wall-mounted waterfall feature joined the party, drenching me from a new and completely unnecessary angle.

"Luke, move!" Anna called out, laughing so hard she could barely stand.

She stepped into the enclosure to help, which would've been heroic if she hadn't immediately hit a button that activated the steam feature. Thick mist engulfed us both.

"Wait, maybe this one?" She pressed something else.

A sudden blast of icy water erupted from the foot-massage jets at ground level, hitting us like we'd personally wronged them.

"THAT'S NOT HELPING!" I yelled, my voice echoing off the tile like I was in a cave.

We were both soaked, fumbling blind in the steam, water attacking us from every possible direction. Anna's shoulders shook with laughter as she groped for the panel. "There's got to be an off switch—"

"You'd think!"

Finally—*finally*—she found the central "OFF" button.

We stood there, dripping and gasping. Water pooled at our feet. My hair was plastered to my forehead. Anna looked like she'd just survived a shipwreck.

We looked at each other.

And completely lost it.

"Where—" I gasped between laughs, flinging open cabinet doors. "Where in the world are the towels? How are there *no towels* in this bathroom? Why does Topher have an ottoman but no towels?"

Anna tried to wring out her shirt. "Maybe the ottoman *is* the towel?"

"That's not how furniture works!"

I was freezing now, teeth starting to chatter. I desperately looked around for the climate controls. My eyes landed on the expansive mirror above the sink, backlit by these subtle, fancy embedded lights.

Voice-activated. Had to be.

"Mirror," I commanded, "show controls."

The mirror rippled.

Then it became a video call screen.

And there was Topher. In a suit. In what looked like a very serious boardroom full of very serious people.

His eyes went wide. "Luke? Anna?" He took in our drowned-rat appearances. "Why are you calling me from my guest bathroom? And why do you both look like you fell in a pool?"

I couldn't even speak. I was laughing too hard. "Wrong... button..."

Anna doubled over. "We were just... we were trying to..." She wiped tears from her eyes. "Your fancy mirror!"

Someone in the background of Topher's call leaned into frame, clearly confused. Topher held up a finger—*one moment*—and turned back to us with a smirk. "You know, I've taken a lot of weird calls in my career, but this is a first. Not gonna lie, Luke, this is exactly the kind of chaos I expect from you."

"Happy to deliver," I managed.

Anna waved at the screen. "Enjoy your meeting!"

"Oh, I will." His grin widened. "Try not to destroy anything else."

The screen went dark.

There was a knock at the door. "Tornado warning's over," Tom called through. "You're free to leave the bathroom."

I glanced at Anna. Damp hair clinging to her face, cheeks flushed, eyes still sparkling with laughter. She looked like she'd just emerged from some beautiful disaster, radiant and completely unaware of how hard she was making this for me.

I looked away fast, clearing my throat.

We squelched our way out into the hallway, leaving a trail of water like a crime scene. Anna turned to me, that small, devastating smile playing at her lips. "Well. That was an adventure."

Adventure. Sure. Let's call it that.

"Yeah," I said, rubbing the back of my neck. "Not exactly a relaxing evening."

She laughed—soft, genuine—and it hit me square in the chest. I should've been relieved the storm had passed. Instead, all I could think about was how close we'd been in that bathroom. How easily she'd let me in. How thoroughly I was falling for her, whether I was ready for it or not.

"Definitely one for the books," I said. "Thanks for making it memorable."

"Anytime." Her grin turned playful. "Just maybe no more touch screens."

"Deal."

I walked her to her bedroom door, hyperaware of the silence, of how little space there was between us.

"Goodnight, Anna," I said quietly.

She smiled, one hand on the doorknob. "Night, Jacques."

There was a beat. Just long enough for me to wonder if she'd say something else, if I should say something else.

But then she slipped inside, and the door clicked shut.

I stood there like an idiot for a second before heading to my own room. I closed the door and leaned against it, exhaling hard.

I wasn't thinking about call sheets or upcoming press tours. I wasn't performing for anyone.

Instead, I was replaying her laughter, the way her eyes lit up even in the middle of a tornado scare. It struck me that, despite the absurdity of the night, I felt more alive than I had in months. Maybe longer.

I changed into dry clothes. The room's luxurious bedding called to me. As I sank into the mattress, my thoughts drifted to Anna's wit, her resilience, and her ability to turn even the most mundane moment into something memorable. I wondered if she felt the same calm I did now, finally safe and dry after the storm.

The faint hum of the generator lulled me to sleep. My dreams weren't filled with lines to memorize or paparazzi flashing in my face. Instead, they were scattered with laughter, storm-lit skies, and Anna's sweet voice.

I woke the next morning to a pounding at the door.

The housekeeper's voice trembled with urgency. "Mr. Luke, Mr. Luke," she yelled. "There's been an accident. Where is Ms. Amato?"

27

ANNA

I SHOT OUT OF BED, my heart pounding as I stumbled into the hallway. "What accident? What happened?"

Last night had been wonderful. Knowing that Luke was in the room next to mine made it hard to fall asleep. Every sound, every creak of the house, seemed charged with an energy I couldn't ignore. I couldn't stop replaying the evening in my mind, the laughter we shared, the moments when the tension between us felt almost tangible. Excitement buzzed under my skin, keeping sleep just out of reach.

When I finally drifted off, it felt like minutes before I was jolted awake by the housekeeper Joan's voice, trembling with urgency.

She was standing in the hall with three men I'd never seen before. Her face filled with relief as she spotted me. "Oh, honey, I'm so glad you stayed here last night. A tree destroyed the cottage. If you'd been there, you could've been killed."

Her words hit me like a brick. Without thinking, I bolted past her, my feet barely touching the stairs as I flew down them. When I reached the front door, I froze. The massive limb of a neighboring oak had crushed the roof of the cottage.

Luke was close behind me. Our eyes met, and a shared realization passed between us. Madame Aphrodite's eerie warning about a falling tree echoed in my mind, her words now hauntingly prophetic.

Before I could act, Luke's hands gripped my shoulders, stopping my instinctive dash toward the wreckage. "All my stuff," I blurted, my heart racing. Across the driveway, drenched clothes, books, and personal journals lay scattered and ruined, their sodden forms tiny casualties of the storm.

Thankfully, my laptop was safe in the mansion.

"My sons got here as soon as I called them about the tree," Joan said, her voice tinged with pride as she motioned to the three guys behind her. They huddled together, arguing over the best way to use a rusty old saw they'd dug out of someone's garage. It didn't take a professional eye to see that this trio wasn't exactly licensed. Just a family doing their best to help out in a pinch.

One of her sons wiped his brow. "We moved out what we could save, but don't go in yet. The bedroom took the worst hit. There was a lot of paper in there."

Paper. My chest tightened. My ninety-nine rejection letters, each one a symbol of my resilience, all gone. I swallowed hard, trying to find a way to feel relieved. Shouldn't this be freeing? A fresh start? But instead, it felt like a punch to the gut.

I crouched near the soggy remains of what used to be my life. A warped notebook sat on top of the pile, its pages swollen and curling like they were giving up. My clothes were soaked through, and the colors had started to bleed, seams unraveling. Everything felt precarious, on the verge of disintegrating, like one more gust of wind could scatter it all down the block.

I moved closer to the sodden pile of belongings, and I sank to my knees, struggling to process what this setback meant for me.

"Anna, breathe," Joan said, her voice comforting. "We'll help with whatever you need. Your clothes from yesterday? All cleaned and waiting inside. Wear those for now."

I nodded, my voice caught in my throat. "Thank you, Joan."

Luke's voice was low but sure. "The most important thing is that you're okay. Everything else? Just stuff."

Joan chimed in optimistically, "The homeowner's insurance might cover some of it."

I appreciated her attempt to soften the blow, but I knew how long insurance claims could take to process.

"Where will you stay while they're fixing things up?" Joan asked.

"With my aunt and uncle," I said.

But Luke was already shaking his head. "What do you mean? You'll stay here."

My eyes flicked to his. "It's okay. My family lives close by. They'll have me."

Luke wasn't backing down. "You can stay here," he insisted, his tone half-playful, half-serious. "Think of all the space you'll have to write." Then, more earnestly, "Please, stay."

The words hung in the air, and for a moment, I considered staying. But then the familiar knot of fear tightened in my chest. Fear of rejection. Fear of stepping into something that might only hurt me in the end. What if I stayed, and it ended up being more about convenience for him than anything real?

I shook my head, trying to steady my voice. "I can't. My aunt and uncle have plenty of room."

It was safer this way. Safer to walk away than to risk hearing him say later that I'd overstayed my welcome.

A flicker of disappointment crossed his face, gone so quickly I wondered if I'd imagined it. He masked it with humor. "Right, now that you mention it, the place might be a bit cramped."

My phone buzzed.

"It's my aunt." I turned away to answer. "Aunt Dolores, a tree destroyed the cottage."

"What? That's terrible. Are you okay?"

"I'm fine, but I need a place to stay. Can I stay with you until I find another place?"

Her hesitation was thick with guilt. "We've got the Gibson family staying with us. Their house was destroyed. They've got six kids, and the bedrooms are full. But you're always welcome here. You can crash on the couch."

My chest tightened. I hated being a burden. For a moment, I longed for the comfort of my mom—the one person who'd have made me feel safe and cared for.

Forcing my voice to stay light, I backtracked. "No problem. I'll figure something out. Don't worry about it, okay?" I hung up before she could respond, ignoring her call when she tried again.

Taking a deep breath, I turned back to Luke. "The guest room at my aunt's house is full. She said I could stay on the couch."

Luke frowned, his gaze intense. "You shouldn't have to sleep on a couch, especially after this." He gestured toward the debris. His voice softened. "Stay here. You can have your own room. Or twelve."

I hesitated, the knot in my chest tightening. But then I swallowed hard, forcing myself to push through it. "Are you sure? I don't want to get in the way."

He stepped closer, his voice earnest. "Right now, the only thing that matters to me is making sure you're okay. We'll figure the rest out."

My chest tightened for a different reason this time, tears threatening to spill. But I couldn't cry. Not now. Not in front of him again. I looked around at the wreckage, at the chaos that mirrored the mess in my head. "Okay," I murmured, almost like I was testing the word. "Thank you."

Luke nodded, a small smile playing at the corners of his mouth. "Good. You'll see, it's the right call."

I didn't know why he was doing this, but it didn't matter. I was grateful it was Luke standing there, offering me more than just a roof over my head. Somehow, of all people, he made me feel like maybe I wasn't as alone as I thought.

28

LUKE

ANNA HAD AGREED to stay with me. A rare win, though the responsibility now felt heavier than I'd anticipated. As I watched Joan's sons pack what remained of Anna's belongings into soggy boxes, it hit me how much her life had been upended. It wasn't just her roof that had been crushed; it was her sense of stability.

I glanced at my phone. Missed call from Topher. Great. When I called back, he answered almost immediately. "Luke, do you have a moment to discuss the neighborhood drama you've caused?"

I sighed. "Topher, a literal tree fell on the cottage where Anna was staying."

"I know. Her aunt reached out, by the way. Lovely woman, but she wanted to know if you're 'a heartbreaker.'"

I pinched the bridge of my nose. "Her aunt called *you*? How does her aunt even have your number?"

"I went to high school with Anna's cousin. Anyway, she asked if I thought you were 'stable.' Stable. As if you're a stallion up for auction."

"Fantastic," I muttered. "Did you tell her I'm a paragon of emotional stability?"

"Not exactly. I said you're *mostly* harmless, except when someone cheats on you and you punch their co-star in the jaw."

"Topher—"

"Kidding. She has no idea who you are. Listen to me carefully. Do not, under any circumstances, mess this up. Her aunt already sounds like she's ready to send a cousin with a baseball bat to 'sort you out.'"

I groaned. "Anna's staying here because her roof caved in. That's it. I'm not exactly proposing marriage."

"Good, because based on that shower incident, you can barely handle bathroom appliances," Topher quipped.

"Wow, thanks for the support."

"Anytime," he said breezily. "Keep your head down. No unnecessary complications, no bad press."

I rubbed my temples. "She's a friend who needs help."

"Sure, sure." He was unconvinced. "But just in case, I told her aunt that if anything goes wrong, I'll personally fly down to New Orleans and drag you back to LA."

"Looking forward to it," I muttered, hanging up before he could get in another dig.

I turned back to the house and saw Anna's belongings being unceremoniously dumped into a box. Something in me twisted at the sight. This wasn't how someone's life should look: wet, crumpled, and shoved into a cardboard rectangle.

Before I could stop myself, I threw open the window and yelled, "Don't toss anything. Bring it inside. Carefully."

Joan's sons looked startled but nodded, quickly adjusting their approach. I stepped back, shaking my head. Why was I getting so worked up over this?

Because Anna deserved better, that's why.

An idea struck, and I grabbed my phone again. My stylist answered on the second ring. "Darling, tell me you're finally ready to refresh your look."

"Not me," I said quickly. "I need a wardrobe for someone else. A woman. Casual, functional, but nice. And nothing with price tags that scream 'Hollywood.' Think casual and approachable. And fast."

"Say no more. I'll keep it chic but understated. This will be my priority. Give me the sizes for your friend, and I'll call in the orders to stores down there."

THE NEXT MORNING, after a restless night and one too many cups of coffee, I wandered into the kitchen, needing something to distract me.

My thoughts kept circling back to Anna. I couldn't shake the image of her standing in the wreckage of her cottage, soaked to the bone, trying to salvage pieces of her life with that unshakable determination in her eyes. She hadn't asked for help. Didn't even hint at needing it. But it was obvious.

I wasn't used to caring for someone else. Not like this. I'd spent so long being managed myself that stepping in for someone else felt unfamiliar. Uncomfortable, but not in a bad way. Maybe it was because Anna didn't want anything from me. No demands, no expectations. Just honesty.

A knock at the front door pulled me out of my head.

Delivery people arrived with garment bags and boxes. I directed them toward the guest room closet, watching as a mini department store unfolded before me. I peeked inside one of the bags, marveling at my stylist's ability to curate perfection with almost no instruction. Then I caught a glimpse of a price tag and winced.

Approachable. Casual. Right. If you lived in a luxury magazine spread.

A few minutes later, Anna appeared in the doorway, hair still damp from a shower, wearing borrowed clothes that didn't quite fit but somehow still worked. Her eyes landed on the neatly arranged wardrobe. She froze, gaze sweeping from one designer label to the next.

"What is this?" she asked, her voice cautious.

"Just a few things," I said, trying to sound nonchalant. "I figured you might need replacements for the stuff you lost."

She picked up a T-shirt, her jaw dropping when she saw the tag. "Two hundred dollars for this? For a plain white T-shirt?" She rifled through the rack, pulling out a pair of jeans. "Three hundred for these? Luke, this is insane."

I shrugged, trying to keep it light. "They're just clothes."

She held up a sleek black dress next, her eyebrows shooting up. "Two grand for this? Where exactly am I supposed to wear it? A royal ball?"

I ran a hand through my hair, realizing how this looked. "I told my stylist to keep it simple, casual," I said defensively. "Clearly, she and I have different definitions of that."

Anna's disbelief melted. "Luke, I can't accept this. It's too much."

My chest tightened. The last thing I wanted was for her to feel like she owed me something. "We have brand deals, so this stuff is basically free," I said quickly. "After everything that's happened, you shouldn't have to stress about stuff like this. And you should be taken care of, treated like a queen."

She set the dress down, her fingers brushing the fabric as she glanced at me. "Why are you doing this?"

Her question caught me off guard. Why was I doing this? Because seeing her struggle made something inside me twist, and I wanted to make things easier for her, even in small ways. But how could I explain that without sounding like an idiot or a chauvinist?

Instead, I led her to the desk I'd had set up by the window of another guest room, complete with a new notebook and a stack of her favorite pens. "That," I said softly, "is because you need a space to write. And the clothes are because you deserve to feel like yourself again."

For a moment, she stared at me, her expression unreadable. Then, she wrapped her arms around her chest and let out a sigh. "You're impossible."

Impossible. That's what Sienna used to call me. But when Anna said it, it didn't sound like an insult It was endearing. "So I've been told."

The desk was nearly identical to the one in her cottage, down to the arrangement of the pens and notebooks. Her fingers brushed over the surface, and her expression shifted into something almost wistful.

"This feels like home." Her words were barely above a whisper, but the words hit me harder than I expected. I'd been trying to fix things with grand gestures, but all she needed was a sense of normalcy. Of belonging.

And as I watched her hand tracing the edge of the wood, it struck me how much she'd been holding back. The fear of taking up space, of letting someone help, mirrored my own. Maybe that's why I'd pushed so hard.

I thought of her wall of rejection letters, now gone. She'd carried them like armor, and now that they were destroyed, I wasn't sure how she felt about it. I didn't want to poke the wound, but maybe this was my chance to say what had been swirling in my head.

"You know," I began carefully, leaning against the doorframe, "those rejection letters being gone... maybe it's a fresh start. You don't have to quit at one hundred."

She looked up at me, the corner of her mouth lifting into a determined smile. "No, I think that means this story, my hundredth, will be my masterpiece."

She was extraordinary, plain and simple.

A smile crept onto her face. "You've got good taste. Even if you're terrible at understanding budgets."

I grinned. "That's what they all say."

She shook her head, but a warm smile lingered. She walked to her bedroom, to the closet full of new clothes, and swept her hand gently over the sleeve of a cashmere sweater. Then, she looked up at me with something happier in her eyes.

And that's when it hit me. I didn't just want her to feel at home *here*. I wanted her to feel at home *with me*.

It wasn't just about giving her space to heal, write, or find herself.

It was about us. Together.

The thought was terrifying, exhilarating, and utterly undeniable. She made me feel like the best version of myself—the real me, not the polished version Hollywood paraded around. And I wanted to take a leap of faith, not for a role or a career move, but for her.

I exhaled, leaning against the doorframe of her bedroom as she folded a T-shirt. She glanced up at me, her brow furrowing slightly. "What's up?"

I walked into the room. My voice wavered, but I pushed through. "I need to tell you something."

Her hands stilled, the shirt forgotten on the desk. "What is it?"

I hesitated, my heart pounding, but then I took another step closer. "I don't want just to be the guy you give tours to, or the one who happens to share a roof with you. I want to be more. I want *us* to be more."

For a moment, she didn't move. Didn't speak. The silence stretched, and my chest tightened as the fear of rejection clawed at me. But then, her lips curved into a tentative smile. "You're serious?" she asked, her voice barely above a whisper.

I nodded. "Completely."

Her smile grew, lighting up her whole face. "Then yes."

Relief and joy crashed into me all at once, and I didn't think. I just closed the distance between us. My hand found her cheek, and I tilted her face toward mine. When our lips met, it wasn't hesitant or cautious. It was full of everything I'd been holding back—hope, fear, want.

Her hands gripped my shirt, pulling me closer, and the kiss deepened. The world outside faded away until it was just us, wrapped in a moment I never wanted to end.

When we finally pulled apart, her cheeks were flushed, her eyes sparkling as she looked up at me. "So, what happens now?"

I leaned in, pressing a quick kiss to her forehead. "We figure it out. Together."

29

ANNA

IF A MOVIE STAR—ONE who's not just gorgeous but also funny, sweet, and so protective it makes my heart ache—wanted me for a tour guide (and more), who was I to say no? Twist my arm, right?

For the next ten days, Luke and I were inseparable. It was like stepping into a dream, only better because it was real. Apart from the nights I was hustling at Muses, we explored every corner of New Orleans together, and I'd never been so happy.

It wasn't just his looks. Though let's be honest, those were definitely part of the package. Luke made me laugh, and he also had this way of making every moment feel like an adventure, of turning even the most minor things into something extraordinary.

We started with a swamp tour in the bayou, where Luke slipped into the persona of Dr. Archibald P. Featherbottom, a Harvard professor with an impeccable Boston accent and an even more impressive handlebar mustache. He asked the most absurdly "academic" questions, like, "Do alligators prefer their lobster bisque with or without sherry?" and "Do you think gators ever pause to ponder their place in the ecosystem?"

At the National World War II Museum, he morphed into Trevor, an overenthusiastic tourist from Minnesota in a Hawaiian shirt so loud it could have stopped traffic. He took pictures of everything—including the restroom signs—and exclaimed, "Oh geez, this one's definitely going in the scrapbook" in an accent so thick it fooled the tour guide.

And then there was Pierre Le Pencil, a flamboyant French "artist" who visited the New Orleans Museum of Art. With his beret and comically crooked fake mustache, Pierre sketched a masterpiece titled *Starry Night at a Bourbon Street Karaoke Bar*. A group of tourists gathered around, nodding as if they were witnessing the birth of a new Picasso. I was dying inside, trying not to burst out laughing.

But the disguises and the jokes were just part of it. The real magic was in the quieter moments. When we sat at Preservation Hall, letting the raw, soulful jazz wash over us, or when we swayed to blues at Le Bon Temps Roule, or got lost in the rhythm at Vaughn's in Tremé. And almost every night ended at the Spotted Cat in the Marigny, where the music flowed freely, and I felt like I was falling—into the music, into the city, into him.

Luke was different. Sure, he was still every bit the charming, quick-witted Hollywood star, but there was something more thoughtful about him. I'd catch him watching people when he thought I wasn't looking, like he was studying them, trying to figure out what made them tick.

It happened on the swamp tour when a little boy asked the guide how alligators slept without drowning. The guide had explained their special muscles and floating habits, but Luke had stayed focused on the child, as if marveling at the way children see the world.

At the National World War II Museum, he'd lingered in front of a display about the homefront, reading every word about the sacrifices ordinary people had made. Later, he struck up a conversation with a couple who were visiting from Kansas. They talked about their parents, who'd lived through the war, and Luke listened as if their stories were the most important thing in the world.

Even at Preservation Hall, where most people were lost in the music, Luke's eyes wandered over the crowd. He watched the older man in the corner, tapping his foot with the precision of someone who had probably played jazz in his younger years. He noticed the couple holding hands as if they were the only two people in the room. He noticed *everything*.

And he asked endless questions of everyone, from other tourists, the jazz musicians, the waitstaff, and the guides. "What brought them here? What do they love about New Orleans?"

One night, as we walked home from a late dinner, I finally asked, "What's with all the questions?"

Luke shrugged, slipping his hands into his pockets. "I spent so much of my life in a bubble. People were telling me what I wanted to hear, selling me versions of myself they thought I wanted to buy. Out here, people are real. They'll tell you about their day, their struggles, and their joys. It's grounding."

I smiled, tucking that thought away. He wasn't just seeing people; he was learning from them. And somehow, watching him do that made me want to be better, too. It made me want to be real, to show him all the messy, unpolished parts of myself that I usually kept hidden.

At home, the masks came off, and Luke would shrug out of his Hollywood polish, sometimes literally, changing into my lavender hoodie from Muses like it was his uniform for unwinding. He told me about his dad, the man he admired most in the world, and I found myself sharing stories about my chaotic, love-filled childhood. He wasn't just a movie star; he was a man who made me feel safe, cherished, and seen in ways I hadn't realized I was missing.

It was during these evenings that I began to notice the subtle shifts within myself, too. While Luke immersed himself in preparing for his audition, I found myself drawn to the writing desk he had picked out for me. The desk overlooked the lush garden, its serenity coaxing me to sit down and face a blank page.

At first, it was just scattered thoughts, snippets of dialogue, and raw emotions, but soon, the words started flowing. I used my experiences and emotions to fuel the story, drawing heavily from my life in New Orleans and, without realizing it, my growing feelings for Luke. I felt alive and hopeful. It was like I'd found my voice again, and it was stronger than ever.

One night, my writing was interrupted by a knock at my door. Luke leaned against the frame, his casual confidence matched by the hint of a smirk tugging at his lips. "Get dressed," he said, his tone light but insistent. "I'm taking you out."

"What? Where?" I blinked, caught off guard.

"Commander's Palace," he replied. "I hear that it's one of the most iconic restaurants in New Orleans. Our reservation is in thirty minutes."

This wasn't just a casual dinner; this was an *occasion*. My eyes landed on the black dress Luke's stylist had chosen.

If this wasn't the occasion for it, I didn't know what was.

When I came downstairs, Luke was waiting near the door, adjusting his cufflinks. He was in a tuxedo, and for a moment, I forgot how to breathe. The way the fabric fit him, the effortless charm in his posture. The soft lighting from the chandelier caught the sheen of the black fabric, highlighting the suit's sharp lines.

But then his eyes found me, and the world seemed to shift, like gravity had suddenly changed direction. He didn't speak at first, but the way he looked at me, like I was the only person in the room, made my heart flutter and my cheeks flush with heat.

"You look incredible."

I smoothed down the dress, trying to play it cool. "You don't look so bad yourself."

The drive to Commander's Palace was brief, barely enough time for me to get over the fact that I was on my way to a legendary New Orleans restaurant with Luke Fisher, Hollywood heartthrob. Tom and Hal ushered us into a private room as discreetly as possible, sparing Luke the need to wear sunglasses and a cap.

Scanning the menu, Luke leaned in closer. "What's the standout here? Turtle soup? Crawfish étouffée? Barbecue shrimp?"

I chuckled. "I've never been here, but the turtle soup is supposed to be legendary."

He nodded, a spark of excitement lighting up his face. "Then it's a must."

The ambiance in the private room was warm and intimate, the perfect blend of elegance and charm. As the food arrived, Luke took his first hesitant bite of the turtle soup. After a moment, his eyes widened, and he leaned back dramatically. "Divine."

I leaned in, lowering my voice. "Okay, is Tom trying to pass as a busboy? Because he just rearranged a stack of napkins like it was a security threat."

Luke didn't even turn around. He just smirked and sipped his drink. "He's got a whole system. Blend in, look bored, monitor exits. Occasionally, fluff a bread basket."

I laughed. "Subtle. Very low-profile. If the Oscars ever give out awards for background acting, he's got it locked."

"Don't encourage him. He once shadowed a valet for an hour because he thought the guy looked suspicious."

"What was suspicious about him?"

"He had a man bun."

I snorted into my water.

Luke's smile faded just slightly, enough for something more serious to slip in. He set down his glass and looked at me across the table.

"Truth is... they're not just watching the waiters and busboys here. They're watching for anyone watching us."

I blinked. "Us?"

"You know," he said, his tone light but edged with something serious, "when we figure out how to take this relationship public, we'll have to be careful."

I blinked at him, caught off guard by his choice of words. "Public?" I echoed, my heart leaping with a joy so unexpected it almost made me dizzy. A smile spread across my face before I could stop it, warmth flooding my belly.

He nodded. "It's only a matter of time before someone takes a photo or asks the wrong question. And I... want to be ready for that.

For what it means when we're not just having dinner in a private room. When it's headlines and speculation and the whole mess."

The restaurant buzzed with clinking silverware, bursts of laughter, and the low hum of conversation in the surrounding rooms. But for a second, it all fell away.

"I want to protect this," he said. "Not because I'm scared of what people will say. Because I don't want anything messing with what we've got."

I stared at him, warmth blooming in my chest. Slowly, I reached for his hand.

Something in his eyes eased. "You don't know what it's like to have your love life splashed throughout every paper."

I coughed. "Actually, I do have some experience with that."

Luke raised an eyebrow, clearly skeptical. "Oh, really? When was the last time TMZ camped out on your lawn?"

I leaned forward, propping my chin on my hand. "Not TMZ, but *The Times-Picayune* did a pretty good job of broadcasting my love life to all of New Orleans. My breakup with Beau? Front-page news."

That got his attention. "Wait. Seriously? It was in the newspaper?"

I didn't hesitate at all to open up. He'd shown me in every interaction that I could trust him with my joy and my pain. "After high school, I stayed here at Tulane while Beau headed off to Duke. I genuinely believed we had a future. We'd talk endlessly about how we were going to New York together. But it all came crashing down during our junior year over Mardi Gras."

Memories flood back. Bitter memories.

I sighed. "Mardi Gras is more than just a single day of parades. It's a weeks-long carnival that starts in January. But the crown jewel is the Rex parade on Mardi Gras day itself. It's a big deal. Every year, they have a king and queen. The king is usually an influential older guy, well-rooted in New Orleans social circles. And the queen? Always a twenty-one-year-old debutante, typically a junior in college, and always the relative of a Rex member."

I cleared my throat. "The grand reveal of the royalty happens the day before the parade, on Lundi Gras. *The Times-Picayune* showcases the king and queen's faces on its cover."

I held up my hands for emphasis. "So, picture this. It's Lundi Gras morning. I'm groggy from staying out late watching the Bacchus parade, and I find I've got missed six calls from Beau. Just as I'm trying to make sense of that, my cousins burst in, hugging me, consoling me. I had no clue what was up until they showed me the newspaper."

I sighed deeply. "The king was Beau's dad. And the queen? Reagan. Remember the girl we bumped into at the French Quarter? Her."

Luke leaned in. "I remember."

"The article was gushing about Reagan and her boyfriend, Beau, completely ignoring the fact that he was already with someone else. It read like a Mardi Gras fairy tale, and I was the inconvenient foot-note. Completely erased from the story."

Luke's jaw tightened, his expression darkening. "What a bunch of—"

"Don't worry," I interrupted with a wry smile. "I've already used all the good words to describe it. Trust me, you're not going to come up with anything new." I snorted. "If you read this article, you'd think Reagan was some kind of modern-day saint." I raised an eyebrow at Luke. "While in real life, the only time she's given back is at a store return counter."

He winced sympathetically.

"Just wait. The worst is yet to come. I had barely finished the article when Beau called me. And what he said still stings. 'You knew that we would never end up together. You don't fit into my world.' That he and Reagan just made more sense because she did. I hung up. I never spoke to him again."

The whole city seemed to have read that article. The news that Beau wasn't with me, but with the Queen of Mardi Gras, traveled faster than hot beignets disappearing at Café du Monde. By the after-noon, it felt like every corner of the city, from the French Quarter to uptown, was abuzz with the latest on my love life. And the gossip hadn't been confined to people I knew well. It reached the most unexpected places.

Mrs. LeBlanc, the ever-gossipy mail carrier in Mid-City, who knew everyone's business better than her own, had delighted in sharing the news with my aunt Clara when delivering her post. Maurice, the jovial butcher from Crescent City Meats, gave my uncle Tony not just a leg of lamb but also a side of gossip. Even Sister Marie-Thérèse, usually with her nose buried in a hymnal at St. Louis Cathedral, cornered me after Sunday Mass with a gentle pat and a sympathetic word.

Beau had been the most important relationship of my life, other than my mother. I thought he might be my person, the one I could count on to put me ahead of anyone else. But when he left, it just confirmed what I had always suspected. I wasn't worth staying for, wasn't worth a love that lasted.

Luke's hand found mine across the table, and his touch was gentle. "I see you. And I'm not going to let anyone erase you—not from my life. And for the record, if anyone tries to spin some ridiculous narrative about us, they'll have to go through me first. You're the most unforgettable woman in the world."

My cheeks flushed at his words, the warmth spreading from my face to low in my stomach. I tried to laugh it off, brushing my hair behind my ear. "Well, you know, makeup does wonders." I forced myself to sound light, unaffected, but inside, I couldn't shake the way my heart fluttered.

He shook his head. "It's much more than that. Honestly, any guy would be out of his mind to let you go."

It was one thing to think you were worth it, but having someone else, especially someone like Luke, see it too? It was a revelation. If the world's biggest movie star could see my worth, maybe Beau was the fool all along. And for the first time, I wasn't just acknowledging that intellectually. I was starting to believe it, deep down.

Luke's fingers brushed my hand, sending a shiver racing up my arm. For a brief moment, thoughts of Beau and Reagan just faded away. I could only think of that touch and how unexpectedly electrifying it felt.

But then Tom sidled up, murmuring something into Luke's ear. Luke glanced at me, then mumbled, "I've got to take this call." He pulled his hand back.

I couldn't help but catch snippets of Luke's conversation. "What's the issue?" A pause. "Where is she? And what exactly did she say?"

Feeling guilty about eavesdropping, I scrolled on my phone, pretending to read texts.

But I couldn't miss his voice, thick with irritation: "Look, we don't need lawyers. Just give her what she wants."

30

LUKE

AFTER HANGING UP, it felt like every ounce of energy had been drained from my body. The half-eaten meal in front of me sat forgotten, steam long since faded into the air. I had lost my appetite.

Anna's voice was a soothing whisper. "Everything okay?"

Glancing up, I met her eyes, so full of concern that it nearly bowled me over. Without even realizing it, I began to talk. "That was my manager. My mom's asking for money again."

Anna waited, giving me room to breathe. I sat down at the table. Encouraged by her silence, I pressed on. "It's not the first time. My mom's got a drinking problem."

Sighing, I looked away, a bitter taste in my mouth. "She wasn't always like this. Growing up, she was more of a wild spirit. Met my dad in a bar, got pregnant, and they thought, 'Why not, let's do this.' For a while, she tried playing house. The first time she left my dad and me? I was six. I remember the exact day she came back because it was my seventh birthday party. That time, she stayed only six months before leaving again. My dad and I planned the biggest party ever for my eighth birthday, hoping she would come back for it. She didn't."

I drew in a deep breath, remembering how hope had surged in

me like a tide every time the door opened that day. But my hopes had been crushed again and again. "The next time she came back, I was nine. She stayed for a couple of years, but it just didn't stick. After that, she would come back periodically and stay for a few months."

When I was a child, I never knew what really happened during her absence. "When she'd disappear, Dad would come up with these wild stories, saying she was helping a sick relative or working in an orphanage in Africa. I only found out much later that she was, you know, partying it up. She had inherited some rental properties from her parents. She wasn't mega-rich but had enough to hop around and enjoy life. And when the cash ran low? She'd drop back into our lives, refill the coffers, and then off she'd go again."

Anna's eyes filled with tears. "How could a mom just abandon her son like that? I'm so sorry. Did your dad ever find someone else?"

"Never. Dad was incredible. He always defended her, even though I could see how much it destroyed him every time she left. He was completely in love with her, and she knew it. Used it against him."

A lump formed in my throat, but the words kept coming. "We pretended everything was fine. When it was just me and Dad, I wasn't about to be the one to put that broken look in his eyes, so we never talked about it. Then Mom would come back for a while, and we'd all play pretend, like we were some normal, happy family." I swallowed hard. "Our whole life was a lie."

I paused, gathering my thoughts. "When I got into Brown, my dad was on cloud nine. But leaving him to go off to college? Even though it was only an hour away, that just about broke me."

Anna must have picked up on the conflict in my voice because her tone turned compassionate. "He must've wanted what was best for you. And didn't you mention that you took care of him after hitting it big?"

"Yeah." I rubbed the back of my neck, a sheepish grin forming. "I got into modeling while I was at Brown. Paid my way through college with it."

"Modeling? And then you just jumped to acting?"

I chuckled. "It was quite the journey. In my senior year, I tried out for a play just for fun. It turns out that one of the dads in the audience was a movie producer. He saw something in me. He called it the 'it factor,' and cast me in his next film. That film was *The Boyfriend Test*."

My smile faltered a bit. "After I became a success, the very first thing I did was buy Dad a house. Not just any house—a massive one just outside Boston, where I grew up. Meanwhile, I was in this tiny apartment in Hollywood. Every time things looked up for me, I'd send him more. He... he was so proud. He passed away three years ago."

The empathy in Anna's eyes undid me. "I'm so sorry," she whispered, giving my hand a gentle squeeze.

"Man, I miss him so much. You know, after I bought that house for him, I flew back to surprise him. And guess who was there? Mom." I ran a hand through my hair, remembering my frustration. "Dad and I had this massive argument. I made it clear I wouldn't drop by if she were around. I was such a jerk."

"Luke, you're not—"

"No, seriously. Sometimes I think about it and... Why couldn't I just let him have his moment of happiness?"

"You were just watching out for him. You didn't want your mom to take advantage of him again. It's like you were stepping in his shoes, protecting him the way he always protected you."

I could feel my blood boiling. "And now she contacts me, and it's like she believes we have a normal mother-son relationship, as if she hasn't been absent my entire life. I can't lie anymore. I won't."

"You're right, you shouldn't have to," Anna said gently. "Pretending everything's okay isn't fair to you. You've got every right to feel the way you do, and you don't owe anyone a performance, especially not her. Your feelings, your truth, they matter."

I watched her in the dim light. We'd shared so many moments that made me laugh, but this was different. There was no pretending left between us. No script, no disguise. Just her and me, and the kind of silence that makes you realize what you want.

"You're the first person I've ever told this to." My chest ached. I didn't know when she'd become the person I trusted most, but I knew, without question, that I didn't want it to end.

She gave a small, understanding smile. "My mom always told me, when you split your troubles, they become half as big."

My fingers intertwined with hers. "Anna, meeting you has been the best thing that's ever happened to me."

Her eyes sparkled, and the look she gave me made my heart leap in a way I hadn't known was possible. She squeezed my hand, her voice as tender as her gaze. "I feel the same way."

Time seemed to stand still. All sounds faded, and it was just the two of us sitting close, the warmth of her hand in mine. It was comfortable. She didn't have to say anything, and neither did I. There was something calming in just *being*—no cameras, no scripts, no pretending to be anyone but ourselves. And I realized, as I held her hand, that I didn't want this moment to end.

A knock on the door broke the spell. Hal poked his head in, his expression neutral but pointed. "Sir, they're closing. We need to move."

Anna glanced at me, her cheeks flushing slightly as she withdrew her hand. "Guess we've overstayed our welcome," she murmured with a shy smile.

I sighed, reluctant to leave. "Yeah, I guess we have." Standing, I reached for my hat and glasses.

Hal and Tom flanked us, guiding us toward the private exit. But I barely noticed them. My focus was on Anna.

When she glanced up, catching me watching her, she raised an eyebrow, her lips curving into a teasing smile, and her voice was warm. "What?"

"Nothing," I murmured, shaking my head, but my heart betrayed me. It wasn't nothing. It was everything.

The muggy night air hit us as we stepped outside, but all I felt was the warmth of her presence. The car waited, and as she slid in ahead of me, her hair catching the soft glow of the streetlights, I found myself frozen.

I'd never felt like this before. Not with anyone. The thought hit me hard, almost knocking the air out of my lungs.

I climbed in beside her, the door shutting behind us. She turned to me, her expression curious, and I knew.

I knew I was in love with her.

31

ANNA

THE WORDS WERE FLOWING like they hadn't in years, a rush of creativity I hadn't felt since college.

Back then, it had been different. I'd written a story about my mother, raw and personal, a piece that had won an award and drawn more attention than I'd ever expected. Critics called it "stunning" and "heart-wrenching," and I felt like I'd found my voice. But nothing I'd written since had come close to that.

Until now.

My story had begun to take shape, and I found myself creating a love interest for my superhero protagonist. This character was infuriating and magnetic, someone who challenged the superhero and charmed him in equal measure.

The superhero swooped in, as he always does. The superhero saved her, as he always should.

I didn't even realize what I was doing until I paused, rereading one of my scenes. The vulnerability, the push-and-pull of emotions. It was all so familiar. And yet, the realization didn't scare me. It thrilled me.

I wasn't just telling a love story. I was living one.

32

LUKE

THE ZOOM CALL STARTED EXACTLY as I should have expected: chaotic and slightly unhinged.

The director's face popped onto the screen, his hair wild like he'd been electrocuted, a cigarette dangling from his lips even though he wasn't smoking it. "Luke Fisher, Hollywood's golden boy." He waved a spatula for some reason. "You gonna phone this in, or are you finally ready to act like someone who's seen the inside of a Walmart?"

I blinked. "Good to see you too, Gerald."

Gerald Fargo, the most eccentric man in Hollywood and proud of it, leaned closer to the camera, inspecting me like he was trying to find a flaw. "You look too polished. We need grit. Show me the pain. Show me a man who's been kicked in the nether regions by life and still manages to stand upright."

"Do you want me to act or fight a bear?" I deadpanned, unable to resist.

He grinned. "Same thing."

As weird as the guy was, and he was absolutely the kind of person who'd eat spaghetti for breakfast to make a point, I could tell he liked me. His questions were like those weird riddles a troll asks you before letting you cross a bridge. And for once, I felt ready. I'd spent enough time away from the Hollywood bubble to realize most of it was held together with Botox and delusion. I deserved this role. I could bring something real to it.

The audition went well, I was sure of it, and our conversation afterwards was easy until Anna walked through the background, holding a mug in her hand. She froze mid-step, her eyes widening as she realized she was in the shot. Gerald's eagle eye zeroed in on her instantly.

"Who's that?" he barked, waving his spatula like a weapon. "Is she part of your method?"

Anna's face went bright red. "I'm so sorry," she blurted, holding the mug up like a shield. "I didn't mean to interrupt. I didn't know you were still on a call."

"Relax, sweetheart," Gerald said, squinting at her through the screen. "You're his muse, aren't you?"

"No, no," she stammered, backing out of the frame. "I'm just... I was getting coffee." She disappeared so fast that she almost left a puff of smoke behind.

I pinched the bridge of my nose, trying not to laugh, but unsure how I should describe Anna to the director. "She's my... She's—"

"Not important," he interrupted, pointing the spatula at me. "What *is* important is that you've got the look of a man who's been inspired. That's what I need for this role: love, pain, misery. And also redemption. You can do that, right?" Before I could respond, he slapped his spatula on his desk and said, "You'll hear from me soon. Don't make me regret this."

The screen went black, and I leaned back in my chair, exhaling deeply. As bizarre as it had been, I had a good feeling.

Anna peeked her head back into the room, her cheeks still flushed. "I'm *so* sorry."

"It's fine," I said, biting back a grin. "Honestly, I think you just sealed the deal for me. He liked you."

"So, am I your muse?"

I tilted my head, smiling as I looked up at her. "You're more than that." I reached for her hand, my fingers brushing hers as I gently pulled her closer. She leaned down, her gaze steady but her breath hitching just enough for me to notice. When our lips met, it wasn't the first time, but it still felt new. Every kiss with her was like that. Each one left me feeling like the ground had shifted beneath me, like I was standing on something more solid and yet more thrilling than ever before.

Her lips were warm and soft, a perfect match to the electricity buzzing between us. When she pulled back, her cheeks were flushed, and her smile was just shy enough to make my heart ache.

"Well," she murmured, her voice low but playful. "Guess I really am inspiring."

I laughed, resting my hand on the arm of the chair, unable to look away from her. "You don't even know the half of it."

She stepped back, her fingertips brushing lightly against mine. I sank into the chair, the tension from the call beginning to ease. Gerald liked me. I could feel in my bones that I had the role.

And for the first time, I believed I could balance it all. My career. My love for acting. What I had with Anna.

I didn't have to choose between the life I'd built and the one I wanted.

Maybe I could have both.

33

ANNA

I HAD SIGNED up for this catering gig months ago, back when it seemed like an easy way to make some extra cash.

But that night, standing in a room full of New Orleans' elite, I was seriously questioning all my life choices.

Why did catering companies insist on dressing their staff in the most humiliating outfits imaginable? That's right, I was decked out like a jingling Mardi Gras jester.

Cringing at my reflection in the polished silver serving tray, I adjusted the ridiculous hat perched on my head, its bells tinkling with every movement. The purple, green, and gold onesie, with its puffy sleeves and shorts, topped with a black bow tie, was a peak of indignity. At least the eye mask offered me anonymity.

Marie Antoinette, in her matching jester costume, swished past me with a tray of crab cakes. "Everybody who's anybody in New Orleans is here tonight," she whispered dramatically.

"You're right. I just saw the mayor." I bent slightly, jingling every inch of the way, as a woman in a dazzling fuchsia dress reached for a muffuletta from my tray.

"Ahem," a woman in a black sequined dress said, snapping her fingers in front of my face. "Your tray's as empty as my glass."

I jerked my head back. "Oh, right, sorry about that. Thanks for the heads-up."

"You need to pay attention." The woman narrowed her eyes at me. You'd think I'd stolen the last piece of cake at her birthday party.

"Got it, heading to the kitchen," I mumbled. Behind me, she continued to berate my lack of skill to anyone within earshot. I moved faster, carefully loading a fresh tray with an assortment of meticulously crafted mini-muffulettas. "You got this," I whispered to myself.

But fate, it seemed, had other plans. The first face I saw when I stepped out of the kitchen was none other than the displeased woman, her glare as sharp as the sequins on her dress.

"You finally remembered how to do your job," she sneered. Her talon-like nails darted out to snatch a sandwich, and just as I thought she'd retreat to her lair, she reached for another, her greed tipping the scales of fate.

As she yanked the second sandwich with the finesse of a starved raccoon, she jostled my tray. Trying to salvage the situation, I spun back around, but her sandwich heist had thrown me off balance. My feet tangled, the tray wobbled, and before I could utter, "Please don't sue me," an explosion of muffulettas filled the air.

A mess of olive salad, sesame-seed bread, and deli meats rained down onto the pristine marble floor. The chaos knocked my mask and my jester hat clean off, leaving me standing there, fully exposed and surrounded by fallen hors d'oeuvres—all thanks to her double-sandwich greed.

The room went silent, save for the judgmental whispers and muffled gasps. The muffuletta-loving woman looked down at me with pure disdain, somehow managing to speak clearly through a mouthful of food.

"Utterly incompetent," she declared before turning on her heel with a dramatic flourish, leaving me amidst the chaos I had created.

Flushing with embarrassment, I dropped to my knees to gather the wreckage. "Smooth, Anna," I muttered under my breath. "Really smooth."

"Here, let me help you," said a familiar voice cloaked in an unfamiliar Australian accent. I looked up to see a man in a tuxedo and mask kneeling beside me, his piercing blue eyes unmistakable.

"Luke?" I whispered in disbelief.

He winked and handed me a muffuletta. "G'day, mate. Looks like you've had a spot of bad luck."

I bit my lip to stifle a laugh as he dabbed at the olive salad with a damp handkerchief. "I thought you were going to stay home," I murmured, heat rushing to my cheeks.

"And miss this? Not a chance." He plucked a piece of olive salad off the floor and studied it thoughtfully. "You know, this reminds me of the time Hugh Jackman spilled an entire platter of shrimp cocktail on Oprah's couch. People still talk about it. And look at him—he's thriving."

I snorted. "That didn't happen."

"Okay, fine." He tossed an olive onto the tray with flair. "But imagine if it had? Hugh's got the charm to pull it off. And so do you."

I shook my head, focusing on cleaning the rest of the mess. "I don't think charm fixes this."

"Don't sell yourself short." He crouched beside me with an exaggerated air of importance. "Did you know that Brad Pitt tripped over a waiter and completely took out the hors d'oeuvres table at the Oscars after-party? And Keanu Reeves? He once carried an entire fallen cake out of a gala while bowing to the audience."

"Once again, you're making that up." I tried to suppress the giggles threatening to escape.

"I mean, maybe not *Keanu*, but wouldn't it be amazing if he did that? Anyway, now it's your turn to join the ranks of legends."

I couldn't hold back the laugh any longer. "Great. I'll be the jester author who dropped a full tray of muffulettas on a marble floor. Really iconic."

He grinned, offering me a damp handkerchief to clean my hands. "Trust me, in five years, this will be your quirky success story. Every great writer has one. You're just getting yours out of the way early."

I took the handkerchief, shaking my head as I wiped my hands.

"You're weirdly good at making me feel better about public humiliation. What are you even doing here?"

He shrugged, reaching to pick up a piece of olive salad. "Topher mentioned he had an invitation to this masquerade ball, so I figured I'd follow your advice to see more of New Orleans. Little did I know that I'd be cornered into explaining Australian winters at least four times already. People are *very* concerned about how cold it gets in July."

"Did they ask if the toilets flush backward, too?"

"Twice," he deadpanned, popping the olive into his mouth. "Also informed people that 'shrimp on the barbie' isn't actually a thing we say, which apparently ruined several people's evenings."

I laughed despite myself. "So you came for the cultural exchange?"

"Not exactly." He glanced at me, something shifting in his expression. "I came because I knew *you'd* be here. Been watching you work the room all night, actually. Awe-inspiring waitressing skills right up until the sandwich incident."

"Oh no, you saw the whole thing?"

"I had a front-row seat. You wore that costume well, then wore that muffuletta even better." His grin widened. "I was planning to just admire from afar like a reasonable person, but then I couldn't stay away. Had to abandon a very boring conversation about someone's timeshare in Destin."

My heart bloomed in my chest at his admission that he came to the party to see me. I picked up the last olive and the tray. "Thanks for the save."

He shrugged, a sly look in his eye. "Couldn't let you take all the hits alone."

The olive salad smudged on my sleeve caught my eye. "I'll be back. Just need to drop off this tray and clean up before I start smelling like a deli counter."

I made my way back to the kitchen, carefully balancing the tray as I wove through the crowd. Once there, I set it down with a sigh of relief and inspected the damage to my costume. The olive salad smear wasn't nasty, but it was enough to send me toward the bathroom for a quick rinse.

On my way back from the bathroom, I had to cut through the ballroom. There, a deep voice froze me in place. It was a voice I hadn't heard in years, but one I could never forget.

"Anna."

There he was. Beau. The man who had shattered my heart without a second thought. He looked the same, all casual rich-boy charm with his surfer-dude hair and fitted tuxedo. The rest of the world dropped away.

For years, I had rehearsed this moment in my mind, envisioning what I would say if I ever ran into Beau again.

Never had I envisioned that I would be wearing a jester costume.

"Beau, h-hi," I stammered, my voice barely above a whisper.

"You look... Different." Beau's eyes scanned me from head to toe. The way his gaze lingered on my ridiculous costume made my stomach churn.

Different? *Different?* Was that what we were going with? I swallowed hard, the sting of his casual condescension making my cheeks flush.

"I could say the same," I shot back, surprising even myself. My eyes flicked to his tailored tuxedo and carefully tousled hair. But it was a lie. He looked every bit the polished rich guy he'd always been.

"I heard you're working at that bar," he said smoothly, as if he hadn't just raked me over the coals with a glance. "Muses, right? Still writing, too?"

"Yes, actually," I said, lifting my chin. "And you're back at the family bank?"

He shrugged, his smirk unwavering. "You know how it is. Gotta take over the family legacy sooner or later. Looks like we're both keeping busy."

I wanted to say something clever, but my mind stalled. All those imaginary confrontations, all those rehearsed zingers, and yet I was completely blank.

"Hey, congrats on the engagement," I said finally, my voice stiff.

Beau's smirk faltered. "Yeah, about that... I'm sorry. For how everything ended. You know, my bad."

I blanched. *My bad.* That was his apology? I stared at him, and a hot wave of anger stirred in my gut. My brain scrambled for a retort, but my tongue sat in my mouth like a lead weight.

I could have been a good Southern girl, graciously pretending he hadn't ripped my heart out and stomped on it in front of an audience. But no. The anger won out, and suddenly, I found my voice.

"Yeah, that's right, it is your *bad.*"

Beau's mouth fell open like he'd just been hit with a flying muffuletta.

"Yes, you hurt me," I continued, the words tumbling out with years of pent-up frustration. "And yes, reading about it in the *newspaper* was a cruel way to find out you were cheating on me. And I know you feel pressure from your parents to marry the right person, join the right clubs, and be the perfect heir to the family business. But I remember the Beau who loved art, who dreamed of moving to Paris to paint every day while I wrote."

I paused, my breath catching as his expression shifted to something almost like regret. But I wasn't finished.

"And you know what I've learned? The more you twist yourself to fit other people's expectations, the further you stray from who you are, the more you become a stranger to yourself."

The words hung in the air like beads from a Mardi Gras float—bright, bold, and impossible to ignore. I took a deep breath, feeling suddenly lighter.

Life after Beau had been chaos. My once-promising writing career had stumbled, my dreams felt like they'd gone up in smoke, and for a while, I thought everything was slipping away. But now, standing here, I realized something important: that wasn't the whole story.

So what if I wasn't a published author? *Yet.* The exhilaration wasn't in the recognition or the success; it was in staying true to myself and chasing what mattered to me. And because of that, I was more myself now than Beau, Reagan, or any of their crowd would ever be.

Beau's face twisted into an expression of pure astonishment, and I thought that my words had gotten through to him. Then I noticed he wasn't looking at me anymore.

He was staring at something behind me. "You're—" he began, his voice faltering.

I turned, and there was Luke, standing tall, his smile calm and confident. What shocked me most wasn't his sudden appearance but the fact that he wasn't wearing a mask anymore.

Luke put his arm around me possessively, lifted my chin with his knuckles, smiled down at me, kissed me quickly on the lips, and said, "Hello, beautiful." He then extended his hand toward Beau like they were meeting at a cocktail party. "I'm Luke. And you are?"

"Beau," my ex managed, his voice faint. His handshake was slow, as if he wasn't entirely sure this was real.

The hum of shock rippled through the room like a slow wave. Not everyone could hear what was being said, but now it was clear that everyone was paying attention to us. Heads turned, whispers darted from one cluster of people to another, and gasps punctuated the murmurs as recognition dawned.

"Is that—" someone whispered.

"Luke Fisher? The movie star?" another voice hissed.

Then, somewhere in the crowd, the pièce de résistance: "Wait, he's with *the catering?*"

Luke's arm tightened protectively around my shoulders. "You're good," he murmured, low enough for only me to hear.

I could feel hundreds of eyes pressing on me, but Luke, unfazed as ever, leaned down and kissed me on the top of my head.

The whispers faltered, gasps turned into outright stares, and somewhere, a woman muttered, "I didn't think it was possible to make a jester outfit look chic. Guess I was wrong."

Luke's tone was as smooth as silk. "Thanks for keeping Anna company." He pulled me in a little closer in an easy, possessive gesture. "She's one of a kind, isn't she?"

Beau blinked, clearly at a loss for words. "Uh, yeah. I guess so."

"She fits into my world perfectly," Luke added, his voice loud and clear, carrying a gentle, almost awestruck tone that made my cheeks flush. His words hung in the air, undeniable and deliberate, leaving the room buzzing.

Suddenly, Reagan appeared, gliding to Beau's side with her usual icy poise. Her gown glittered like she'd been dipped in diamonds, but her eyes, darting between Luke and me, gleamed with something less refined: jealousy.

"Wait," Reagan said, her lips curling into a disbelieving smile as her gaze locked on Luke. "You're *with her*?" She gestured vaguely at me as if I were a misplaced umbrella. "*That's* what's happening here?"

Luke raised an eyebrow, his grin widening. "Guess it's my lucky day."

Reagan laughed, a sharp, humorless sound. "Oh, I get it. This is one of those ironic things. You know, like performance art or a publicity stunt. Very Hollywood."

"Not a stunt," Luke said smoothly, his tone unbothered. "Just good taste."

Reagan huffed. "You're *Luke Fisher*. You could literally date *anyone*."

Luke tilted his head as if giving her statement serious thought, then shrugged. "True. But why settle for just *anyone* when I can have Anna?"

I could practically see Reagan's brain short-circuiting as she struggled to keep her composure.

Luke, ever the master of timing, grabbed my hand with an easy confidence, signaling it was time to go. He threw one last look over his shoulder at Beau, his grin bordering on smug. "Nice meeting you, Bob."

"It's Beau. Beau," my ex stammered, his face a shade of crimson I didn't know was possible.

"Ah, my mistake," Luke said with mock sincerity. "Apologies."

I couldn't help it. I burst out laughing as we walked away. I wiggled my fingers in a cheeky wave. "Take care, Bob."

We were almost out of the door when I looked down at the ridiculous jester costume. "Oh no," I muttered. "I can't just leave. I'm *working*."

Like a fairy godmother, Marie Antoinette appeared out of nowhere, her jester costume jingling. She took one look at Luke, then at me.

"Absolutely not," she said, balancing a tray on her hip like a pro. "If you don't leave with this man right now, I'll personally see to it that you never live it down. Go. Shoo." She waved her free hand dramatically, as if she were warding off a stray cat.

"But I—"

She cut me off with a finger to my lips, her red curls bouncing under her jester hat. "No, no, no. I've got the muffulettas. You've got a movie star. This is not a situation you overthink."

Luke chuckled, glancing at me with an amused expression. "I like her."

Outside, under the glow of the streetlights, Luke stopped and turned to me. "You handled that brilliantly."

I smiled up at him. "I had a little inspiration."

He leaned in, his lips capturing mine in a kiss that was everything Beau never could be: steady, real, and perfect. As the noise of the gala faded behind us, I realized something. Revenge might be sweet, but moving forward with someone who truly saw me? That was even sweeter.

34

LUKE

SHOWING up Anna's ex-boyfriend had been satisfying, no question about it. Watching his face turn as red as a crawfish when he realized I was *with her*? Pure gold.

But I couldn't shake the nagging thought that it might not have been my most brilliant move.

Luke Fisher, a surprise guest at a masquerade ball, stepping out into the open with a beautiful woman on his arm... it wasn't exactly low-profile. People had phones. People posted things. I could practically hear the headlines writing themselves: *Luke Fisher Spotted at Private Ball with Mystery Woman.*

My publicist was not going to love this. Maybe I should have been preparing for the press onslaught. But none of that mattered. Anna had appreciated it, making it worth the trouble that was certainly coming my way.

I had watched her all night in that jester costume. Her smile was incandescent, and I knew that everyone there saw what I did: someone effortlessly gorgeous, lighting up the room.

The drive back to the mansion was quiet but for the hum of the engine and the occasional rustle of her costume. By the time we walked through the mansion's grand doors, the night's earlier chaos felt worlds away.

Anna slipped away as soon as we walked inside the door, murmuring something about needing to change. I watched her retreat, her steps light but purposeful, and decided to head to the library. The oversized windows there had a way of grounding me, framing the night sky like a living masterpiece.

I stood by the largest window, gazing out at the stars. They seemed impossibly bright tonight, almost close enough to touch. I didn't hear her come in, but I felt her presence before I turned.

"Hey." She walked toward me, barefoot, her legs bare beneath a pair of worn jean shorts. An oversized T-shirt hung loosely over her frame, and her hair was piled haphazardly on top of her head, strands already escaping to frame her face. No makeup, no pretense. She was the most beautiful woman I'd ever seen.

Anna drifted toward the largest window. Her face tilted skyward, her expression caught between curiosity and awe.

Without thinking, I walked to her and slid an arm around her waist, pulling her gently against me. She leaned into my chest, her head resting just below my shoulder.

I pointed to a familiar constellation. "Look up there. Do you see Orion?"

She blinked, her brow furrowing as she scanned the sky. "Where?"

I smiled, gently taking her hand to guide her gaze. "Right there, those three stars almost in a straight line. That's Orion's Belt."

For a moment, I thought she might not see it, but then her face lit up. "Oh, there they are."

I noticed the subtle flush on her cheeks, and I wasn't sure if it was just from the events of the evening. I traced an invisible line in the sky. "Now, if you follow those stars upward, you'll find two brighter ones— Orion's shoulders. Below the belt, you'll see two more stars for his feet."

She tilted her head. "So... it's like a giant hourglass?"

"Exactly." I guided her hand again, pointing to a curved line of stars. "And that's his bow. Orion was a hunter who was in love with the goddess Artemis."

As I told the story, I couldn't help but notice the way Anna's expression shifted. She was listening intently, but there was something else, something deeper in her gaze as she looked up at the stars.

I launched into the myth, keeping my tone light and teasing. "Orion was a mortal with a bit of an ego. But he got a little too full of himself, and the goddess Gaia sent a scorpion to take him down. Heartbroken, Artemis put him in the sky so he could shine forever."

"That's beautiful," Anna murmured, her voice soft.

"It is," I agreed, but my focus had shifted from the stars to her. I studied her face, wondering what she was thinking, how she was feeling, and wishing I could hold on to this moment just a little longer. I voiced what I thought she might be thinking about her mother because it was the same thing I thought about my father: "I love the idea of being remembered forever, even after death."

She looked deep into my eyes, then reached up and caressed my face, warming my insides. "I love that too. Do all constellations have stories like that?"

"Most of them. That's what makes the night sky so enchanting."

"How do you know so much about constellations?"

The words spilled out. "It was my dad. During summers or school breaks, we'd spread blankets in our backyard, and he'd point out the constellations to me. He was a classics scholar, so he was familiar with all the stories. He was patient, too, always making sure I could spot the stars, even when it felt like it took forever." I paused, the memories washing over me, the edges bittersweet. "Whenever I look at the night sky now, it takes me back to those moments with him. It's my way of staying connected, I guess."

A strange mix of relief and vulnerability washed over me as I told the story. When was the last time I talked about this with anyone? I wasn't one to open up, especially not about something so personal. But with Anna, I always seemed to do precisely that. It had never happened with any other girlfriend. Certainly not with Sienna, even though I had thought that was love.

I glanced at Anna. Her eyes brimmed with understanding. "That sounds special." She cleared her throat. "It's strange. The ways we hold on to the people we love. I catch myself using my mom's phrases sometimes, as if they keep her here with me in little pieces."

Her words hit me harder than I expected, like she'd reached inside my chest and found the exact place that ached. For a moment, we stood in silence, as if we were both letting ourselves sit with memories we usually kept tucked away.

I shifted slightly, aware of how much I'd let my guard down. This wasn't like me. I didn't open up like this and lay myself bare. Yet, with her, it felt natural. Unforced.

We relocated to a couch, with me pointing out constellations and weaving their myths, and her listening with wide eyes and the occasional question. Now and then, she'd glance at me, and I could feel the space between us growing smaller, even as the universe seemed impossibly vast above us.

After a while, her head began to dip. She fought to stay awake, but I could see the day's exhaustion winning. When she finally drifted off, I gently covered her with a blanket.

The peace of the moment didn't last long. My phone buzzed in my pocket, pulling me back into reality. I checked the screen and groaned.

A series of texts from my manager, Bob, lit the screen:

CALL ME. **NOW.**

Your face is everywhere. In a tux. WITH A JESTER.

I thought New Orleans was a QUIET GETAWAY. Was I misinformed???

The girl is STUNNING by the way. Good job. Who is she?

They haven't ID'd her yet, but it's only a matter of time.

Fisher, what in the name of Hollywood are you doing? CALL ME.

I'm billing you for the stress ulcer I'm developing.

. . .

I STARED at the messages for a moment, imagining the chaos brewing on the other end. Bob was probably pacing a hole through his office floor, possibly clutching a bottle of Tums.

I glanced at Anna, fast asleep under the stars, her face peaceful and calm.

Shaking my head, I murmured, "Worth it."

The world I'd been trying to keep at bay was closing in, and I had no idea how I was going to face it. Or how my relationship with Anna would survive it.

Then, with a resigned sigh, I typed back: **Give me an hour.**

Because for now, this moment with her was mine, and I wasn't ready to let it go.

35

ANNA

THE FIRST THING I noticed was the smell of crawfish.

The second was the unmistakable sound of my Aunt Dolores hollering, "Where's the hot sauce?"

Before I could fully register what was happening, the doors to the library burst open, and my cousin Lucy marched in, holding a tray of corn and sausage. "Good morning, Sleeping Beauty. So, they don't have enough bedrooms in this place, and you have to sleep on the couch?"

I groaned, rubbing my eyes as I sat up on the library sofa, the blanket Luke had draped over me slipping to the floor. "I fell asleep down here, okay?"

Aunt Dolores bustled in just as Lucy was leaving, and my aunt carried a massive tray of crawfish. "Don't worry, honey, we're making do. Now, grab a tray or something useful. Let's head outside. Your cousins are setting up the folding tables."

"Wait, what?" I blinked, still groggy. "Why are you all here?"

Then it hit me. The music, the smell of boiled seafood wafting through the open window. My family had come to throw me a surprise crawfish boil. How very New Orleanian of them. Nothing says *we love you* quite like 30 pounds of crustaceans and a folding table covered in newspaper.

"We couldn't miss an opportunity to see this fancy mansion of yours," Aunt Dolores said matter-of-factly. "And your uncle thought it was a great idea to bring the boil to you since you've been so busy."

"Great idea? You realize this is how people end up on neighborhood Facebook groups, right?"

Aunt Dolores waved a hand. "If anybody complains, we'll just invite them over. Nothing diffuses outrage like a plate of hot crawfish. Grab the hot sauce, and let's go."

I padded into the kitchen, stopping short at the sight of my entire family swarming the backyard like they'd been air-dropped in. Tables, coolers, and crawfish pots had materialized out of nowhere. How had I slept through this?

Luke stepped cautiously into the room, his hair a little tousled, eyes soft when they found mine. "I think our place got invaded." His lips were twitching.

"I'm so sorry," I whispered, crossing to him. "I didn't know they were coming. Go hide upstairs. Save yourself while there's still time."

He smiled, the kind of smile that made my heart stutter. "I think we're ready for a little 'meet the family,' don't you?"

"Normally I'd agree," I said, peeking through the window at the chaos unfolding. "But not my family. Maybe we start small, like just my cousin Lucy or Mary. They're basically normal. The rest of them, especially all together, are like Mardi Gras on espresso."

He chuckled, brushing a piece of hair from my cheek. "I'll take my chances. Though, I did want to talk to you about something. But it can wait."

Before I could ask what, the back door banged open, and my Uncle Ray appeared, clapping Luke on the back with enough force to knock him off balance. "Well, look at this guy. You must be the one who's been keeping our Anna so busy. Welcome to the family boil, son."

Luke straightened, still smiling—somehow. "Uh, thanks. Big fan of seafood."

My uncle beamed. "Grab an apron and make yourself useful." My uncle shoved a gaudy, oversized apron into Luke's hands. The bold, glittery letters read *Pinch Me, I'm Cajun.*

Luke held it up. "This is incredibly sparkly."

Then, my cousin Mary appeared, shrieking as if she'd spotted a rare animal in the wild. "Holy moly cannoli, it's Luke Fisher," she yelled, nearly dropping her tray of drinks. "Lucy, LUCY. Look."

"Oh, for the love of..." I muttered, shaking my head.

Aunt Dolores swooped in, eyes sparkling as she gave Luke a once-over. "Well, aren't you even more handsome in person?" She patted his arm. "Anna, honey, you didn't tell us you were friends with a movie star."

Uncle Ray squinted at Luke. "Wait a second... are you the guy from that movie? The one where you're, uh..." He gestured vaguely with his hands. "Doing all that dramatic running?"

Luke hesitated. "Uh, probably?"

"You know," Uncle Ray continued, snapping his fingers. "The one with the explosions. And the car. Or was it a boat?"

"Yes." Luke nodded.

Uncle Ray nodded sagely. "I knew I recognized you. Great work."

I buried my face in my hands while Luke shot me a grin that said he was absolutely loving this.

More family poured in, hugs and handshakes flying as people jostled to greet Luke. One of my aunts wrapped him in a bear hug, while my cousin James took a selfie with him before he could protest.

"I'm so sorry," I whispered to Luke as Uncle Robby—who hadn't connected the dots—clapped him on the back.

"You here for the crawfish, son?" Uncle Robby asked. "Let's get to the backyard and grab a plate. We've got plenty."

Luke opened his mouth to respond, but Aunt Dolores cut him off. "He's not here for the crawfish, Robby. He's here for *Anna.*"

Someone handed me a tray of hot sausage, and we headed to the backyard, where tables had been arranged.

It didn't take long for Luke to get swept up in the chaos. Within minutes, he was standing by the boiling pot, cracking jokes with my cousins and peeling crawfish like he'd been born to do it. He seemed entirely at ease, wearing the apron as if it were part of his everyday wardrobe.

"Hollywood's not bad at this," Uncle Tony shouted, clapping him on the shoulder.

My grandma Nonna looked him up and down. "You're skinnier in person. Do you eat? Sit down. I'm making you a plate."

Aunt Mona leaned in beside me, her voice low and conspiratorial. "He's a keeper, that one. Down-to-earth, you know? Not like that other one. What was his name again? Ben? Boo?"

"Beau," I muttered.

"Right, him," Aunt Mona said with a cackle. "He was always struttin' around."

Uncle Charlie chimed in from the other side of me. "This one's got a good head on his shoulders. Not like that trust fund guy. Bet that guy wouldn't even know what to do with a crawfish if you boiled it, peeled it, and handed it right to him."

I forced a smile, trying to steer the conversation elsewhere. "Yeah, well, Luke's different."

Uncle Ray leaned over, grinning. "So, Anna, what's it like dating a movie star? Do you get free popcorn every time you go to the theater?"

Before I could answer, Aunt Sharon cut me off. "What about his house? Or does he have more than one? Is one of them a castle? I bet one of them's a castle."

"Sharon, be reasonable," Aunt Dolores interrupted, rolling her eyes. "Castles are expensive to heat. He probably has, like, a yacht or something."

"Does he have a yacht?" Aunt Sharon pressed, turning her full attention to me.

"I don't know," I stammered, but they weren't done.

"Wait, wait," Uncle Charlie added, his tone dead serious. "Is he one of those method actors? Like, if he plays a knight, does he ride a horse everywhere for months?"

"Oh," Aunt Dolores exclaimed, clapping her hands together. "And does he do his own stunts? Because I bet he could. He's got those arms."

"Do you think he could get me a walk-on role in one of his movies?" my cousin Mary asked, her eyes sparkling with excitement. "I'd even settle for background. I can stand in a crowd really convincingly."

I opened my mouth, but no words came out. It was like being stuck in the middle of a popcorn machine, except instead of buttery morsels raining down, it was a barrage of absurd questions.

"Has he met Meryl Streep?" Aunt Mona gasped suddenly, as though it had just occurred to her. "That's the big one, Meryl Streep."

"Does he know how to cry on cue?" My cousin Lucy leaned in with genuine curiosity. "Because I could use that to get out of parking tickets."

At that, I couldn't hold back a groan. "Guys, he's just... a person. Like everyone else."

Uncle Ray raised an eyebrow. "He doesn't seem like everyone else to me. Everyone else doesn't peel crawfish that fast."

"Or look that good doing it," Aunt Sharon added with a wink.

"You're cute together." Mary hip-checked me.

Aunt Mona gasped, her hands flying up to cover her mouth. "Heavens to Betsy, you're dating a movie star."

"I—"

"Don't listen to her. She'll deny it," Aunt Sharon said.

"I'm not denying—"

"Of course they're dating," my cousin Lucy said. "Two beautiful people sharing a house like this? It's like one of those romantic-comedy movies he stars in."

Aunt Mona grabbed my arm, her face serious. "So how serious is this? Because he seems like a keeper."

I nearly choked. "We're... it's still pretty new."

"Anna, you're blushing," Aunt Dolores teased. "That tells us everything."

Uncle Charlie leaned in. "I like him. He's got good energy."

I looked across the yard where Luke was peeling crawfish and laughing with my uncle like he'd been part of the family for years. He caught my eye and grinned. My chest felt too full. He fit here, somehow. In the chaos and the noise and the complete lack of boundaries that was my family, he just... fit.

And watching him there, sleeves rolled up, completely at ease, I realized how much lighter everything felt with him around. How much happier I'd been these past few weeks. How right this all felt, even when my family was being completely overwhelming.

He looked over at me again, and this time he mouthed, *You okay?*

I nodded, smiling despite the interrogation happening around me.

Yeah. I was more than okay.

36

LUKE

I FOUND myself peeling crawfish at a folding table in the backyard, elbow to elbow with Uncle Robby, who kept up a running commentary about his adventures in love, life, and everything in between.

"The secret to life," Uncle Robby announced, waving a crawfish tail for emphasis, "is knowing when to twist and when to pull. Works for crawfish, stubborn jar lids, and getting out of family obligations."

I stared at him. "That's... your secret to life?"

"Got me through three mortgages and two hernias." He pointed the crawfish at me. "You're in with a good one over there, by the way." He nodded toward Anna, who was laughing with her cousins across the lawn.

I followed his gaze, and everything else faded.

She was standing in a shaft of late afternoon sunlight, her head thrown back in laughter at something Mary had said. The golden light caught in her hair, and the way her whole face lit up—man, she was beautiful. Not magazine-cover beautiful, though she was that too. It was something deeper. Warmth that drew people in without her even trying.

She looked over then, like she could feel me watching, and our eyes met across the yard.

My chest tightened. This. *This* was what I'd been missing my whole life without even knowing it. Not the parties or the premieres or the moments that looked perfect on camera. Just... this. A backyard full of people who actually cared about each other.

For the first time in years, maybe ever, I felt like I was exactly where I was supposed to be.

"Luke! You in or what?" Uncle Charlie called out, already tossing a football in the air.

"What am I in for?" I asked, reluctantly tearing my gaze from Anna.

"Touch football. Winner gets first pick at dessert, and Aunt Mona made her famous bread pudding, so the stakes are high."

"The stakes are *very* high," Uncle Ray confirmed solemnly. "That bread pudding is delicious."

Within minutes, I was being tagged by a ten-year-old who had apparently been training with the Saints, while Uncle Steve provided play-by-play commentary like we were in the Super Bowl.

"And Fisher goes down! Taken out by Little Michael! The crowd goes wild!"

Anna was on the other team, and she was *competitive*. When she intercepted a pass clearly meant for Uncle Charlie, she did a victory dance that had everyone howling.

"That's my girl!" Aunt Sharon yelled.

"Showoff!" I called across the lawn, grinning.

She stuck her tongue out at me, and my heart did something stupid and complicated in my chest.

Yeah. I was completely gone for this woman.

Two plays later, I caught a pass and dodged around Mary, heading for the makeshift end zone (Uncle Ray's cooler), when Anna came out of nowhere and tagged me so hard I stumbled.

"Gotcha, movie star," she said breathlessly, eyes sparkling.

"That was an *aggressive* tag," I said, laughing.

"Bread pudding's on the line. No mercy."

By the time Anna's team won (she caught the winning touchdown, naturally), I was sweaty, grass-stained, and happier than I'd been in months. Maybe years.

I grabbed a beer from the cooler and was about to rejoin the group when I overheard two of Anna's aunts talking near the porch.

"Do you think this means Anna will move to Hollywood?"

"Not a chance. After everything she's been through, that girl's never leaving New Orleans. Not even for a Hollywood star."

"I know you're right. New Orleans girls like Anna don't leave home. This place is in their bones."

The words landed like a punch to the gut.

I stood there, beer forgotten in my hand, as the implications sank in. I'd been thinking—maybe not consciously, but somewhere in the back of my mind—that if I got the part, if things between us kept going this well, maybe Anna could come with me. She was a writer. She could work from anywhere, couldn't she?

But what if she couldn't? What if she wouldn't?

What if I asked her to choose, and she chose New Orleans over me?

I tried to shake it off and rejoin the chaos. Uncle Steve was attempting to teach the kids how to have a watermelon-seed-spitting contest, demonstrating his technique with the enthusiasm of an Olympic coach. At the same time, Aunt Mona stood behind him, shaking her head and muttering about "teaching children bad manners." The energy was infectious.

But those words kept echoing. *That girl's never leaving New Orleans.*

How could I ever ask her to leave this behind? Her family, her city, everything that made her *her*?

Then, a shout from across the yard shattered the moment.

"Anna! You're famous!"

37

ANNA

I STARED at the photo on my aunt's phone. It was me.

"At least they got my good side," I winced. Might as well look on the bright side.

Luke's mouth twitched. "That jester hat is doing you a favor."

"Right?" I managed a weak laugh. "Very flattering angle."

But my thoughts were already racing ahead to what this meant: headlines screaming that we didn't belong together. That he was Luke Fisher, and I was just... me.

And once he saw those headlines, once the world started pointing out how mismatched we were, would he start to see it too?

"Anna." My Nonna's voice cut through my spiraling thoughts. She was squinting at someone's phone. "You're on the internet. Does this mean I need to friend you on the Facebook now? I don't even know my password."

"Nonna, you don't need to—"

"Your cousin posted a casserole recipe last week, and I couldn't comment. This is important, Anna."

Aunt Mona appeared at my elbow, peering at the photo over my shoulder. "The jester costume really brings out your eyes," Mary added helpfully.

Uncle Charlie squinted at the screen. "Says here you're a 'cater-waiter.' Isn't that what we used to call waiters?"

"It's fancier," Aunt Sharon explained. "Hollywood fancy."

I needed air. Or a locked room. Preferably both.

I mumbled something about needing water and escaped to the kitchen, gripping the counter as I tried to catch my breath.

"Anna?" I looked up to find Luke in the doorway, his expression concerned. "Can we talk about this? I'm so sorry."

"It's not your fault—"

"It is, though." His jaw tightened. "I took off the disguise. I should've thought this through better."

I stared at the photo on my phone again. Me in that ridiculous jester costume. The headline reduced me to a *cater-waiter*, like that was the most interesting thing about me.

"What happens now?" I asked quietly.

Luke stepped closer, his hand warm on my arm. "What happens now is that my team steps in. My publicist and my manager are the best in the business. This is what they do. We'll control the narrative, make sure the story's accurate. I promise, Anna, we'll handle this."

His voice was steady, reassuring, but I could see something flickering behind his eyes. Something that looked almost like... fear? Was he worried that *I* was going to bail?

His hand tightened on my arm. "I'm worried you'll realize this isn't worth it. The paparazzi, the headlines, people dissecting every part of your life..." His voice cracked slightly. "I wouldn't blame you if you decided it was too much."

My heart twisted. This wasn't the confident movie star I'd gotten to know. This was just... Luke. Vulnerable, uncertain, and terrified that I was going to walk away.

I reached up, covering his hand with mine. "Do you really think a little fan craziness is going to scare me off? After everything?"

"It's not just fan craziness. It's everything else, too."

"I know what it is." I squeezed his hand. "And I'm still here. The press doesn't scare me. That's not what matters."

He exhaled like he'd been holding his breath. "I care about you,

Anna." His voice dropped lower. "So much. And I need you to know that. I need you to know that your feelings are the only thing that matters to me."

The lump in my throat grew. "I care about you, too. And I'm not going anywhere."

His mouth curved into a small, relieved smile. "I'll do everything I can to protect you from this." His hand brushed a strand of hair behind my ear, the gesture so tender it made my chest ache. "I promise."

Man, he was sweet. Standing here in my kitchen, worried about *me* when his entire team was probably having a collective meltdown. Looking at me like I was the one who might break his heart, when the tabloids would probably spend the next week explaining in excruciating detail why we didn't belong together.

But the way he was looking at me, the way his thumb was tracing absent circles on my arm, I realized something: I really, really liked him. More than I'd let myself admit. And if he thought a few invasive headlines were going to change that, he clearly didn't know me very well yet.

From the backyard, Uncle Charlie's voice boomed: "Alright, folks, I think we've overstayed our welcome! Let's give these two some peace!"

"We're not leaving yet!" Aunt Mona protested. "There's still king cake!"

"There's *always* king cake, Mona. We can take it to go."

I heard the sounds of my family beginning to pack up: coolers being dragged across the grass, chairs folding, Nonna issuing instructions about who was driving whom home.

Luke glanced toward the back door, then back at me. "Should we go say goodbye?"

We walked out together, and I felt his fingers tighten around mine as my family spotted us. But instead of the scrutiny I'd been expecting, I saw Uncle Ray give Luke an approving nod. Aunt Sharon winked at me. Even Nonna, who never approved of anything, patted my cheek and whispered, "He's a good one. Don't let the internet people scare you."

One by one, they hugged us both, packed up their things, and filtered out through the side gate. Uncle Charlie was the last to leave, clapping Luke on the shoulder.

"You take care of our girl," he said.

"I will," Luke promised.

When the gate finally clicked shut, the backyard fell quiet. The sun was setting, casting everything in golden light. Luke's hand was still in mine.

"That wasn't so bad," he said softly.

"No," I agreed, squeezing his hand. "It wasn't."

He pulled me closer, and I let myself lean into him, breathing in the familiar scent of him, soap and something warm and distinctly Luke.

"We'll figure this out," he murmured against my hair. "Together."

And standing there in the fading light, surrounded by the remnants of crawfish boil and family chaos, I believed him.

Whatever came next, we'd face it together.

And that was enough.

38

LUKE

As USUAL, Bob Reardon turned what should've been a crisis management session into a stand-up routine at my expense.

"Explain this to me like I'm five," my manager began, "You're supposed to be out of sight, prepping for your role, and instead, you're... what? Helping out the Crescent City's favorite girl-next-door?"

I sighed, pacing the length of the library. "I'm dating her, Bob."

There was a beat of silence, then a slow, drawn-out "Ohhhh." He let the word hang in the air like a bomb about to go off. "So, we're just fully leaning into this rom-com life now? That's the vibe we're going for? Because I gotta tell you, Luke, the studio's gonna *love* this."

"It's not like I planned it," I shot back, stopping to lean against the bookshelf. "It just... happened."

"Uh-huh." Bob's tone was flat. "And what exactly 'happened'? Did you trip and fall into her arms? Was there a jazz band playing in the background? Please tell me there was a jazz band. It'll round out this love story for the press."

"Can you not?" I groaned, pinching the bridge of my nose. "She's not just some girl. She's... she's incredible, okay? And yes, I'm in love. Happy now?"

I mean, I hadn't told Anna that I loved her yet, but I knew it was how I felt.

There was a pause. "Wait. The way you just said that... Have you told *her* this?"

"Not... exactly."

"Not exactly?"

"I mean, not in those specific words, no."

Bob let out a bark of laughter. "Oh my. Fisher, are you telling me I'm the first person hearing this? Your *manager* gets the 'I love you' before your girlfriend does?"

"It's not—that's not how—"

"This is amazing. This is peak Luke Fisher. I'm putting this in my memoirs." He was full-on cackling now. "Chapter Seven: The Time Luke Fisher Told Me He Was In Love Before Telling The Actual Woman."

"Are you done?"

He was not.

"Do you want me to call her? Break the news? 'Hi Anna, Luke's manager here. Just wanted to let you know he's in love with you. He told me first, obviously, as one does.'"

"I hate you."

"You love *me* too? Fisher, you're really spreading it around today. Does Anna know she has competition?"

"Did you want to do some actual planning for how we're going to talk to the press about this?"

"I just want to get this straight: instead of focusing on nailing the role of a lifetime, you're living out a Hallmark movie subplot in the heart of New Orleans?"

"It's not a Hallmark movie," I muttered, though even I had to admit it sounded like one.

"Right, because in a Hallmark movie, you'd be a small-town baker trying to save the family business, not a movie star hiding from the paparazzi. My bad."

"Bob, I don't need this right now," I replied.

"Fine, fine," Bob relented. "But you'd better get ahead of this,

Luke. The world already knows you're dating someone outside the Hollywood bubble, and the headlines aren't slowing down. You, my friend, are a walking tabloid headline. With a plot twist."

I sighed, glancing at my phone as notifications lit up the screen like a fireworks show. "I know, Bob. Trust me, I know."

"Good. Because if you're going to do this, you'd better be sure she's worth it."

I paused, thinking of Anna. "She is."

Bob groaned. "Let's get Mabel on the line. That publicist of yours has already texted me eighteen times, and one of them was just a picture of a fire emoji."

Seconds later, Mabel's shrill voice cut through the call. "Luke Fisher. Tell me this is all some elaborate prank, and I'm not currently spinning a strategy for *you* and a Mardi Gras jester."

"Mabel—"

"No, no, let me paint the picture for you. Hollywood's golden god, *Luke Fisher,* spotted at a gala in New Orleans with someone *not* wearing couture, not from a famous family, and not part of a PR-approved power couple. How am I supposed to spin this? You've officially broken the algorithm."

"Mabel." I tried to suppress a laugh. "It's not that big of a deal."

"Not that big of a deal?" she repeated, her voice climbing an octave. "Luke, you're dating someone who was dressed as a jester. Do you know what the internet can do with that? Meme factories are already running at full capacity. *We are trending on platforms I didn't even know existed.*"

I shook my head. "Okay, so how do we handle this?"

"How do we handle this?" Mabel scoffed. "Step one: We lean into the romance angle. Mysterious New Orleans date? The public eats that up. Step two: We hope to high heavens that the jester costume doesn't overshadow your charm. Step three—Bob, are you listening? —We need to get ahead of this before some blogger does."

Bob chimed in with a chuckle. "Mabel, you're scaring the poor guy."

"Oh, please," she shot back. "Luke, I don't scare you, do I?"

"Not at all." I smiled faintly. "I find this level of panic oddly endearing."

"Good. Because if you're serious about her, we're going to need a whole new playbook. And if you're not serious..." She trailed off ominously, leaving the threat unspoken.

"Oh, he's serious," Bob said, and I could hear the grin in his voice. "He loves her."

There was a beat of silence, then Mabel's tone completely shifted. "Wait. What? Luke Fisher is in *love*? That's... that's actually really sweet."

"Can we not make this a thing?" I said.

"No, no, this is absolutely a thing," Mabel said. "Bob, are you tearing up right now? Because I'm tearing up."

"Little bit," Bob admitted.

"Our boy's in love," Mabel said, and I could practically hear her pressing her hand to her heart. "I need a moment. This is like watching your kid graduate."

"Are you two done?"

"Never," Bob said. "I'm putting this in the group chat."

"Don't you dare—"

"Too late. Sent."

Mabel laughed, then I heard her take a breath, switching gears. "Okay, okay. Back to business." Her voice shifted into crisp publicist mode. "This is actually perfect from a narrative standpoint. A love story between a movie star and a regular woman. The public will eat that up. But we need to control the rollout."

"Agreed," Bob said, all business again. "The 'cater-waiter' angle is condescending and needs to be corrected immediately."

"She's an author," I said, unable to keep the pride out of my voice. "An award-winning author. She's brilliant and talented, and she comes from this hilarious and huge New Orleans family that's been here for generations. And... she's just amazing."

There was a pause.

"Oh, he's got it *bad*," Mabel said softly. "And for the record? I like her already. Anyone who's got you this smitten is clearly something special."

Bob cleared his throat. "We're going to make this the feel-good story of the year. Luke's in love with this woman, and we're going to make sure everyone falls in love with her too."

Mabel broke in. "Luke? If you see a camera, smile like you just won an Oscar."

"Got it," I replied.

"Good luck, Romeo." Bob's voice was brimming with amusement.

I hung up, and from the other room, I could hear Anna humming to herself. My phone buzzed again, and I glanced down at the screen. A text from Topher lit up: **You're trending, bro.**

I stifled a groan, slipping the phone into my pocket.

I walked back to the couch where Anna was sitting, her face half-lit by the soft glow from the window.

I stepped closer, brushing a hand lightly against her arm. "How about tomorrow we take a break from all this? Just you and me. No phones, no headlines. Let's make a day of it."

She tilted her head, her brow furrowing slightly. "Are you sure? Don't you have to... I don't know, do some crisis management?"

"Mabel and Bob have it handled," I said, squeezing her hand. "Right now, all I want to do is to be with you."

Her lips curved into a small smile, and she leaned into me, resting her head against my shoulder. "Okay. That sounds really nice, actually."

I pressed a kiss to the top of her head, breathing in the familiar scent of her shampoo. Outside, the world was probably buzzing with speculation and gossip and hot takes about us. Reporters were probably already staking out Muses. The tabloids were sharpening their knives.

But sitting here with Anna tucked against my side, her hand in mine, her quiet humming resuming as she relaxed, none of that noise mattered.

Yeah, once the reporters figured out where we were staying, it might get complicated. But as I looked down at her, seeing the trust in her eyes when she looked back up at me, I knew one thing for sure.

She was worth it.

All of it.

39

ANNA

IT WAS the kind of perfect day you never wanted to end.

After the whirlwind of media chaos, Luke and I were given strict instructions: lie low, but, if we chose to go out, stay disguised. The publicist hinted at the possibility of future public appearances together, but for now, discretion was key. No one knew we were staying at Topher's mansion, which made sneaking in and out relatively easy.

I'd taken a few days off from Muses to avoid the inevitable crush of curiosity. Marie Antoinette had texted me a picture of the crowd crammed into the bar, standing room only, people hoping to catch a glimpse of Luke or at least hear some gossip.

The media frenzy didn't appear like it would let up, either. The paparazzi had unearthed every awkward high school and college photo of me they could find. There were even interviews with people I'd never met, all claiming some intimate connection to my life.

Luke's publicist had pulled off a minor miracle. Public opinion was shockingly positive, with headlines hailing me as a "regular woman" who had "caught the eye of a Hollywood heartthrob." Newer headlines identified me as a writer, highlighting the award I'd won in college.

Still, the constant noise felt suffocating. That's why the day after everything broke, Luke and I went wandering through City Park, and both of us had to wear disguises.

We started at the Sculpture Garden, where Luke pretended to narrate each piece like a museum tour guide.

"And here we have *Stick Man Contemplates Existence*," he said, gesturing dramatically to a minimalist piece. "A poignant commentary on the futility of waiting in line for coffee."

I laughed so hard I nearly tripped over my own feet. "Stick Man deserves better than that."

"Oh, absolutely. Stick Man deserves a beignet."

From there, we rented a pedal boat. Luke insisted on doing all the work at first until he quickly realized pedaling wasn't as easy as it looked.

"You're enjoying this too much." He panted as I lounged back, my feet nowhere near the pedals.

"Maybe a little," I teased, dipping my fingers into the cool water. "But hey, you're the one who wanted to steer."

By the time we made our way to the Café du Monde stand near the art museum, we were sweaty, a little sunburned, and laughing. We split an order of beignets, and powdered sugar stuck to both of us as the breeze scattered it like confetti.

"This is what heaven tastes like," Luke said through a mouthful, his grin boyish and carefree.

"Powdered sugar and fried dough? Sounds about right."

"You've got some right there." Luke gestured vaguely at my face.

"Here?" I asked, swiping my cheek.

"No, the other side."

I swiped again, and he grinned. "Still missed it."

"You're the worst." I couldn't stop laughing.

Before I could attempt another pass, Luke leaned in, his hand cupping my chin gently as his thumb brushed over my cheek. The moment felt electric, his touch sending a wave of warmth through me. His eyes met mine for the briefest second, something unspoken passing between us.

"There," he said, his voice lower now, his thumb lingering a second longer than necessary. And then, he kissed me. Soft and sweet, his lips warm against mine. It wasn't a long kiss, but it was enough to leave me tingling, my skin humming with the aftershocks. "Got it that time."

After we ate, we wandered the paths around Big Lake, pausing now and then to admire the view. Luke bought a watercolor from a street artist, a painting of the iconic live oaks draped in Spanish moss.

"These trees remind me of you." His voice was low, gravelly.

I tried to laugh it off. "What, because I'm old and creaky?"

"No." He stepped closer, and I could see the warmth in his eyes. "Because you're beautiful. And no matter how hard the wind blows, you stay rooted."

My face flushed. We held hands, and everything felt easy and natural.

As the afternoon stretched on, we sprawled on a picnic blanket under one of the park's massive live oaks. The air was warm, the light dappled through the leaves, and for a moment, it felt like we were the only two people in the world.

Well, the two of us, plus Tom and Hal leaning against a tree, arms stiff, clearly ready to tackle anybody who recognized Luke.

Luke leaned back on his elbows, watching the clouds drift by. "This," he said, his voice quiet, "is perfect."

I glanced over at him, taking in the peaceful expression on his face. "It really is."

But perfect days don't last forever.

On our way home, Tom turned onto Topher's street, and my heart sank before the car even stopped. The driveway was now a frenzy of noise and movement. A cluster of paparazzi swarmed the gates like wasps, cameras raised, lenses glinting like weapons in the afternoon sun.

The car hadn't even come to a complete stop before flashes lit up the windows.

I froze, every muscle in my body going tight. My chest clenched, like my lungs had forgot how to work. "Oh no."

Luke let out a slow sigh, already reaching for the sunglasses on the dashboard. Tom drummed his fingers against the steering wheel as if it were a countdown, and Hal slid out of the car, his jaw tight, motioning for the photographers to back up.

Hal cleared a path, barking orders like a drill sergeant as Tom inched the car through the sea of flashing cameras. The gates finally creaked open, and we slipped inside just long enough for them to slam shut behind us.

Inside, I tried to shake off the unease. I opened my laptop, thinking some writing might distract me, only to be greeted by an email I hadn't expected.

"Unfortunately, this piece is not a fit for us at this time."

The rejection stared back at me. I hadn't even remembered submitting the short story, a historical fiction piece about a failed revolution in 19th-century Poland. But seeing it rejected now stung more than I wanted to admit.

This wasn't supposed to be the hundredth rejection.

I exhaled.

"Hey."

I looked up to see Luke standing in the doorway, his eyes lingering on me with a tenderness that made my breath catch. "What's wrong?"

I turned the screen toward him, waving vaguely at it. "Another rejection. I didn't even remember submitting this story. It's just, I don't know. It's silly."

"It's just one rejection," he said gently. "You're better than that."

His kindness hit a nerve I didn't know was raw.

"It's not just one rejection. It's my hundredth rejection. You don't get it," I snapped before I could stop myself. "You don't know what it's like to put your whole heart into something and have people tell you it's not good enough."

His jaw tightened. "I do know what that's like, Anna."

The silence that followed was thick and immediate; his words echoed louder than either of us had expected. Shame surged through me almost instantly.

"I'm sorry," I whispered, stepping toward him. "I didn't mean that. I just..." My voice cracked. "I'm tired of feeling like I'm not enough."

I wrapped my arms around him, resting my cheek against his chest. He hesitated for a second, then pulled me closer. I listened to the steady rhythm of his heartbeat. His hand moved gently up and down my back.

"You're incredible, you know that?" he murmured, his voice low and soft against my hair. "I wish you could see yourself the way I see you. You don't have to be perfect for anyone. You're already enough."

His words hit me squarely in the chest, leaving me breathless for a moment. I swallowed hard and whispered, "I'm sorry. I didn't mean to take it out on you."

He tilted my chin up, his gaze meeting mine. "You don't need to apologize. I get it, Anna. I really do. I mean, I know rejection, too. Hollywood's built on it. For every role I get, there are ten I don't. For every glowing review, there's someone saying I'm overrated."

I reached up to touch his face, my fingertips brushing his cheek. "You're one of the good ones, Luke."

He smiled faintly. "And don't forget that you're one of the good ones, too."

The tension in my chest began to ease as his words sank in. For a moment, the world outside didn't matter. The rejection emails, the headlines, the noise. It was just the two of us, wrapped in a kind of understanding.

He pressed a gentle kiss to the top of my head, his lips lingering there. When he pulled back, his hands slid down my arms slowly, his thumbs tracing small circles that made my breath catch.

"You're going to finish this book." His eyes searched mine. "And when you do, the world's going to see what I already see. That you're brilliant and talented and absolutely incredible."

"You make me believe that," I said quietly. "When I'm with you, everything feels possible."

"I mean it." He tucked a strand of hair behind my ear, his touch so tender it made my chest ache. "I believe in you, Anna. More than you know."

I reached up and covered his hand with mine, holding it against my cheek.

He leaned down to kiss my forehead, then the tip of my nose, making me laugh despite the emotion welling up inside me.

"There's that smile," he murmured, his own widening.

For a moment, we just stood there, close enough that I could feel the warmth of him, see the flecks of gold in his blue eyes. The rest of the world felt very far away.

His phone buzzed in the silence, cutting through the moment. He glanced at the screen, and something in his expression shifted. It was so subtle that I thought I'd imagined it.

"Everything okay?"

"Yeah." He smiled and tucked the phone back into his pocket. "Just Bob checking in. I should probably call him back before he sends out a search party."

"Of course." I stepped back to give him space. "Go ahead."

He squeezed my hand once more. "I'll just be a few minutes. Why don't you pick something to watch? I'll be right back."

"Okay."

I stayed by the window, staring out into the night, that brief flicker of unease still twisting in my chest.

Maybe everything *was* fine.

So why did it feel like it wasn't?

40

LUKE

THE TEXT ARRIVED JUST a moment ago, and I already knew it would change everything.

It's official. You got it, baby. Filming starts in a week. Call me.

My manager's words were still glowing on the screen, but I couldn't bring myself to respond. Not yet.

I paced the kitchen, phone still in hand, trying to breathe around the knot tightening in my stomach. This was it. The role I'd fought for, reshaped myself for. The role that could redefine my entire career.

And I got it. So why did it feel like the floor had shifted under me?

I had kept glancing at Anna throughout our day at City Park, trying to memorize how she looked, with her hair catching the sunlight, her smile wide and unguarded. She made everything feel perfect.

And now, everything was about to change.

How was I supposed to tell her I'd be leaving soon? I knew what I had to do. She said she would never leave New Orleans, but what was holding her here? I had to ask her to come with me. But uneasiness flickered in my stomach.

What if she said no?

I rubbed the back of my neck. I thought about how she'd leaned against me by the lagoon, the smell of her hair mingling with the warm scent of the oaks, and I couldn't shake the ache in my chest.

Before I could even process it, my phone buzzed again. This time it was an actual call. I sighed, knowing I couldn't dodge Bob for long. I answered, holding the phone to my ear as I leaned against the desk. "Hey, Bob."

"Hey? *Hey*? That's all I get?" Bob's voice boomed through the speaker. "You, my friend, just landed the role of a lifetime. Gerald Fargo is over the moon. He's telling everyone you're 'a walking metaphor for the tragic comedy of existence' or some artsy nonsense like that. Translation: you crushed it."

I shook my head. "Well, I'm glad my helping-my-girlfriend-dressed-as-a-jester moment landed with him."

"Landed?" Bob scoffed. "No, it soared."

"Well, I'm glad he's thrilled," I said, rubbing the back of my neck.

Bob caught the hesitation in my voice. "What's this tone I'm hearing? Don't tell me you're second-guessing this."

"No, I'm not," I replied quickly, though the tightness in my chest disagreed. "It's just... the timing's complicated."

"Ah, let me guess," Bob said, his voice dropping into mock seriousness. "The timing involves a certain New Orleans jester-slash-girl-next-door? Listen, I get it. She's great. But, Luke, this is Hollywood. Opportunities like this don't wait. You can't afford to get tangled up. You've got a week to prep, and then it's showtime. No distractions."

I wanted to argue, but the words caught in my throat. Bob sighed, lowering his tone. "Look, I'm not saying don't be happy, okay? But don't forget what got you here. Don't lose sight of that. You can't have it all, buddy. Not in this business."

"I hear you," I said, though my chest tightened even more. "I'll figure it out."

"You'd better," Bob quipped. "And hey, if it's any consolation, Fargo thinks you're a genius. So, there's that."

I forced a laugh. "Yeah, thanks for the pep talk, Bob."

"Anytime, Romeo."

I shoved the phone back into my pocket just as Anna walked into the kitchen. "What was that about?" she asked, tilting her head.

I hesitated, then forced a grin. "Just Bob. Trying to find me something else to audition for. You know how he is."

Her brow furrowed slightly, concern flickering in her eyes. "What about the audition with Gerald Fargo? Did Bob say if it went okay?"

I hesitated, the truth sitting heavily on my tongue. "Not yet," I lied, forcing a grin. "Bob's just... Bob. Always trying to find the next thing for me to chase."

She studied me for a moment, her expression unreadable, before nodding. "Okay," she said softly. "But are you sure you're alright? You seem... I don't know, off."

My chest tightened, and before she could press further, I pulled her into a kiss. Her hands slid to the back of my neck. The kiss was sweet, warm, and everything I needed. But as it ended, the heaviness in my chest didn't lift.

I brushed a strand of hair from her face and tried to smile. "I'm fine." The words felt thin, hollow.

As she turned back toward the window, humming, I stood frozen, watching her. My heart raced for all the wrong reasons. *She deserves better than this,* I thought, the doubt gnawing at the edges of my mind. *She deserves the truth.*

The words from Bob and the text replayed in my head. One week. How could I leave now? The thought of living away from her felt impossible.

I wouldn't be able to keep the truth from her for much longer. And as I stood there, staring at her, the realization hit me like a gut punch: *I might have landed the role of a lifetime, but what if I lost Anna in the process?*

41

ANNA

SOMETIMES, when everything feels too good to be true, you start looking for the cracks. Even when they're not there.

Luke had been acting weird last night after he got the text from Bob, and that morning, he seemed distracted and quieter than usual, as if something was weighing on him. I'd caught him scrolling through his phone in the kitchen last night. Usually, he'd crack a joke about my coffee-making skills or launch into some absurd Hollywood anecdote, but today? Nothing.

I tried to focus on my routine, but my stomach tightened with every passing minute. *This is it,* I thought, the familiar doubt creeping in. *He's pulling away. I knew it was too good to last.*

I wandered into the living room, my coffee mug warm in my hands. Luke was leaning against the counter, his eyes fixed on his phone. He glanced up, and for a second, his expression was unreadable. Then he sighed, running a hand through his hair. "There's something I need to tell you."

My heart sank, bracing for the worst. "Okay," I said, my voice steadier than I felt.

He hesitated, then held up his phone, his lips curving into a cautious smile. "I got the part."

Relief flooded through me. "Luke, that's amazing!" I set my mug down and threw my arms around him, practically bouncing with excitement. "You got it! You actually got it! This is incredible!"

He hugged me back, but his grip didn't feel as tight as I expected. When I pulled away to look at him, ready to see that brilliant smile of his, his expression faltered. His eyes flicked to the side as if avoiding mine.

"Wait." My excitement dimmed slightly. "What's wrong? This is what you wanted, isn't it?"

"Filming starts in LA soon." There was sadness in his eyes. "I'll have to leave in a week."

And there it was. The other shoe dropping. I nodded, doing my best to keep my expression positive. "Oh. In a week." The words felt like they were scraping against my throat.

Luke stepped closer, grabbing both of my hands in his. "Anna, come with me. Bring your laptop, write, and explore. It'll be fun."

His blue eyes met mine, steady and sure, but also nervous.

My heart thudded hard. He was offering everything: partnership, adventure, love. The life I used to imagine but never thought I could have.

And for a flicker of a second, I thought maybe I could do it. Maybe I could leave. Pack my bags, get on a plane, start over in the sun instead of the shadows of this city.

But then my chest tightened. My throat constricted. The air around me went thin. I tried to take a breath, but it caught halfway, shallow and fast. My pulse roared in my ears. All I could see was water—rising, dark, endless.

Not again. Not leaving.

"I don't know," I whispered, forcing a shaky smile. "You've got a life in LA. I don't want to get in the way."

"Anna." He took both my hands in his, his thumbs brushing across my knuckles. His voice dropped, becoming softer, more vulnerable than I'd ever heard it. "I love you."

My breath caught. Everything seemed to stop. The tick of the clock on the wall, the hum of the refrigerator, my own heartbeat.

"You—what?"

"I love you," he said again, his eyes never leaving mine. "I'm completely in love with you."

Tears sprang to my eyes. This was everything I'd wanted to hear. The words I'd been waiting for, without even realizing how badly I needed them.

"I love you too," I whispered, the confession breaking free. "Oh, Luke, I love you so much."

His face lit up, relief and joy flooding his features. He pulled me closer, his forehead touching mine. "Then come with me. We'll figure it out. Whatever you need, whatever makes you happy. We'll make it work."

I wanted to say yes. I wanted to be brave enough to leap.

But fear still had its grip on me.

"I can't," I whispered, my voice breaking. "I can't leave New Orleans. My family, my friends, my job. My whole life is here. I'm sorry. I love you, but I just can't."

The light in his eyes dimmed. His hands were still holding mine, but I could feel the distance growing between us even as we stood inches apart.

His face fell, but he recovered quickly. "You said you would never leave here, and I should have listened. I'll be back soon to see you. I'll get a break, and I'll come visit."

"Yes," I said quickly, relief washing over me even as tears threatened to spill. "Yes, I want to stay together. I want to make this work. We can do long distance, right? People do it all the time."

I don't know why I was so scared to leave this city. What was holding me back? I was a grown woman after all.

But Luke wasn't making me face my fears. He was saying it could work long distance. Hope flooded through me. We could stay together, even if we couldn't be in the same place. I smiled and kissed him, hoping it would push away the ache in my chest. His lips were warm and steady.

When the kiss ended, he smiled and pressed his forehead to mine. "We'll talk every day."

Over the next few days, we both threw ourselves into our work. Luke disappeared into his preparations for the role, spending hours on Zoom with his acting coach and meticulously memorizing his lines.

And me? I wrote.

Even though I had received that dreaded hundredth rejection, this superhero story begged to be finished. Every time I tried to step away, to convince myself it wasn't worth it, I found myself pulled back, powerless to stop the words from flowing.

I sat at the desk in the guest room, wholly immersed in my work. Draft after draft poured out of me, and the words felt alive.

Luke and I stole time together when we could. He brought me coffee while I wrote, and I sat quietly in the library while he ran lines, our fingers intertwined even when we weren't talking. Small moments that reminded me why I'd fallen for him in the first place.

One afternoon, I was so deep in a chapter that I didn't hear Luke approach until his hand gently touched my shoulder. "Okay, close your eyes," he said, tugging me by the hand through the mansion's hallways.

"If you're leading me into a prank, I swear..."

"Just trust me."

I closed my eyes, letting him guide me. We stopped, and I heard the creak of a door opening. "Okay, beautiful, open your eyes."

I blinked. We were standing in one of the smaller guest rooms, but it had completely transformed. A blanket fort was constructed over the bed and couch, with string lights draped inside, creating a soft golden glow. A laptop sat in the middle, cued up to what looked like a classic movie.

"What is this?" I asked, my voice catching slightly.

"You said you've been stressed about your writing, and I've been stressed about the shoot, so..." He rubbed the back of his neck, suddenly looking uncertain. "I thought we could just hide from the world for a few hours."

I turned to him, my chest tight. "You built a blanket fort."

"Is it stupid? It's stupid, isn't it? I just thought, you know, we were talking about how we're both only children and never built blanket forts with our siblings, that..."

I kissed him before he could finish, pouring every ounce of gratitude and affection into it. When I pulled back, he looked dazed.

"It's perfect," I whispered.

We crawled inside, the blankets creating a cozy cocoon around us. Luke pulled me against his chest, one arm wrapped around my shoulders as we settled in to watch some black-and-white comedy from the 1940s that had us both laughing within minutes.

Halfway through, Luke's fingers traced absent patterns on my arm. "Anna?"

"Hmm?"

"When I'm in LA... I'm going to miss this. Just being with you."

I tilted my head to look at him. "I'm going to miss it too."

"We'll make it work, though, right?" His voice was vulnerable. "This isn't just, I mean, it's not just because we're stuck in the same house, or—"

"This is real." I sat up slightly, cupping his face. "What we have is real."

He searched my eyes for a moment, then nodded, relief washing over his features. "Yeah. Yeah, it is."

He pulled me back against him, pressing a kiss to the top of my head. We stayed like that for hours, wrapped up in each other and our little fort, the world outside temporarily forgotten.

And for those few hours, I let myself believe that distance wouldn't change anything.

42

LUKE

THE DAY before I was set to leave for LA felt surreal. My suitcases sat half-packed in the corner of the bedroom, a physical reminder that this was really happening. In less than twenty-four hours, I'd be on a plane and leaving Anna behind.

I'd been trying not to think about it too hard by throwing myself into last-minute preparations, triple-checking my script notes, anything to avoid the hollow feeling in my chest. But every time I looked around the room and saw Anna perched on the edge of my bed, watching me pack with running commentary, it hit me how much I was going to miss this. Miss *her*.

"You're bringing *that* shirt?" she asked, pointing at a faded t-shirt I was folding.

"What's wrong with this shirt?"

"Luke, it has a hole in the armpit."

"It's a *small* hole. Character-building hole."

"It's a hole that says, 'I've given up.'" She grabbed it from my hands and tossed it toward the trash can. "You're a movie star. Act like it."

"Hey!" I retrieved the shirt. "This is vintage."

"Vintage hobo, maybe." But she was grinning, her eyes sparkling with mischief.

I shook my head, smiling despite myself, and went back to packing. I reached for the lavender hoodie draped over my chair. "Remember when you gave this to me?" I asked, holding it up.

Her expression softened. "You're taking it with you?"

"Of course I am." I folded it carefully and placed it on top of everything else in the suitcase. "I'll take this with me wherever I go."

She bit her lip, her eyes getting a little shiny. "It's just a hoodie, Luke."

"It's not just a hoodie." I sat down beside her on the bed, taking her hand. "It smells like you. And when I'm in LA missing you at three in the morning, I'm going to put this on and pretend you're there."

"You're going to make me cry before you even leave."

"Sorry." I kissed her knuckles. "But it's true."

She leaned back on her hands, watching me fold another shirt with what I'm sure was terrible technique.

"You're doing it wrong," she observed.

"There's a wrong way to fold a shirt?"

"You're creating wrinkles. Future Luke is going to be very disappointed in Present Luke's folding skills."

"Future Luke will have a maid who knows how to iron."

"Future Luke sounds lazy."

I looked over at her. The afternoon light streaming through the windows catching in her hair, the easy smile on her face, the way she looked completely at home here in my space, and for a moment, I just had to stop and appreciate her.

"What?" she asked, catching me staring.

"Nothing. Just... I'm going to miss this."

Her smile softened. "Miss my superior folding critiques?"

"Among other things." I sat down beside her on the bed. "Your terrible coffee. Your off-key humming."

"I do *not* hum off-key."

"You absolutely do." I pulled her closer, pressing a kiss to her temple. "And I'm going to miss it so much." She leaned into me, quiet for a moment. Then, I continued. "So... Bob and Mabel want us to go out tonight. Apparently, we need to 'show the world our love story' and be seen looking happy and in love."

"A public date?"

"Yeah. Dinner at Commander's Palace. They've already tipped off a few friendly photographers." She looked up at me. "Nothing too intense. Just us being us, but with an audience."

"That sounds... romantic?"

"About as romantic as a dentist appointment," I admitted.

"Well, when you put it that way, how can I resist?" She wrapped her arms around my neck. "Our last night before you leave, and we're performing for photographers. Very us."

"We'll make it fun," I promised, nuzzling against her. "And after, it's just you and me. No cameras. No performance. Deal?"

"Deal."

COMMANDER'S PALACE WAS STUNNING, all white columns and Victorian elegance. We were seated at a prime table near the window, perfect for the photographers lurking outside, and Anna looked gorgeous in a deep blue dress that made her eyes shine.

"Smile," I murmured as our waiter approached. "We're madly in love, remember?"

"Right. Madly." She took a sip of water, her eyes sparkling with mischief. "Should I gaze adoringly at you? Laugh at your jokes even when they're not funny?"

"My jokes are always funny."

"See, that right there—" She gestured with her fork. "That's the kind of delusion I'm supposed to find charming."

I grinned. "You do find it charming."

"Debatable."

The waiter arrived with our appetizers, and I reached across the table to take her hand, very aware of the cameras outside. But when her fingers laced through mine, and her smile crinkled the corners of her eyes, I forgot about the photographers entirely.

"You know what's weird?" she said, leaning in conspiratorially. "This is actually kind of fun. In a surreal, we 're-performing-our-relationship-for-strangers kind of way."

"It's the absurdity," I said. "Makes everything feel less real."

Her smile faltered slightly. "Yeah. Less real."

We ate and talked, and on the surface, everything looked perfect. We laughed at the right moments, held hands across the table, and played our parts beautifully. At one point, Anna told a story about Uncle Charlie's latest crawfish contraption that had me genuinely cracking up, and the photographer outside got his shot of me laughing, her beaming, both of us looking like the perfect couple.

But as dessert arrived—bananas foster that Anna insisted we share—she set down her spoon and looked at me.

"Can I be honest about something?" she asked quietly.

"Always."

"I hate this." She gestured vaguely at the window, the cameras, the performance of it all. "Not being here with you. That part's great. But... all of this? Having to prove our relationship to strangers? I want our love to be ours. Just for us. Is that selfish?"

Relief flooded through me. "Not even a bit. I was thinking the same thing."

"Really?"

"Anna, I don't want to share you with the world. I don't want our relationship to be a headline or a photo op or some narrative Bob and Mabel are managing." I squeezed her hand. "I just want you. The real you. The one who makes terrible coffee and hums off-."

She laughed, her eyes getting shiny. "Again, I do not hum off-key."

"You absolutely do. It's adorable."

"Well, you eat your sandwiches with the turkey on top of the cheese. Like some kind of monster. And you're completely unapologetic about it."

"There's a right way and a wrong way to eat a turkey sandwich, and I will die on this hill."

"You're ridiculous."

"And yet you're going to miss me."

"I will," she said softly, her laughter fading into something more tender. "I'm going to miss you so much."

"I'm going to miss you every single day." I brought her hand to my lips, kissing her knuckles. "But we'll make it work. I'll call you so much you'll get sick of me."

"Impossible."

"Anna." I looked at her thoughtfully. "I love you. That doesn't change just because I'm in LA. You're it for me. You know that, right?"

Her eyes were definitely shiny now. "I love you too. So much it scares me sometimes."

"Scares you?"

"That this is too good. That something's going to take it away from me." She swiped at her eyes, laughing self-consciously. "Gosh, I'm being ridiculous."

"You're not." I stood up, pulling her to her feet and into my arms right there in the middle of the restaurant. Let the photographers get this shot. "You're not being ridiculous. And nothing's taking me away from you. Distance is just... distance. It doesn't change how I feel."

She buried her face in my chest, and I held her tight, breathing in the scent of her hair, memorizing the feeling of her in my arms.

When we finally pulled apart, she was smiling through her tears. "We should probably leave before I completely ruin my makeup."

"You look beautiful either way."

"Smooth talker."

We left the restaurant hand in hand, ignoring the flashes from the cameras, and drove home in comfortable silence. When we got back to the house, Anna turned to me in the doorway.

"Thank you," she said. "For tonight. For understanding."

"Always." I kissed her softly. "Get some sleep. You've got writing to do tomorrow."

"And you've got a plane to catch."

"Exactly. We're both busy, important people." I grinned.

She shoved me playfully, and I caught her hand, pulling her in for one more kiss.

When she finally went upstairs, I stood in the hallway for a long moment, the silence of the house pressing in around me.

The morning came too soon. As Hal loaded my bags into the car, Anna stood in the doorway, arms wrapped around herself against the early chill. I walked over to her slowly, neither of us quite ready for this moment.

"Call me when you land?" she said, her voice small.

"The second the plane touches down." I pulled her into my arms, holding her tight. "I love you."

"I love you too."

The car idled in the driveway behind us, waiting. I kissed her one more time, trying to memorize everything about this moment. Then I forced myself to let go and climbed into the backseat.

The car started to pull away, and I turned to watch her through the back window, standing there in her pajamas, getting smaller—

"Stop! Stop the car!"

Anna's voice cut through the air. Hal hit the brakes before we'd even reached the end of the driveway, and I spun around, my heart leaping into my throat.

She was running toward the car, clutching a paper bag. Hope surged through me like electricity. *She changed her mind. She's coming with me. She's—*

I threw open the door before she even reached us. "Anna?"

She skidded to a stop, breathless, holding out the paper bag. "I made you a sandwich for the plane."

My heart, which had been soaring, settled into something softer. "You made me a sandwich?"

"Yes. And before you ask—" She was trying to catch her breath, a smile breaking through even as tears filled her eyes. "The turkey is on TOP of the cheese, just like you like it. You weirdo."

I started laughing, even as my own eyes burned. I took the bag from her and pulled her into my arms. "You made me a sandwich?"

"It's a long flight," she said against my chest. "And airplane food is terrible. And I just—" Her voice cracked. "I needed to do something. To take care of you one more time before you leave."

I held her tighter, this ridiculous, wonderful woman who'd sprinted barefoot down the driveway to make sure I had lunch. "I love you so much."

"I love you too." She pulled back to look at me, tears streaming down her face, but smiling. "Don't let it get squished."

"I'll guard it with my life."

"And text me when you eat it so I know you didn't throw it away."

"I would never throw away a sandwich you made."

She laughed, then started crying harder. I cupped her face in my hands, wiping away her tears with my thumbs.

"Come with me," I whispered. "It's not too late. Just get in the car. We'll figure everything else out."

She closed her eyes, fresh tears spilling over. "I can't. I'm sorry. I just—I can't."

I wanted to understand. I wanted to ask her why, what was holding her here so tightly that she couldn't take this leap with me. But looking at her, I knew pushing wouldn't change anything.

"Okay," I said softly. "Okay."

She loved me. I had to hold on to that. Even if I couldn't understand why she was so scared to leave, even if it hurt like crazy, she loved me.

"I'll call you the second I land," I promised.

"You better."

I kissed her one more time, trying to memorize everything—the taste of her tears, the way she held onto my jacket like she couldn't let go, the sound of her breath hitching.

Then I got back in the car, clutching the paper bag like it was something precious.

As Hal pulled away, I turned to watch her through the back window. She stood in the driveway, barefoot and beautiful and heartbroken, getting smaller and smaller, until the car turned the corner and she disappeared from view.

I looked down at the sandwich bag in my lap. There was writing on it in her handwriting: *I love you. Come back to me.*

I stared out the window, the streets of New Orleans blurring past. I was chasing a dream of this blockbuster movie, but what if I'd just walked away from the only reality that mattered?

43

ANNA

LUKE and I were killing this long-distance relationship thing.

Seriously, we could write a book. Teach a class.

The first day he was gone, deliveries started arriving at my door like clockwork. Every hour, on the hour, a new surprise.

Nine a.m.: Flowers. Purple tulips, my favorite, with a note that said *Missing you already.*

Ten a.m.: A box of books from Octavia Books, an independent bookstore I'd mentioned once in passing. He'd remembered. Of course, he'd remembered.

Eleven a.m.: Reese's Peanut butter cups. An entire case of them. The note read: *For emergency writing fuel. Or just regular fuel. I don't judge.*

Noon: More flowers. That time, sunflowers, bright and ridiculous, which made the whole kitchen look like a meadow.

By three p.m., the mansion looked like a florist shop had exploded, and I was crying-laughing on the phone with Lucy.

"He's either the most romantic man alive or his assistant is really good at their job," she said.

"I'm choosing to believe it's him."

"Anna, no man coordinates hourly deliveries without help."

"Let me have this, Luce."

The next day, more flowers arrived—orchids this time, delicate and beautiful. The card said, *Still missing you. Also, my assistant says I need to pace myself or I'll go bankrupt.*

That night, my phone rang at exactly 10 p.m. That was our agreed-upon call time, because apparently, we were the kind of couple who scheduled calls now.

"Hey," Luke's voice came through, warm and a little tired. "How's my favorite author?"

"Caffeinated and slightly buried under flowers," I said, curling up on the couch. "How's my favorite movie star?"

"Exhausted. Gerald had us do seventeen takes of the same scene today because he said my 'emotional aura' wasn't aligned with the lighting."

"Your... emotional aura?"

"Direct quote. He also made us all do trust falls before filming because he wanted to 'cultivate ensemble energy.'"

I bit back a laugh. "Did it work?"

"One of the stunt guys caught me. Very bonding. Very weird." He paused, and I could hear him shifting, probably settling into bed. "Tell me about your day. Please. I need to hear about something normal."

"Nonna called me today because she couldn't figure out how to 'follow you on the Instagram.' Turns out she was trying to friend-request your IMDb page. She's very upset it won't accept her."

He laughed loudly, and the sound made me so happy. I continued, "And, apparently, Thanksgiving planning started today. In July. There was a forty-five-minute argument about whether shrimp goes in the gumbo or if that's 'an abomination against Cajun ancestors.'"

"Oh no."

"Oh yes. Uncle Ray was on team shrimp. Aunt Dolores was team chicken-and-sausage-only. Things got heated. Someone invoked Nonna's authority, but she refused to weigh in, said it would 'cause a family civil war.'"

He laughed. "Please tell me it ended peacefully."

"It did not. They brought samples to Muses today. Made everyone do a blind taste test."

"You're kidding."

"I wish I were. They had labels. 'Gumbo A' and 'Gumbo B.' They took notes. Uncle Ray brought a clipboard, Luke. A *clipboard.*"

"Which one won?"

"That's the thing—everyone loved both. Said they couldn't choose. So now we're having two gumbos at Thanksgiving."

"I love your family so much."

"They're insane."

"They're perfect." His voice softened. "I miss them. I miss you."

"I miss you too." I pulled my knees up to my chest. "But hey, we're doing okay, right? This whole long-distance thing?"

"We're crushing it," he said. "Though I have to admit, talking on the phone isn't quite the same as having you here."

"I know." I closed my eyes, trying to picture him. "But we'll figure it out."

We talked for another hour, about everything and nothing. He told me about the other actors, about the insane schedule, about how Gerald kept insisting they do "character work" that involved interpretive dance. I told him about my writing, about the chapter I was stuck on, about how Nonna had asked me again if she needed to "get the Facebook" to follow his career.

"Okay, so walk me through the plot point you're stuck on," he said finally. "Maybe I can help."

"You're tired. You don't have to—"

"Anna. I want to. Tell me."

So I did. I explained the scene I'd been wrestling with for days, how my main character needed to make a choice but neither option felt right, how I'd written myself into a corner.

"What if," Luke said slowly, "she doesn't choose? What if the whole point is that she's stuck because she's waiting for permission to want both things? Like, maybe the answer isn't choosing between them, but figuring out how to have both on her own terms?"

I sat up straighter. "Oh my gosh."

"What?"

"That's it. That's exactly it." I was already reaching for my laptop. "Luke Fisher, you're a genius."

"I have my moments." He sounded pleased. We stayed on the phone for another twenty minutes, neither of us wanting to hang up, until he finally yawned so hard I could hear it through the speaker.

"Go to sleep," I said softly. "You have an early call tomorrow."

"I know. I just... I like talking to you."

"I like talking to you, too."

"Good night, Anna. I love you."

"I love you too. And Luke?"

"Yeah?"

"Thank you for the flowers. All of them. This place looks ridiculous."

"That was the goal." I could hear the smile in his voice. "Sweet dreams."

When we hung up, I sat there for a moment, phone still warm in my hand, staring at the orchids on my bedside table.

We were doing okay. Better than okay.

We were going to be fine.

I opened my laptop and started writing, Luke's words still echoing in my head. The scene flowed easily now, my character finally finding her way forward.

Yeah. We were definitely going to be fine.

44

LUKE

WEEK TWO IN LA, and I was starting to find my rhythm. The early call times, the endless takes, Gerald's increasingly bizarre directing notes—it was all becoming familiar in a way that felt almost comfortable.

What made it bearable? Anna.

Every morning, I woke up to a text from her. Sometimes it was just a photo. Maybe her coffee mug, the sunrise over New Orleans, her laptop open with a new word count she was proud of. Sometimes it was longer.

Wrote 3,000 words today. Your plot advice unlocked something.

Be brilliant today. I believe in you.

Gerald sounds unhinged. Channel that chaos.

I saved every single one.

On day ten, a massive box arrived on set, addressed to me. The entire crew gathered around as I opened it, curious about what could require a box that size.

Inside: six king cakes. Each from a different bakery, with little notes taped to the boxes explaining which one was which. "Gambino's—the classic," "Randazzo's—Nonna's favorite," "Dong Phuong—

my fave." Beneath them were pralines wrapped in wax paper, chicory coffee, Roman candy, and, at the very bottom, approximately seven pounds of Mardi Gras beads in purple, green, and gold.

The note on top read: *Since you can't come to New Orleans yet, I'm sending it to you. Share with the crew. Love, A.*

"Oh my gosh," one of the camera operators said, already reaching for a praline. "Is this from New Orleans?"

"My girlfriend," I said, unable to keep the pride out of my voice.

It had been a long day. We'd been filming since five a.m., running the same scene over and over until everyone was exhausted and cranky. But the second that box opened, the entire energy shifted.

Within minutes, the beads were everywhere. The grip team was wearing them. Gerald had at least fifteen strands around his neck and was dramatically catching beads people tossed at him like he was on a parade float. Someone started playing zydeco music from their phone. The king cakes were demolished in record time, and heated debates broke out over which bakery was superior.

"There's a baby in this piece of cake!" someone shouted, holding up the tiny plastic figurine.

I stood back, watching the chaos unfold, and pulled out my phone to take a video. The stunt coordinator was trying to teach one of the actors how to "throw like you're on a float." Someone had put beads on one of the cameras.

I sent the video to Anna: **It's like Mardi Gras here. The crew is obsessed. You're officially their favorite person.**

Her reply came immediately: **I can see Gerald wearing 30 strands of beads. This brings me joy.**

I called her immediately.

"They loved it," I said when she picked up. "Like, *loved* it. Morale completely shifted. You just saved us from a very grumpy afternoon."

Her laugh was warm and bright. "I'm glad. I was worried it was too much."

"Too much? Anna, Gerald is still wearing the beads. Thank you."

"This seemed like the next best thing to being there."

"I miss you too. So much."

THE DAYS BLURRED TOGETHER, but Anna was woven through all of them.

One night, three weeks in, we FaceTimed for two hours. She was in her pajamas, hair piled on top of her head, glasses sliding down her nose as she leaned over her laptop.

"Okay, so this character," she said, gesturing at her screen. "She's brave, right? But she's also terrified. How do I show both at the same time without it feeling contradictory?"

"Make her hands shake," I said immediately. "But have her move forward anyway. Bravery isn't not being scared. It's being scared and doing it anyway."

She stared at me. "How are you so good at this?"

"I play pretend for a living. It's transferable."

"Don't diminish what you do. You're beyond talented."

"And you're helping me be a better actor." I shifted my phone so I could see her better. "I was telling Gerald about your main character yesterday—the way she overthinks everything but still takes risks—and he said it gave him ideas for my character's internal life."

"Wait, you talk about my book on set?"

"All the time. Everyone knows about it now. They're all planning to buy it when it's published."

"*If* it's published."

"*When*, Anna. When."

Another week passed. More texts. More calls. More voice messages left in the middle of the night because we couldn't wait until morning to share something.

Voice message from Anna, 1:23 a.m.: "Okay, so I was thinking about your scene tomorrow—the one where you have to cry on command? Don't think about something sad. Think about something you love and then imagine losing it. That's what always gets me. Anyway, good luck tomorrow. You're going to be amazing."

I used her advice. Nailed the scene in two takes. Gerald literally applauded.

A month in, I called her after a particularly brutal fourteen-hour day. I was exhausted, covered in fake blood from a stunt that had gone slightly wrong, and missing her so much it physically hurt.

"Hey," she said softly when she answered. "Rough day?"

"How'd you know?"

"I can hear it in your voice." A pause. "Tell me about it?"

So I did. I told her about the stunt that took twelve takes, about Gerald's increasingly cryptic notes, about how I'd forgotten my lines twice and felt like an idiot.

"You're not an idiot," she said firmly. "You're tired. There's a difference."

"I just... I want to be good at this, Anna. I want to prove I deserve this role."

"Luke." Her voice was gentle but insistent. "You already deserve it. They cast you because you're talented. Because you're perfect for this. One bad day doesn't erase that."

I closed my eyes, letting her words sink in. "I love you."

"I love you too. Take a shower, eat something, and get some sleep. Tomorrow will be better."

"Yes, ma'am."

"And Luke?"

"Yeah?"

"I'm really proud of you. Even on the hard days. Especially on the hard days."

Six weeks in, and we had it down to a science. Morning texts. Evening calls. Voice messages throughout the day. She sent me photos of her writing progress. I sent her videos from the set (the ones Gerald approved). We traded playlist links. She mailed me books she thought I'd like. I sent flowers on random Tuesdays just because.

"We're really good at this," she said one night, her face pixelated slightly on my phone screen.

"We are," I agreed. "It's not the same as being together, but—"

"But we're making it work."

"Yeah. We are."

She smiled at me through the screen, and even though she was 1,800 miles away, even though I couldn't touch her or hold her or kiss her, it felt like enough.

For now, it felt like enough.

"I love you," I said.

"I love you too. Now tell me about Gerald's latest insane note. I need a good story for Lucy."

And just like that, we fell back into our rhythm. Talking, laughing, supporting each other across the distance.

We were killing this long-distance thing.

45

ANNA

I WAS FINALLY FINISHED with my book. I sat at my desk, staring at the final draft of my superhero story. It was the first thing I'd written in years that felt like it had any real heart. The first thing since the story I wrote about my mother in college.

But the ending of this story, in which the heroine finds strength in admitting her fears, left me uneasy.

How could I write about bravery when I couldn't even summon enough courage to send this out?

With a sigh, I closed my laptop, telling myself it wasn't ready. After one-hundred rejections, maybe it was time to give up. I was tired of chasing after dreams that only ended in disappointment.

Luke had called every night since he left. His world now felt galaxies away from mine, and he always seemed so busy.

The sound of my phone jolted me from my thoughts. His name lit up the screen.

"Anna." His voice was warm and familiar, and for a second, it felt like no time had passed.

"Hey," I said, forcing a casual tone. "You're calling early. What's the occasion?"

He chuckled. "I got a break. They're resetting a scene for the fifth time because the sun isn't cooperating. But hey, it gives me time to call my favorite person."

"Flattery will get you everywhere. If you keep this up, I might even let you buy me dinner the next time you're in town."

"Deal. So, how's your story going?"

"I just finished it, actually," I admitted.

A muffled voice in the background cut me off. "Luke, we need you on set in two."

"One second," he shouted back, his voice straining as he returned to me. "Sorry, what were you saying?"

I hesitated. "I thought of the best plot twist, and I—"

"Luke, wardrobe needs you for adjustments," another voice shouted.

He groaned. "Seriously? Sorry, Anna, go ahead."

"It's fine," I said, trying to hide my frustration. "You're busy."

"No, no, I want to hear this," he insisted. "Tell me."

"I left bread crumbs all throughout—"

"Luke, are you ready to run it again?" a third voice cut in.

I heard him fumbling with something on the other end.

"I've got to go," he said, his voice rushed, the warmth edged out by exhaustion. "I'm so sorry. But I want to hear about it next time, okay? I mean it."

I smiled faintly, even if something in me wilted a little. "Yeah. Of course."

There was a pause, like he didn't want to hang up either but didn't have a choice.

"Hey," he added, softer now, "I'm happy we talked. I miss you."

My heart clenched. "I miss you, too."

There was a long pause. "So...any chance you've changed your mind about moving out here? The weather's beautiful, and we'd get to see each other more."

My breath caught. I couldn't believe that he was bringing this up. I was a bit annoyed because I'd given him my answer numerous times, and it was always the same.

I just couldn't, and I don't know why he wouldn't take no for an answer. I mean, everything inside me wanted to say yes. But fear tucked my words tight. "Luke, I can't."

He paused, and I wondered what was going through his mind. Was he annoyed at me? I could practically feel it through the miles that separated us. But when he finally spoke, his words were calm, "Gotcha. No worries. You take care, okay?"

I whispered, "You too."

Click. The call ended, and I was enveloped in silence. I stared at my phone, the emptiness settling like cold water in my chest.

The next night was the first when he didn't call. All I got was a brief text: **Love you! Miss you!**

"Have you heard from him?" Marie Antoinette's voice cut through the clatter of the bar the next night as she slid a tray of glasses onto the counter.

"Yes," I said, wiping down the counter with more force than necessary. "He's fine. Busy."

"Uh-huh. And is that why you're reorganizing the liquor cabinet by color? Because he's *fine*?"

I paused, glancing at the neat rows of bottles I'd just arranged by label gradient. "It was bothering me."

"And the coasters?" she asked, gesturing to the perfectly aligned stack I'd been straightening earlier.

"They were uneven," I mumbled, going back to scrubbing.

She sighed, tapping her perfectly manicured nails on the counter. "Anna, you're stress-cleaning."

"I'm not stress-cleaning."

"Step away from the sponge. You're practically polishing the wood off this bar. What's really going on?"

"Nothing," I said quickly. "I'm just keeping busy. Like Luke."

"Mm-hmm." She was clearly unconvinced, but too polite to press the matter further. "Well, if you run out of things to rearrange, I've got some receipts you can alphabetize."

I shot her a glare, but her smirk softened it.

"I mean it," she added, her tone kind this time. "Whatever's bugging you, it's okay to admit it, you know."

But I wasn't ready to say it out loud. I didn't want to voice the fear that Luke and I were drifting apart. Not yet.

Later, alone in my apartment, I opened my laptop again and stared at the story. The words blurred on the screen, their meaning hollow now, like something vital had been drained from them.

This is what I got for letting my guard down. I should've known better. I'd convinced myself that things could be different, that I could let someone in and not end up hurt.

But I was wrong.

Tears pricked the corners of my eyes, and I blinked them back. Superheroes don't cry, and I didn't have time to feel sorry for myself. Instead, I saved the draft, closed the laptop, and told myself I'd feel better tomorrow.

46

LUKE

I SAT IN MY TRAILER, the script balanced on my knee, untouched. Gerald's last note bounced around my head like a bad song stuck on repeat.

"You're holding back. Again. I need more from you, Luke. You're not a sad accountant who's late filing taxes. You're a man who's just lost his family. Cry harder, darn it."

Gerald was in a Hawaiian shirt covered in flamingos, paired with mismatched plaid shorts, and was holding a megaphone for no apparent reason, despite standing five feet away.

I knew he was right when he accused me of holding back. My performance felt hollow, as if I were going through the motions without truly engaging.

I felt something in New Orleans. Now, it was like I'd forgotten how.

I wanted to talk to Anna. No, I needed to talk to Anna. She had a way of making me believe I could do anything, even when I doubted myself. She didn't need to do anything extraordinary to make me feel better. Just hearing her voice, her steady, calm voice, would be enough.

She got me in a way no one else ever had.

And I missed her so badly, it was killing me. It wasn't just the big things I missed. It was the little things, like the way she'd hum when she was concentrating or the way she'd wrinkle her nose when she didn't believe me.

She put herself out there in ways I never could, even if she thought she was failing.

But I felt like something was wrong. A few nights ago, we had been so busy on set that I didn't get to call her. And she sounded sore when we finally got in touch. I hated the times when we fought.

I wanted to remind her how amazing she was, to tell her how much she inspired me, even if she'd roll her eyes and call me dramatic.

She picked up on the third ring, and her voice sounded harried. "Hello?"

"Hey," I said, leaning back in my chair, trying to sound casual. It was the time we had arranged to speak, so I was a bit miffed that she sounded like she was in the middle of something. "Caught you at a bad time?"

"Kind of," she admitted, the clatter of glasses and muffled voices in the background immediately giving her away. "What's up?"

"You said that you finished your story. Are you going to send it out?"

"Maybe," she said curtly. I could hear the hum of a blender whirring and the hiss of a soda gun in the background. "I haven't decided yet."

"What's stopping you?" I asked, hoping to draw her out.

"Nothing," she said. "Hey, can we talk later? Someone just—"

There was a loud crash on her end, followed by her muffled voice. "No, Trevor, the keg goes on the dolly, not your shoulder. It's not CrossFit."

Another voice chimed in, faint but distinct: "Marie Antoinette, I swear, if you call me Cinderella one more time..."

A sharp bark cut through the chaos, and someone shouted, "Why is there a dog in the kitchen? Who brought a dog in here?"

"Sorry, Luke," Anna cut in, sounding exasperated. "I have to go.

We're short-staffed, and someone just spilled grenadine all over the napkins. Again."

"Yeah," I said, trying to keep my disappointment in check. "Sure. Talk later."

The line went dead before I could say goodbye.

I stared at my phone, the silence in the trailer settling over me like a heavy blanket.

She was pulling away. Maybe this was what I got for thinking I could have both her and my career.

I'd opened up more to her than I ever had with anyone. I'd told her about my mom leaving, about the nights I spent wondering why the people I loved most seemed to reject me. I'd let her see the parts of me I usually kept hidden, trusting her with the pieces I was afraid to show the world.

And now? It felt like those pieces weren't enough. It felt like I wasn't enough. But maybe, I thought bitterly, that wasn't a shock. After all, when had anyone ever stayed with me?

I tossed my phone onto the table and picked up the script, forcing myself to focus on the lines. But the words felt heavier with every page I turned.

"Luke," a PA called, her voice strained. "They need you on set. Gerald's, well, he's pacing. With the megaphone."

I groaned, dragging myself up. By the time I stepped onto the set, Gerald was mid-rant, waving the megaphone like a conductor directing an off-key symphony.

"Luke," he shouted, even though I was only a few feet away. "Darling, sweetheart, you're killing me. And not in the emotional, award-winning way that I want."

I sighed, stepping into position. "What do you need, Gerald?"

"What do I need?" he repeated, lowering the megaphone to clutch his heart dramatically. "I need you to dig deep, to channel grief, despair, heartbreak. Right now, you're giving me *meh*. And I cannot work with *meh*."

I clenched my fists, frustration bubbling under the surface. "I'm trying," I gritted out.

"Trying isn't good enough," Fargo shouted, flinging his arms like someone swatting a swarm of bees. "This isn't community theater, Luke. You're not playing Tree #2 in a middle school musical. We need *emotion!*"

From somewhere behind the monitors, a crew member stifled a laugh, and Gerald whirled on them. "Do you think this is a joke? Do you think *art* is a joke?"

I rolled my shoulders, taking my mark. Gerald's eccentricity was infamous, but today he had taken it to another level.

"Okay, everyone, places," Gerald shouted into the megaphone again, though no one had moved. "Let's try this again. And Luke? Give me *Oscar-bait tears,* or so help me, I'll send you back to the student-run ditties of Brown's Production Workshop."

I should have known better than to let my guard down and fall in love. Now, all I was doing was proving I wasn't enough. For Anna or this role.

As the assistant director called for another take, I planted my feet and gripped the script tighter. I would get through this, one way or another. But it felt like the things I cared about most were slipping further out of reach.

47

ANNA

THE CROWD at Muses was pure madness.

The bar buzzed with chaos. Drinks were flying off the counter, orders piling up, and one of the bartenders was arguing about whether grenadine was a garnish or a vibe. Short-staffed again, I'd volunteered for another shift. It wasn't like I had anything better to do. Not writing, that was for sure.

I hadn't opened my laptop in days. Why bother? The stories weren't good enough, and neither was I. It was easier to focus on something tangible, like pouring drinks and wiping down counters, than staring at a blank screen and waiting for inspiration that never came.

And then there were the questions.

"What's Luke up to these days?" a regular named Dave asked as I poured his usual gin and tonic. "Still dodging paparazzi?"

I forced a smile. "Something like that."

"Hey, Anna," one of the college kids at the end of the bar called out. "Your boyfriend is that actor, right? The one with the abs?"

I rolled my eyes. "Sure, but I'm pretty sure he also has a face and a career."

Marie Antoinette, sliding in next to me to grab a fresh tray of glasses, smirked. "You should print out an FAQ sheet for these people. 'Yes, he's famous. No, I won't introduce you. And for the love of vodka, stop asking if he's single.'"

I groaned, gripping the edge of the bar for support. "I think I liked it better when people just ordered their drinks and left."

By the time my shift ended, I was exhausted. All I wanted to do was kick off my shoes and collapse, but my phone buzzed with a call.

Luke.

The calls had been shorter lately, more strained, like we were both walking on a tightrope. He'd been short with me, snapping sometimes over things that didn't matter, and I wasn't any better. My patience was thin, my words meaner than they needed to be.

But I still answered every time.

Because as much as the tension between us hurt, the silence would've been worse. I told myself that these calls were a lifeline, even if they felt more like a reminder of everything we weren't saying.

I was scared that it was just a matter of time before he broke up with me. It was inevitable, as much as I didn't want to face it. I didn't know when it had shifted, when the easy rhythm we'd once had turned into this push and pull of strained pleasantries and unspoken frustration.

But every time his name lit up my screen, I felt the same knot in my chest. Part of me wanted to let it go to voicemail, to avoid the inevitable stumbles and sighs. But I couldn't bear to miss the chance to hear his voice, even if it wasn't the voice I knew.

So, I took a breath, plastered on a smile he couldn't see, and answered.

"Hey."

"Hey." His tone carried that edge of tiredness I'd come to expect. "How was your day?"

"Busy," I said, tucking my legs under me. "I picked up an extra shift at Muses."

"Another one?" he asked, and I couldn't tell if it was concern or judgment in his voice.

"Yeah, another one," I said flatly. "It's not like I've got anything else going on."

There was a pause, and I could almost hear him piecing together what I wasn't saying. "What about your writing?" he asked finally.

I closed my eyes, already regretting where this was going. "I haven't had time for that. Work's been too busy."

"Anna, come on," he said, his voice tinged with frustration. "You're a writer."

"Well, maybe I'm not a writer anymore," I retorted, the words escaping before I could stop them.

"That's not true, and you know it,"

"Excuse me?" I said, sitting up straighter. "What do you know about it, Luke? You're out there living your dream, doing exactly what you want to do. You have no idea what it's like to pour your heart into something and get nothing in return."

"That's not fair. You think everything comes easy for me? You have no idea what it's like on set, how hard I have to work just to prove I belong there."

"Yeah, well, at least you've made it," I shot back. "I'm stuck, trying to keep my head above water, and you're halfway across the country telling me I'm not trying hard enough."

His breath caught, and then he replied, "I can't understand why you can't come to LA."

"What did you expect me to do, Luke?" I said, my voice shaking. "Drop everything?"

There was a pause, just long enough to hurt, before he replied. "You're stuck, Anna. Stuck in that bar, stuck in your head, stuck in your own pity party," he said, his words turning sharp. "And you want to blame me for leaving? Maybe you should look at yourself. Ask why you won't leave New Orleans."

He made it sound so simple, like moving was just a plane ticket and not an unraveling of my entire life. He didn't understand that leaving wasn't just hard for me, that it felt impossible.

I was angry that he still didn't get it. That he refused to hear me when I said no, when I said I wasn't ready.

I wanted to tell him that I wasn't trapped here—I chose this city. I stayed because it's the one place that feels like home, because I know what it means to lose everything. But the words wouldn't come. My chest was tight, my breathing shallow. Fear and anger tangled until I couldn't tell which was which.

One beat passed, then another. When Luke finally spoke again, his voice was quieter, but it landed like a blow. "Maybe this isn't working."

I froze, the words slicing through me. "You're right," I murmured, though every part of me wanted to scream the opposite. "It's not."

Neither of us said anything else.

The call ended, and I sat there staring at the phone, my heart pounding in my chest.

I'd always known it could end this way.

But knowing didn't make it hurt any less.

48

LUKE

THE PHONE WAS STILL in my hand, my call with Anna barely disconnected, and already I was second-guessing everything I'd just said.

Maybe this isn't working.

What in the world had I been thinking?

I'd wanted her to fight for me, but she didn't. She didn't even try.

I dropped the phone on the table and leaned back against the trailer wall, staring at the ceiling. The conversation played on a loop in my head, every word cutting deeper.

I didn't call her every day because I had to. I called her because I wanted to. Hearing her voice was the only thing keeping me sane.

But it wasn't enough for her. I wasn't enough.

It wasn't like I'd hidden anything. She'd seen me. All my flaws, my doubts, the cracks I kept hidden from everyone else. And what did she do with that? She decided the real me wasn't enough to fight for.

I shoved the script off the table, letting it fall to the floor. I remembered the director's notes from earlier: "You're holding back, Luke. You're not connecting."

I was holding back. But what good had it done to open up? It had only left me exposed, raw, and now alone.

I rubbed a hand over my face. My chest tightened, and for a moment, I thought about calling her back. Apologizing. Telling her I didn't mean it.

But then what? More silence? More excuses? More refusals to ever come to LA?

I glanced down at the script, the pages splayed across the floor. One of the lines stared back at me, underlined in red ink by Gerald Fargo himself: *"A hero doesn't quit when the world falls apart. He fights harder."*

I barked a humorless laugh, shaking my head. A hero fights harder. Sure.

But I wasn't a hero.

I stood up and grabbed the script, shoving it back onto the table. A knock on the door interrupted my thoughts, and the assistant director spoke. "We need you on set now."

I stared at the door for a second, then squared my shoulders. If I couldn't be enough for Anna, maybe I could at least be enough for this role.

It was all I had left.

49

ANNA

Luke and I were over.

But it was impossible to avoid him because he was everywhere I went.

On my phone. In every headline. Smiling next to an endless parade of starlets, each more beautiful than the last.

Every time I opened social media, there was Luke Fisher, larger than life. My stomach twisted as I scrolled through the comments, each one worse than the last.

"A movie star and a model? Shocking."

"Another day, another co-star hookup. Hollywood Bingo, anyone?"

"Guess he's not still with that bartender from New Orleans. No surprise there."

Each statement felt like a slap, a reminder of what I already knew: I didn't belong in his world. I never had. But then, my inner voice, always a little too eager to kick me when I was down, piped up.

Did I push him away first? Was I too scared to let him in?

I was leaning against the bar at Muses one afternoon, trying to drown out the doubts, when Marie Antoinette burst into the room like a whirlwind. She was still in costume from giving a tour of the French Quarter, and it made her entrance very dramatic.

I sighed, holding up my phone so she could see. It was a photo of Luke, looking devastatingly handsome as always, smiling next to his ridiculously gorgeous co-star on some red carpet. "Look at this. He's with her now."

She peered at the screen, her painted eyebrows rising dramatically. "Oh, please." She tilted her head as if evaluating a fine painting. "Her smile? Too many teeth. She probably gargled with glitter before the photo op. Completely fake."

I let out a small laugh, despite myself. "She's perfect."

"And you're you." She grabbed my phone and set it face down on the bar. "Which is infinitely better. You know, breakups are the universe's way of saying that you're destined for a better story."

"Who said that?"

"Me," she said. "I said that. Now stop stalking him and tell me why you haven't submitted that story yet. Or better yet, explain why you're still wearing that tragic 'woe-is-me' expression when you could be living your best life."

"It's not that simple," I protested.

She rolled her eyes. "It *is* that simple. Are you seriously going to sit here wallowing all night, or are you finally going to submit that story and stop being a coward?"

"I'm not a coward," I said, though my voice wavered, betraying me.

My friend crossed her arms, tilting her head with a smirk that was equal parts sass and challenge. "Really? Because from where I'm standing, it looks like you're scared to live your life."

"Excuse me?" I sat up straighter.

"Oh, please." She paced around the room like she was delivering a monologue. "You had Luke Fisher. Freaking Luke Fisher. And you let him walk away. For what? Your fear of rejection? Guess what, sweetheart? You already rejected yourself."

"Wow, thanks for the pep talk." I shot back, my cheeks burning.

"Don't thank me yet. You haven't earned it." Her hands were on her hips. "You're scared of rejection? Welcome to the human experience. But newsflash, Anna: living in this pity party isn't safe. It's just sad."

Pity party. That was the same thing that Luke had said to me. I opened my mouth to retort, but no words came out. Marie Antoinette had a way of cutting right to the truth, and whether I wanted to admit it or not, she was right.

"Here's the deal." She sat down next to me and patted my hand like a benevolent queen. "You can either keep scrolling through those articles like some self-punishment ritual, or you can do something about it. Submit the story. It's the best story you've written since the one you wrote about your mother when you were in college. Take a risk. If you fail, you fail. But at least you'll know you tried."

The comparison hit me like a punch to the chest. My mother. That story had been raw, personal—it had meant something. And after that, what had I done? I'd spent years writing safe pieces. Fiction, sure, but stories where I could hide behind dystopian worlds or other countries or other times. Stories where rejection didn't feel personal because *I* wasn't really in them.

But this story? This was me. My life. My messy, complicated feelings laid bare on the page, even if the names were changed.

The last time I'd put myself out there like this, I'd written about my mother. And now, years later, I'd finally written something personal again. And I was terrified. Terrified of rejection.

I blinked back tears. My one chance at making something of myself was sitting on my computer, abandoned and gathering digital dust.

She spoke again, "Luke asked you to go to LA, right?"

My voice caught. "He did."

"Then why didn't you go?" She pressed, her tone sharp as she accepted a patron's payment, then slammed the register drawer shut. The sound echoed between us. She took a breath, her voice lowering as her gaze met mine. "You're scared because of your mom. Losing her in Katrina broke something in you. It made you believe that leaving New Orleans would cost you everything. You've been punishing yourself ever since."

I shook my head, my voice barely a whisper. "I'm not scared."

She shook her head. "Say it again. Loud enough for the people in the back."

I tried, but the words came out thin, uncertain. "I'm not scared."

She held my eyes. "Okay, fine. You're scared, Anna. And that's allowed. But it doesn't mean you have to turn around and walk away from something good. You're honoring your mom by living, not by standing still."

I was speechless.

Marie Antoinette patted my hand gently. "Don't let fear run your life."

I exhaled, nodding. "I understand."

And I did. A flicker of courage pushed past my sorrow. The first glimmer of a choice: to stay *and* move forward, without losing the past.

50

LUKE

THE TRAILER DOOR creaked as I slumped onto the worn couch, staring at the crumpled script in my lap. The day on set had been brutal. Gerald had lost his patience hours ago, barking orders into his ever-present megaphone: "Luke, you're killing me here. Where's the pain? Where's the heartbreak? You look like you just lost a parking spot, not your family."

My co-star, Brielle, had started avoiding me entirely. I couldn't blame her. Her publicist's stunt of planting those photos to make it look like we were a couple had caused a lot of tension. I'd called Mabel, furious, demanding she fight back against the narrative. But the damage was done, and now Brielle was done with me, too. Earlier, she'd stormed off, muttering, "Keep your drama off my brand."

To top it off, the production team had pulled me aside to deliver an ultimatum: *"If you can't nail the monologue tomorrow, we're cutting it. We need to move on."*

I sat in the suffocating silence of my trailer, scrolling through my texts with Anna. Her words felt like a lifeline, even if they were from weeks ago. I typed *I miss you*, but my thumb hovered over the delete button.

I stared at the unsent text, then at my reflection in the mirror. The perfect Hollywood image stared back: tousled hair, chiseled jawline, just the right amount of exhaustion to look rugged. I felt sick.

The phone buzzed, and I answered without checking the caller ID. It was Bob. "Luke, great buzz about you and Brielle. People are eating it up. Chemistry off the charts."

"It's all fake," I spit out, my voice cracking. "None of it matters."

Bob paused, and I could feel his confusion through the phone. "Uh, what?"

I didn't wait for an answer. I hung up and threw the phone across the trailer, watching it bounce harmlessly off the padded wall.

I chose this, I thought bitterly. *I chose my career over Anna. I thought I could have it all, but I'm still pretending.*

A knock on the door pulled me out of my spiral. "It's open," I called hoarsely.

Topher stepped inside, dressed in a bespoke suit. He looked like he'd just closed a billion-dollar deal, which, knowing him, he probably had. "You look rough, man," he said, dropping into the chair across from me. "And not in the 'gritty, tortured artist' way. More like the 'guy who spent the night locked in a vending machine' way."

I shot him a look. "Thanks for the pep talk."

He smirked. "Hey, I call it like I see it."

I tried to brush him off. "I'm fine."

"Fine?" he repeated, raising an eyebrow. "You're about one bad take away from a meltdown. You're spiraling. And it's not because of this movie. You're miserable because you left Anna."

"I don't—"

"You've been running your whole life." He leaned forward. "Hiding behind fame, charm, and that 'aw-shucks' smile of yours. And now you're too scared to stop running. But guess what? You can fix this. It's not too late to stop acting like an idiot." He slapped me on the back.

"But, Toph, I asked her to move to LA with me, and she rejected me. Why would she stay in New Orleans? It's a place of heartbreak for her. It's where she lost her mother. I mean, she can write from anywhere."

Toph shook his head. "Look at it from her point of view, man. She's probably terrified. Look at what happened the last time she tried to leave. Her mother died in that evacuation nightmare. That kind of trauma doesn't vanish."

I blinked, taken aback. "Trauma," I echoed.

"That's right. Love isn't always moving forward. Sometimes it can mean just standing still and surviving."

For the first time, it hit me. Not just intellectually, but in my bones. Anna wanting to stay in New Orleans didn't mean she didn't care for me. It was a lifeline she couldn't let go of.

Topher let the silence hang for a moment before clapping his hands and standing up. "Okay, enough brooding. I've got a meeting to crush, and you've got lines to learn. So figure out what you want, Luke. Seriously."

He gave me a pointed look, adjusted his tie, and strode out the door like he'd just delivered the keynote speech at some Fortune 500 conference.

I sat there for a while, staring at the door.

51

ANNA

THE RIVERFRONT WAS QUIET, save for the gentle lapping of the Mississippi against the bank.

I hadn't been to this spot in years. It had been since before Hurricane Katrina, when my mom and I used to sit here and talk about everything and nothing. I could almost feel her beside me, her hand resting on mine, her voice calm.

The memories came rushing back, and I let myself cry.

I cried for her, for the years I'd spent wishing she were still here. I cried for Luke, for the chance I'd had and thrown away. I cried for the fear that ruled my life, keeping me from reaching for anything I truly wanted.

I stared out at the water, the rhythmic sound of the waves soothing the ache in my chest. Marie Antoinette's words echoed in my head. *You already rejected yourself.* And *don't let fear run your life.*

She was right. I'd spent my whole life running from rejection instead of fighting for what I wanted.

The humid New Orleans air curled the edges of the printed pages in my lap, and I smoothed them absently as I read through my story again.

It wasn't just a superhero story. Not really.

I'd written about a hero finding strength in vulnerability, but as I flipped through the pages, I saw myself there too, in every moment of doubt, every battle fought in silence. I'd written about my fears of failure, of opening up, of rejection.

And I'd written about Luke.

Not as a flawless hero swooping in to save the day, but as someone who showed me the beauty in being real. He showed me New Orleans—my city, my home—from a perspective I'd never known before: not just as a place that shaped me, but as a place I could finally honor *and* choose to leave.

The pages reflected everything I'd been too afraid to admit, even to myself, how fear of rejection had controlled so much of my life, keeping me from ever truly putting myself out there. But the real revelation? Rejection wasn't the worst thing. The worst thing was never taking the chance at all.

My eyes burned, and I was done crying.

Mom's voice echoed in my mind: *You can do anything, Anna. You just have to try.*

I pulled out my phone and logged into my email. My manuscript was ready, attached, and waiting, but my fingers hovered over the send button.

What if it wasn't good enough?

No. I was done letting fear win.

I took a deep breath, pressed send, and watched the email disappear into the digital void.

The weight I'd been carrying for weeks began to lift, like a storm finally breaking apart to let sunlight through. I stood and looked out at the river, the golden rays of the sun spilling across the water in soft, shimmering light.

A breeze brushed past me, gentle and freeing, as if the world itself was whispering: *It's time to stop being afraid.*

Feeling lighter, I sat back and opened Instagram to scroll mindlessly, but a notification from *Entertainment Tonight* popped up on my feed. Against my better judgment, I tapped on it. The video auto-played: Luke walking on an LA street, flanked by Tom and Hal, his hoodie pulled up.

Not just any hoodie. *My hoodie.*

The lavender Muses hoodie, oversized and a little worse for wear, with that faint stain from the rum-and-Coke spill. My heart stopped.

The reporter's bubbly voice played over the clip: "Luke Fisher was spotted ahead of his big premiere."

The camera zoomed in as a paparazzo called out, "Luke, what's the fashion statement here?"

He stopped mid-stride and gave one of those charming, lopsided grins that could sell a million movie tickets. "No fashion statement. Just something that makes me happy."

I froze. *Happy?*

The reporter pressed further. "Is it sentimental? A gift?"

Luke paused, his gaze flickering to the camera as though weighing how much to say. Then, with a half-shrug, he added, "You could say that. It's from someone who means a lot to me."

Someone who means a lot to me. Means. Present tense.

The reporter's voice chimed back in as the video cut to a studio shot. "Well, there you have it. Luke Fisher, Hollywood heartthrob, keeping it real. In lavender."

I stared at the screen, my heart racing. Of all the things he could've worn, he chose *that*. The thought sparked something deep inside me, a flicker of hope I didn't know I still had.

Maybe he missed me as much as I missed him.

Sure, it was scary. He might reject me outright. But I was done letting fear hold me back. I was done letting fear keep me trapped in New Orleans.

I missed him more than I wanted to admit. But I wanted to challenge my fears. Whatever came next, I was ready to face it.

52

LUKE

YESTERDAY'S SHOOT had been a disaster.

I slept, but not well. It was the kind of restless sleep where you wake up feeling just as tired as when you went to bed.

Today, I had to nail it. Not just for Fargo or the crew, but for myself.

By the time I got to the soundstage, the usual buzz of activity surrounded me—lighting adjustments, hushed conversations, the clatter of equipment. The final scene was on the schedule, the one I'd been botching all week.

I walked onto the set during a break and picked up the script I'd discarded the night before. The lines stared back at me, mocking me. It wasn't just about the words, though; it was about what they represented.

You're miserable because you left Anna. Topher's words rattled around my brain like an unwelcome guest.

He was right. I'd spent my life hiding behind roles, using them as armor against anything real. With Anna, it had been different. She didn't care about the Hollywood shine. She saw me. The real me.

I ran my fingers over the edges of the script, trying to focus. It felt like something was pressing against my ribs. What was the point of fame if I couldn't be with her?

My phone buzzed on the chair next to me. I glanced at the screen and froze.

Saw you on ET. Nice hoodie.

My heart leaped. The hoodie. Her lavender hoodie from Muses. The one she'd given me that night at the bar to help me escape unnoticed.

I typed a response, my thumbs flying over the screen.

It's the most comfortable thing I own.

Her reply came almost instantly. **Comfortable enough to wear on national TV? Bold choice, Fisher.**

I chuckled as I wrote my response: **Hey, good enough to escape from a bachelorette party at Muses, good enough for me.**

I stared at the screen, the corner of my mouth twitching into a smile. For the first time in weeks, I felt lighter. Her text was simple, playful, but it hit me harder than any line I'd delivered on set.

She was still there, in my life, even if it was just a text.

The assistant director's voice pulled me back. "Five minutes, Luke."

I nodded, tossing the script onto a nearby chair. I didn't need it anymore.

When the cameras started rolling, I drew a deep breath, letting the air settle in my chest. The lights bore down on me, hot and unrelenting, but they didn't feel suffocating.

I poured everything I had into the scene. Every ounce of pain, doubt, and longing. Every moment with Anna that had changed me. The fear of never being enough, the regret of leaving her, the vulnerability she'd taught me to embrace—it all fueled my performance.

My voice cracked on the emotional high point, my hands trembling as I delivered the monologue. For the first time, I wasn't performing. I wasn't hiding behind a character.

I was real.

When the director finally yelled, "Cut," the soundstage erupted into applause. Gerald jumped out of his chair, his signature megaphone in hand, but this time, he didn't use it.

"Now *that's* what I'm talking about," he exclaimed, clapping. "Perfection, Luke. You've got it."

The applause surrounded me, but it felt distant and muted. I managed a nod and a brief smile, but my thoughts were elsewhere.

I grabbed my jacket and keys, ignoring the congratulatory pats on the back as I walked off set. This wasn't a victory.

It wasn't the role or the fame I wanted.

It was Anna.

She was the first person to make me feel like I didn't have to pretend. And I'd let her go. I'd asked her to come to LA with me, and when she didn't, I was hurt. I had been so conceited that I assumed it was all about me, that she didn't love me enough to leave New Orleans. So, I hadn't asked the right questions, questions that would have shown me that it was fear that kept her in New Orleans. So, instead of what I should have done as her boyfriend and helped her face those fears, I left. I ran away.

The realization hit me hard, but this time, it didn't leave me hollow. It left me determined.

I stepped out into the cool night air, the city lights shimmering like distant stars.

This time, I wasn't running away.

I was going to fight for her.

53

ANNA

I SPRINTED through the crowded Chicago terminal, dodging a man in a Hawaiian shirt pulling a rolling suitcase that probably hadn't rolled properly since the Clinton administration. My lungs burned, and my bag bounced against my hip with every step, but I couldn't stop now.

My flight from New Orleans had landed late, and I had exactly fifteen minutes to make it to Gate C15 for my connection to Los Angeles.

I couldn't believe I was flying across the country to tell Luke Fisher how I felt. The thought alone made my stomach flip.

What if I got there, and he didn't feel the same? What if he thought I was just some desperate, clingy girl who couldn't let go?

But I'd spent too much of my life running from fear and rejection. Not this time.

The terminal was a blur of announcements, fast-walking travelers, and the ever-present smell of overpriced coffee. My heartbeat pounded louder than the chaos around me as I zigzagged past people, clutching my boarding pass like it was a lifeline.

My phone buzzed in my pocket. I fumbled to answer while dodging a family with an alarming number of suitcases.

"Hi, Anna, this is Luke's assistant," the cheerful voice chirped on the other end. "I'm returning your call. Luke isn't in LA right now. He finished shooting early, and he's traveling. I think he's in Atlanta today."

The words hit me like a slap, and my feet slowed to a stop. "Atlanta?"

"Yeah, I believe that's where he is. Should I pass along a message?"

"No," I managed, swallowing the lump forming in my throat. "No message."

I hung up, staring blankly at the bustling terminal around me. What was I even doing? Flying to LA for someone who wasn't even there? My stomach twisted as the doubts I'd been suppressing all day rose to the surface.

This was a mistake. A stupid, impulsive mistake. I should turn around, go home, and pretend this whole thing never happened.

My pace slowed to a walk as the energy drained from my body. My grip on my printed boarding pass loosened, and for a second, I considered crumpling it and walking away. What was the point?

But something kept me moving forward, one step at a time, until I rounded the corner and reached the gate.

That's when I saw the hoodie.

54

LUKE

THE LAST THING I wanted was to end up stranded in Chicago when I was so close to getting back to Anna. I adjusted my sunglasses and tried to focus on Hal, who was scanning the gate area with his usual vigilance. Tom stood a few feet away, arms crossed, doing the same.

My phone buzzed, and relief flooded me. Finally, there must be some news. Topher's name flashed on the screen.

"Hey," I said, stepping aside with Hal shadowing me protectively to avoid the flow of foot traffic.

"Don't get too excited," Topher said. "I just talked to someone at Muses. Anna's not in New Orleans."

I froze. Hal's head turned slightly toward me, picking up on my shift in body language. "What do you mean she's not there?"

"She went on vacation. They thought maybe New York or North Carolina. I don't know. They weren't exactly chatty about it."

Vacation? My grip tightened on the phone. "You're kidding me."

"I'm not," Topher said. "I know this throws a wrench in your grand gesture, but—"

"But nothing," I retorted, running a hand through my hair. "Why didn't anyone tell me this before I bought a plane ticket? My assistant tried to route me through Atlanta, of all places."

"Atlanta?" Topher let out a dry laugh. "That's the worst way to get to New Orleans. You've been flying all day to go in circles."

"Yeah, thanks for the geography lesson," I bit back, pacing the terminal as irritation churned in my chest. "Maybe I should've taken Gerald Fargo up on his offer to fly on his private jet."

"You think?" Topher deadpanned. "You've been running on adrenaline and bad ideas for weeks, Luke. Maybe it's time to sit down and think this through."

"Think this through?" I stopped short, glaring at a row of plastic airport chairs in Gate C16 as if they were to blame for my situation. "I've been thinking about nothing else but Anna. She's all I've thought about since I left."

"Then maybe focus that energy on finding her, not snapping at your only ally," Topher said. "I'm on your side. But maybe this detour is a sign to slow down and figure out your next move."

A detour. Right. As if I hadn't already wasted enough time running in the wrong direction. I pinched the bridge of my nose and exhaled. "I'll figure it out. I'll find her."

"Good luck," Topher muttered, clearly skeptical. "You're going to need it."

I hung up and shoved my phone back into my pocket, my heart pounding. She wasn't in New Orleans. What was I supposed to do now?

I glanced at the departure board, half-expecting some divine sign to tell me what to do next. Nothing. My eyes flicked to Gate C15, where a crowd of passengers was gathering.

And that's when I saw her.

55

ANNA

LUKE WAS STANDING at the gate opposite mine, the lavender hoodie I'd given him stretched over his broad shoulders. Even with the ridiculous hoodie and sunglasses, I recognized him instantly. Of course I did. He was the person I was running through this airport for.

As he looked at me, the chaos of the airport seemed to fade away. My breath caught.

I'd spent so long telling myself that I could never leave New Orleans, that I wasn't ready, that love was for people who had their lives figured out. But here I was, in a crowded airport, heart pounding in my chest, walking toward the one person who made me want to face my fears.

He pulled off his sunglasses, and I finally saw his eyes—those amazing blue eyes.

I moved toward him, my feet walking me across the bustling concourse like they had a mind of their own. Okay, maybe I was running.

"Anna?" He stepped forward, his smile breaking slowly across his face.

"Luke." I was breathless as I came to a stop in front of him. "What are you doing here?"

His gaze held mine, steady and unflinching. "I was on my way to New Orleans to tell you that you don't have to leave. I'm coming to you. I'm done running. From everything. From myself. From you. What are you doing here?"

A laugh slipped out. "I was on my way to LA. To tell you that I don't want fear to hold me back anymore."

His smile widened, warm and full of something I hadn't dared to hope for. For the first time in weeks, I felt like I could breathe again.

"I almost didn't come," I admitted. "I kept second-guessing myself. Telling myself that maybe I was too late."

"But you did come," he said, and those three words unraveled something I didn't realize I'd been holding onto.

"I did," I whispered. "Because I'm not afraid to leave New Orleans to be with you. Because home is wherever you are."

His gaze was tender as he reached for my hand.

And just like that, the noise of the airport came rushing back, but it didn't matter. We'd both shown up. At the exact same airport. At the exact same time.

56

LUKE

I'D FLOWN HALFWAY across the country to tell her how I felt, but now that she was standing right there, I couldn't speak. All I could think was how much I'd missed her. Every moment apart had felt like a piece of me was missing.

She wasn't on vacation in New York or North Carolina. She was on her way to see me.

My heart stuttered. "Home is wherever I am?"

She nodded, her eyes shining.

That gave me the courage to stop holding back. "Remember that day in the French Quarter at Napoleon House? You said you wanted one person to put you ahead of everyone else, the way your mom did. I want to be that person." I smiled, my nerves unraveling a little at her expression—open, hopeful.

Her gaze flicked to my hoodie. "You wore my hoodie. Great disguise." She crossed her arms with a smirk.

I hesitated for a moment, then I figured, if I was going to do this, I wasn't going to do it halfway. I took off my baseball cap and glasses. A few people nearby gasped and whispered, but I didn't care. Right now, there was only one person I cared about.

Behind me, I heard Hal mutter, "Oh, here we go," followed by

Tom's resigned sigh and the telltale click as they both moved into high-alert formation.

Anna laughed and loosened something tight inside me. I wanted to hear that sound for the rest of my life.

"Sir," Hal's voice cut through the moment, professional but strained. "You're causing a crowd."

I glanced over my shoulder. A small group of travelers had stopped to watch, phones out. Tom was already positioning himself to block the worst of it.

"Let them watch," I said, turning back to Anna.

"This is going on TikTok," Tom muttered.

"It's already on TikTok," someone in the crowd called out.

Hal pinched the bridge of his nose. "I don't get paid enough for this."

I didn't wait another second. I stepped forward, closing the small distance between us. My hands found her waist as I pulled her close, right there in the walkway between Gate C15 and C16. The world around us seemed to fade—the hurried announcements over the intercom, the click of suitcases against the floor, the smell of airport food.

And then I kissed her.

It wasn't perfect. A baby wailed in the background, a group of college kids yelled something about going viral, and I was sure more than a few people had just snapped a photo. But all that mattered was Anna.

When we finally broke apart, she looked up at me, her cheeks flushed and her smile wide. "Well," she said, her voice teasing but breathless, "that's one way to make a scene."

"I don't care about the scene." I looked in her eyes and brushed a strand of hair from her face. "I love you. And I'm not running from that anymore."

"I love you, too." Anna leaned into me. We weren't at either of our destinations yet, but standing there in the middle of a busy airport, I'd finally found my way back home.

57

ANNA

SIX MONTHS LATER

I DIDN'T GET to 101 rejections.

That was my first thought when I saw the email. It sat at the top of my inbox, the subject line screaming in bold: **Congratulations! Publishing Offer for Your Manuscript.**

My heart stopped. Then started. Then stopped again.

This had to be a mistake. A spam email from a robot that wanted to sell me fake editing services. Or worse, a cruel prank from the universe.

But, no, it was real.

I opened the email with trembling fingers, my eyes scanning the words so fast they blurred together. Bidding war. Multiple offers. Film-rights interest. My stomach flipped.

I reread it, this time more slowly. Then again. My superhero story —the one I almost didn't send out, the one I thought no one would ever care about—wasn't just going to be published. It was going to be made into a movie.

Before I could process the rest, my phone rang.

"Anna." It was my agent, her voice bright and bubbly. "I just got off the phone with another editor. It's official—a bidding war. And—wait for it—Gerald Fargo bought the film rights."

"Gerald Fargo?" I blinked.

"That's the one. And guess what? He wants Luke Fisher for the lead."

My jaw dropped. "Luke?"

"Fargo thinks your boyfriend's perfect for the role." My agent's words tumbled out faster than I could keep up. "I told him you might have notes, of course. It's your story, after all."

"Notes?" I echoed dumbly. My brain was lagging, stuck somewhere between *bidding war* and *film rights.*

"You're a superstar, Anna," she said before hanging up, leaving me alone with my thoughts.

I sank onto the couch, my phone still clutched in my hand, my mind racing. A published novel. A famous director wanting to buy the movie rights. A movie star boyfriend.

What was my life?

58

LUKE

"HONEY, I'M HOME," I called out, grinning like an idiot as I burst through the front door of our house in New Orleans.

Anna jumped up from the couch, and before I knew it, she was in my arms, her momentum nearly knocking me off balance. Her face was glowing, her eyes wide with excitement. "You're starring in a movie based on my book."

I didn't think. I just kissed her. The kind of kiss that made the world disappear, where everything else faded into the background. Her lips were velvet against mine. Every single time I kissed her, it reminded me just how much I loved doing it.

When we pulled back, her cheeks were flushed, her smile breathless. I brushed a lock of hair from her eyes. "Do you realize what this means?" I asked. "We're officially a Hollywood power couple now."

She rolled her eyes, but her lips twitched into that smile I could never get enough of. "It's just a small story, Luke. Nothing glamorous."

"Small?" I stepped back, feigning offense. "Anna, it's incredible. Fargo said he hasn't been this excited about a script since *Apocalypse Tomorrow*."

Her jaw dropped. "You talked to him?"

"Of course. He called me," I said, trying not to sound too smug. "Said he loved the emotional depth, called it *Marvel Universe meets Eternal Sunshine.*"

Anna blinked, stunned. "He said that? About *my* story?"

"Yours," I confirmed, squeezing her shoulder. I let out a breath, stepping back just enough to look at her thoroughly. "It's crazy. A year ago, I was killing myself to land anything decent. Then I nailed the role in Fargo's last movie so hard that I haven't had to audition since. Now, I can pick my projects and write my ticket. But this? Your story? This feels different."

Anna's cheeks flushed, and she shook her head, laughing. "You make it sound like *The Godfather.* It's just a superhero story."

"Not *just* anything," I said firmly. "It's raw, real. The emotional depth, the way you capture fear and strength—it's why people are obsessed with you." I gestured vaguely to her phone, where everything my PR team published on social media about our relationship was met with fanfare. "The way they talk about you, Anna, it's like you're their hero."

She ducked her head, embarrassed. "That's an exaggeration."

"Not even close." I leaned in, catching her eyes. "Being with you hasn't just made my life better, it's made *me* better. People see it. I see it. You've changed me."

She tucked a strand of hair behind her ear. "So, what now?"

"We keep splitting our time between New Orleans and Hollywood. This is working. We've found a balance. You keep writing, I keep acting, and we figure it out as we go."

Her lips quirked up into a grin. "That's a plan?"

"It's the only one that matters," I said, brushing her hair back gently. "Besides, I guess I'll be playing your hero now."

Anna leaned closer, her voice warm and her eyes full of love. "You already were."

I kissed her again. Because I could, because she let me, and because every time I did, I felt like I was exactly where I was meant to be.

59

ANNA

TWO YEARS LATER

THE GOAL WAS SIMPLE: pick up crawfish from the seafood market for the Amato family boil and get out before anyone noticed Hollywood's most recognizable movie star—or, even worse, his bestselling author wife.

Luke and I stood out, but not in the way you'd think.

Luke adjusted his floppy sun hat, a gaudy Hawaiian shirt barely covering his broad shoulders, and oversized sunglasses perched crookedly on his nose. "Do I look inconspicuous?" He tugged at the brim of the hat.

I stifled a laugh. "If by inconspicuous, you mean someone's eccentric uncle who just won the lottery, then sure."

He tugged the rim of my baseball cap lower over my face. "You know, you're my favorite wife."

We'd been married for six months, but I still loved hearing him call me his wife. "I'm your only wife."

He grinned and started helping me load bags of crawfish into our driver's car, the pungent aroma wafting through the humid air.

That's when it happened.

"Hey. Aren't you...?" A man holding a glossy magazine with Luke's face plastered across the cover froze mid-step, squinting at us.

I opened my mouth to speak, but Luke was quicker. Sliding into a deep Southern drawl, he grabbed my arm. "Nope. Just a couple of tourists lookin' for the airboat tours."

The man tilted his head. "Airboat tours?"

"Yes, sugar," I chimed in, batting my eyelashes dramatically. "Now, if you'll excuse us, we're late for our swamp adventure."

The man's brow furrowed, but he shrugged and walked off.

"Swamp adventure?" Luke teased. He pulled off his sunglasses and hat as we climbed into the car.

"Oh, like 'just a couple of tourists' was your finest performance," I shot back.

He grinned and shook his head. "Aunt Dolores better appreciate the effort we put into this."

"She will. Speaking of, when are we telling her she's going to be a great aunt?"

"After her first beer," Luke said with a decisive nod, the corners of his mouth lifting into that lopsided grin that still melted me.

"Our life is perfect," I murmured, leaning into him. Luke kissed me, and it still sent a thrill straight through me, as if it were the first time.

But the truth is, life isn't perfect. I mean, we still get rejected.

Luke didn't get Sexiest Man Alive—again. He lost to some smoldering British actor with cheekbones so sharp they probably came with a warning label.

But hey, we'll take the Oscar instead—Best Actor for the role based on my book. Gerald Fargo snagged Best Director. It turns out Hollywood loves superheroes with emotional depth, after all.

And me? I didn't win the Pulitzer Prize for my second novel, a sprawling tale about love and loss in the aftermath of Hurricane Katrina in New Orleans. But I made it to the finals of the National Book Award. I'll take it.

Rejection stings a lot less when you know you're still winning.

So, life's rejections haven't disappeared—they never do. But now they're just small moments, not overwhelming fears. We have our wins, and we have each other.

I finally have the love and fulfillment I was once too afraid to hope for. I finally feel like someone's most important person. And not just anyone. Luke Fisher's.

And I'm ready to face life's rejections and joys with him by my side. Because at the end of the day, those wins—Oscars, National Book Awards, finally making Aunt Dolores a great aunt—are sweet.

But the best win of all? We're together. And that's a story worth living.

THE END

Celebrity Love in New Orleans (complete series)

Scandalously Yours
Starfully Yours
Suddenly Yours
Secretly Yours
Suitably Yours (free novella)

Thank You

In love with New Orleans? Sign up for my newsletter and get a free novella, Suitably Yours.

About the Author

Katie Talbot writes romantic comedies about sassy, smart heroines. Her debut five-book series, *Celebrity Love in New Orleans,* is set in the city she calls home. Originally from Nebraska, she now lives in the Big Easy with her husband and three wonderful children.

ACKNOWLEDGMENTS

This is the first romantic comedy book I've ever written. I started it right after the COVID pandemic began, and there are probably a few words that look the same, but most of it is very different from where I started. There are so many people, so many editors, that I checked with throughout the journey from unreadable to (hopefully) readable.

To my writing group, Amy Page, KC Newbury, and Elyse Haynes, with whom I first started working when this was in an earlier draft. You all have been instrumental in keeping me on track. Amy, you are a publishing guru and coach extraordinaire. Everything I learned about publishing, I learned from you. KC, you know plot better than anyone, and I am in awe. Elyse, you are sweet and hilarious, and I am enjoying watching your journey as a successful sweet rom-com writer.

To my editor, Whitney Jones of Empowered Writing, who was so helpful.

And to my readers: Thank you for giving this story a shot! I hope you laughed more than you rolled your eyes.

And last but certainly far from least, I would like to thank my children—P, L, and MV. I'm proud and grateful to be your mother. To P, our kids (and I) hit the jackpot with you. Thank you for being my biggest fan. To my parents, for always fostering my love for reading. Thank you!

Stay smart, stay sassy,

Katie